EIGHT DAYS A WEEK

EIGHT DAYS

A WEEK

a novel by

Larry Duplechan

Boston ♦ AlyCat
an imprint of Alyson Publications, Inc.

Typeset and printed in the United States of America.

An AlyCat Book, published by Alyson Publications, Inc.,
40 Plympton Street, Boston, Massachusetts 02118. First published
in 1985 by Alyson Publications, Inc., as a trade paperback original.

First edition: October 1985
First AlyCat edition: May 1995

5 4 3 2 1

ISBN 1-55583-605-4 (previously ISBN 0-932870-84-8)

Backup Vocals

The author would like to thank:

Bob Knox, for saying, "Why don't you write a gay love story?" Ruth Keller, Bonnie Besonen, Eric Dodson, and Jowanna Dove for their encouragement during the early drafts of this book. Barbry Laurie Myown for (among other things) reading the finished draft and saying, "Yes, you are a writer." Allen ("Try to mention that I'm not gay") Esrock, who read the first hundred-some-odd pages of the first draft, and thrashed it; this is a much better piece of work for his having done so. Sasha, for publishing this book, and letting it be. Tom Robbins, whose *Even Cowgirls Get the Blues* is my favorite novel and the shining standard to which I ever aspire. Michael Smith, who published my first short story. Jim Yousling, of In Touch, Inc., who published my first nonfiction article. Michael Denneny of St. Martin's Press, for his continued encouragement and criticism. Michael Franks, for recording the *Passion Fruits* album, to the sound of which much of this book was written. The Crystals, the Ronettes, the Shirelles, Darlene Love, and the Shangri-las, to the sound of whose records much of my life has been lived. Chris Myers, for being my biggest fan. Perry Hart (my "Snookie"), and the "regulars" down at the Cabaret California, for the summer of '79 ("Those were days of roses").

And, of course, my Mister. For everything.

Chapter 28 is dedicated to the memory of Pick's, one of L.A.'s last great coffee shops, home of the best $3.95 steak-and-eggs breakfast — and, bar none, the finest waitresses — in town. R.I.P. 12/09/84.

Much love and a great big kiss — MWAH!

L.D.

Album Notes

Eight Days a Week is a period piece. The bulk of the story is set in the summer of 1979, which, while not so very many years ago, was nonetheless a very different time. Jimmy Carter was still president; John Lennon was still alive. Dance music was called "disco" then. And nobody had ever heard of AIDS.

Eight Days a Week is also a love story. The story includes vivid descriptions (at least I hope they're vivid) of acts of gay love that have, in light of the current gay health crisis, been termed unsafe according to recent safe-sex guidelines. It is my feeling that to impose a 1985 AIDS consciousness upon 1979 gay characters would be like writing a Civil War epic and refusing to mention slavery because the majority of Americans no longer hold slaves.

I would, however, like it understood that we at *Eight Days a Week* neither advocate nor encourage slavery.

Neither do we advocate or encourage unsafe sex.

You get the picture?

Yes, we see.

*This is dedicated
to the one
I love.*

"Mama said there'd be days like this."
—The Shirelles

It is Snookie's hypothesis that people in show business are actually in the "I'll show you" business. As in "You'll see! I'll show you! I'll show you all!" Meaning that anyone who will voluntarily, and of his own free will, endure the life of a performer — the humiliating auditions, the ruthless club owners, the ridiculous hours, not to mention the million-to-one odds against even modest success — has definitely got something to prove to somebody. I tend to agree with that. I refuse to believe it is merely coincidence that so many performers are known to have had perfectly excruciating childhoods. And not just Monroe, the beautiful orphan child, or Barbra, the big-beaked ugly duckling. Ask any performer. The lounge singer going into his umpteenth rendition of "Feelings." The third gypsy from the right in the Oxnard dinner theater production of *A Chorus Line*. The up-and-coming young comic waiting for his big three minutes at the Comedy Store. Easily four out of five performers will admit to a childhood that shouldn't happen to a dog. And I'd venture to guess that the odd one out of five has either managed to suppress some truly wretched memories, or is lying through his teeth.

My mother, Clara, likes to say that the first words I ever spoke were "I'll show you." I think she's kidding.

Still and all, by the time I was seven years old, I knew I wanted be a star — had to be a star. A singing star.

Clara was a singer, and a good one, as was her mother before her. In fact, my very earliest childhood memory is of Clara's voice lifted in song. Oh, and a beautiful sound it was.

Clara is a born singer. She has one of those voices that can make you cry and clutch your heart and rend your garment, just by singing, "Oh." She could have moved Satan himself to tears with "Sometimes I feel like a motherless child, a long way from home." Clara's is a voice that, even when singing a happy song, has, at its core, at its very center, a trace of melancholy. Just the tiniest tang of a tear swelling at the corner of its eye. A certain sadness that's impossible to catch, impossible to put your finger on. Something that can't be touched; only felt. Billie Holiday had it. Mahalia. Mama Cass. A few others. And Clara.

I've always felt that, had she been so inclined, Clara could have been a great jazz vocalist. Carmen Macreaish, a bit of a Betty Carter edge, but with that thing, that sadness, that catch in the voice. That little cry of pain that made Clara's rendition of "My Life Will Be Sweeter Someday" one of the most requested songs on testimony Sundays at the First New Ship of Zion Missionary Baptist Church. That made Clara the toast of the gospel music concert circuit for as long as she chose to be part of it.

Clara could have been a contender. She could have been Newport and Kool Jazz at the Bowl. One or two tasteful albums a year on Pablo and respectful reviews in *Down Beat*. But, no.

"Lord," she would say when the subject was broached, by her friends and, years later, by me, "I couldn't do that. Me? Singin' the blues? Naw," she'd say, ladling pancake batter onto the griddle in expert circles. "I couldn't sing the blues."

Clara had very definite ideas about church singers leaving church singing for the greener financial pastures of popular music. Within the context of this subject, Clara invariably described the singer in question as having foregone "the Lord's music" in order to go out into "the world" and sing "the blues."

Which is not to say that Clara did not recognize, appreciate, and enjoy the particular genre of Afro-American popular music known as the Blues. Indeed, she did. Clara owned and treasured several original Bessie Smith 78s, some extremely rare "Leadbelly" 45s and a gaggle of Joe Williams LPs. Oh, yes, Clara knew her blues from her jazz from her r&b from her rock 'n' roll, even her Motown from her Stax/Volt from her Sun Sessions, as well as anyone I've ever known.

We are, after all, discussing a woman who named her firstborn son after Johnnie Ray, the singer, because, she claims — and I see no reason to doubt her word — I was conceived while the automatic record-changer on the hi-fi replayed "The Little Cloud That Cried," over and over.

It is because of Clara that I began at a very young age to pay attention to what many would consider trivial facts about pop records. Who produced it. Who's playing harmonica in the background. What were the Shangri-las' names. When Clara informed me that it was a young man named Lou Rawls singing harmony vocal with Sam Cooke on "Bring It On Home to Me," I felt privy to delightful secrets. When she told me that the group called the Crystals on "He's a Rebel" was not the Crystals at all, but Darlene Love (with whom Clara had sung in church choirs not so many years before), overdubbed four or five times, I was hooked.

(One result of this love of trivia is a long-standing pet project of mine to write the *Johnnie Ray Rousseau Idiosyncratic History of Rock and Roll*, in which I intend to pass off my personal tastes and opinions as Holy Writ, committing to print everything I know, think, believe, and feel about American popular music. And, believe me, there's plenty — I see two or three sizable volumes, boxed, like Proust.)

Still, when Clara spoke of Sam Cooke leaving the Soul Stirrers to record "You Send Me" and "Chain Gang" and "Everybody Loves the Cha Cha Cha," becoming rock's first real (as some *Billboard* magazine hack would later term them) crossover artist, she would invariably cluck her tongue, like the disapproving mom she was, and say, "There's another one gone to sing the blues." I don't believe she's ever truly forgiven Aretha for leaving the Reverend C.L.'s church choir, the *Amazing Grace* album notwithstanding.

But for all her adamant firmness concerning separation of church and stage, Clara loved pop music. Other kids' mothers could lullaby and good-night themselves blue in the face; Clara bounced pudgy toddler me upon her knee to the tune of "Willie and the Hand Jive" and "Who Wears Short-Shorts (Johnnie Wears Short-Shorts)." Clara kept the radio on all day long as she washed and ironed and cleaned and cooked. Cool cats like Hunter Hancock and Magnificent Montague spun the hits for Clara and me; and Clara sang along, her sparkling alto mounting on the wings of a dove and soaring through the house. Oh, that I should someday sing as well on a stage as Clara sang in her kitchen.

14

Oh, I sang along too.

And I learned early on that Clara had shared at least some of her magic with me; that I, too, had talent.

Once, when I was about six years old, I heard my Aunt Ruth tell my mother, "that child" — meaning me — "that child has got a *voice*, Honey." I was singing along with the stereo at the time — "This Is Dedicated to the One I Love" by the Shirelles, if memory serves me (it usually does).

Another time, I overheard Ruth say (properly sotto voce, but I heard), "He may not be pretty like little David, but he sure is smart — and he's got that *voice*, Honey."

My brother David was a beautiful child — he was four at the time — with smooth cream-colored skin (David took after the Creole side of the family), huge green eyes, and jet black hair that formed a nimbus of curls around his head. (My own hair was — and is — a nondescript brown and incurably nappy.) Our childhood roles were easily cast: I was the smart one, David the pretty one. Family and friends who were properly impressed when I was speaking full sentences at fifteen months and reading Dr. Seuss aloud at two, cooed and clucked and made over David like he was the newly discovered cure for acne. "Clara, that child should be on the teevee," people said of David. Total strangers stopped on the streets and said, "Lord, look at that pretty child!"

It wasn't that I was an ugly child, exactly. I was merely a plain child. My head was just a bit too large for my body, my teeth just a tad too big for my face. "You'll grow into them," Clara said. I was short for my age, thin, and rather delicate-looking. I was an unbeautiful child doubly cursed with a painfully acute appreciation for physical beauty: I knew it and envied it when I saw it.

15

And as if that weren't enough, I had David, as pretty an albatross as ever hung around a young boy's skinny little neck.

In addition to being beautiful ("Lord, that one's gonna break some hearts when he grows up," people said), David was also what Clara and Lance and seemingly everybody in those days liked to call "all boy." As in, "Clara, that little David is *all boy*." The inference, of course, was that I was considerably less than all boy. David was a natural athlete. He could play just about anything involving fast-moving spheres, and play them all well. While I, on the other hand, grew so weary of being told I threw like a girl that I developed an all-encompassing aversion to team sports (I break out in hives at the sight of the name Voit), and to this day I will not, under any circumstances, throw a softball.

I alternated between worshipping my baby brother and wanting him dead.

By the time I was twelve, as David grew taller than me, and more handsome by the minute (and became a little league pitching star to boot), I was singing along with the Beatles (Paul was my favorite — I thought he had the most beautiful eyes), and with Barbra Streisand.

"I'm the greatest star," I'd sing to my full-length bedroom mirror, "but no one knows it." With feeling. With conviction. With choreography. After one viewing of *Funny Girl*, I became fascinated with Barbra. I blew weeks of allowance on seeing *Funny Girl* over and over, until I could recite every line, recreate every move — a one-boy cult. When Barbra said: "You think beautiful girls are gonna stay in style forever? I should say not! Any minute now, they're gonna be out — fiNISHED! Then it'll be my turn," my mind substituted the word "boys" for "girls," and I was momentarily uplifted.

When she sang, "Oh my man I love him so," a lump came unbidden to my throat, and tears came to my eyes. When Omar Shariff took Barbra into his arms, and held and kissed her, I stood gladly in her period high-heeled shoes.

I began to emulate Barbra. I learned all her songs — at the time, I could still sing in her key. When I adopted Barbra's wacky-Brooklyn-Jewish-girl speech and manner, and began crossing my eyes just a bit, no one seemed particularly alarmed. Unusual behavior indeed for a twelve-year-old colored boy from South Central L.A. but then, I'd always been considered an unusual child. Clara did step in, nail clipper in hand, when I decided to grow my fingernails as long as Barbra's.

In Barbra I found a hero. She wasn't pretty, either. (When she appeared on *The Ed Sullivan Show*, singing a rendition of "Cry Me a River" that made me clasp my hands over my mouth in awe, Clara — who seldom commented negatively on anyone's looks — said, "Look at that child's *nose!*" and all Lance had to say was "Lord, that girl *ugly!*") But Barbra had talent. She had a *voice*, Honey.

And although I was not naive enough, even then, to believe that talent was as desirable as physical beauty, I knew talent was all I had. I wasn't good-looking; I wasn't all boy; and, by the time I was thirteen or so, I was beginning to understand the extent to which I was different from other boys of thirteen or so; different far beyond just throwing like a girl. Still, I was smart (straight A's, excepting an occasional B in conduct and consistent C-minuses in Phys. Ed.); and (Aunt Ruth's words rang in my ears like an anthem) I had a *voice*, Honey.

I had to be a performer. What else could I do? I had to become a star. Nothing less would do. I didn't just want stardom like you want the new Stones album, or a coconut macaroon in the middle of the night. I needed it, like a diabetic needs insulin. I could taste it, like salt on the Santa Monica breeze, like the bite of a radish on the back of my tongue. I hung on to the dream of it as to the sides of the last lifeboat named *Titanic*.

The only thing I'd ever wanted nearly as much, for nearly as long, was a boyfriend. A lover. A husband. Some impossible combination of Tab Hunter, Rick Nelson, and Steve Reeves. Someone who'd see my big head, my big teeth, and my skinny little body, and love me anyway. As early as twelve or thirteen years old, I assumed that someday I'd meet a man, fall in love with him (and he with me — Omar fell for Barbra, didn't he?), settle down, and live happily ever after.

Which reminds me of something Mick Jagger used to say: "You cain't always git whut chu wownt."

Which reminds me of something Clara used to say: "Be careful what you pray for — you just might get it."

Which brings me (rather abruptly, I know) to the summer of '79. When I first tasted success. And Keith Keller.

"By the way, where'd ja meet 'im?"
—The Shangri-las

The first time I saw Keith, I must admit I didn't really take much notice. Because he was sitting at the very back corner table in the shadows and was, therefore, very difficult to see clearly. Because he left before I could get close enough to him to take a good look. Because he was with a woman and, even in the shadows, looked off limits. And because, to tell you the truth, I had already set my sights on somebody else.

It was a Friday night; it would have made a perfect hot August night of the Neil Diamond variety, had it not been the middle of July. It was after the third set. We were, at the time, playing three sets a night, Friday and Saturday nights at Tom Sawyer's, this perfectly claustrophobic little club down in Venice.

"We" were me and the Boize, my sometime backup band. The Boize weren't strictly a band at all, let alone mine; just some freelancing musicians Snookie managed to scrounge up when I decided one fine day that I needed a band.

Ladies and gentlemen, allow me to introduce the Boize:

19

On drums, David "Mr. Moto" Miamoto; tall and thin as bamboo, third-generation Japanese-American, and a religious believer that Ginger Baker was God.

On Fender bass and backup vocals, Jeff Bonomo; "Bobo" to his friends. Bobo was the official sex object of the outfit. He was Sal Mineo handsome, with Roger Daltrey's *Tommy — The Movie* physique; and his glands secreted a musk that magically moistened the lower labia of any healthy hetero female specimen within a two-mile radius. He broke an average of a heart an hour, as he was happily, faithfully married to a very sweet girl named Gina with thick thighs, something of a moustache, and a way with linguini. Snookie had a long-standing, unrequited crush on the Bobo. Not me; I knew an incurable heterosexual when I saw one. Or so I believed at the time.

On guitar and backup vocals was one Steve Hicks. Circa 1976, somebody told Hicks that he looked like Peter Frampton, and Steve has been grinning and shaking his mane of long blond hair like a bloomin' idiot ever since. The boy could play some guitar, though.

And of course, there was Snookie on keyboards and backup vocals, and little me on lead vocals and heavy drama.

As I've said, the Boize (except for Snooks) weren't really *my* band, but times were hard (as always) for musicians. So when I lucked up on a paying gig, the Boize did a pretty fair imitation of being mine.

Tom Sawyer's just barely qualified as a paying gig. Just barely. Although the owners of Tom Sawyer's seemed to believe they were running some cool, hip underground cellar full o' noise whose outward funkiness was part and parcel of its charm, Sawyer's was in reality what we in show business like to call a hole — whose outward funkiness was part and parcel of its overall funkiness. The atmosphere of Tom Sawyer's was disturbingly similar to that of a bat cave. As you may or may not remember, the summer of '79 was as hot and damp as three months in the steam room at the "Y" (though not nearly as much fun), and Tom Sawyer's was a tiny, cramped, darkly paneled room with no air conditioning, and almost no light — I believe there were some rather exotic strains of mushroom growing in the corners — also no liquor license. Only domestic beer and some truly pedestrian wines were served at Sawyer's. There wasn't even a stage; just a decrepit spinet piano in perpetual need of tuning, and a barely passable sound system. That the owners of Sawyer's should fancy the room a nightclub at all was the very height of presumption. That there were customers there at all was, to me, amazing beyond words.

I was doing a rather eclectic act in those days. We did some originals, mostly Snookie's. (He's a pretty good tunesmith, Snookie is. A song of his was getting some airplay on the New Wave stations a couple of years ago — "Hot Creamy Monkey Fucks" — maybe you heard it.) We did some Top 40: "I Want You to Want Me" by Cheap Trick and Blondie's "Heart of Glass" (yeah, I know; but it was a very hot song at the time). And also just about anything else that tickled my highly ticklish fancy: "Tonite Tonite" by the Mell-o-Kings (I do love doo-wop), "Remember Walking in the Sand" (with the audience joining in on finger-snaps), even the occasional obscure show tune (the "Plastic Jesus" song from *Cool Hand Luke*). We did some Elvis, some Motown, a bit of Bacharach, and David — you name it. I even encored with "Lydia the Tattooed Lady" for a while. We threw together some pretty interesting sets in those days, let me tell you.

For the record, we never once played "My Sharona" — I rather liked it, but Moto wouldn't touch it with a ten-foot drumstick — or anything by the Bee Gees, by unanimous decision.

Sawyer's has long since gone the way of all flesh. It has since been a four-square Fundamentalist church, a lesbian cruise bar, and a Scientology center, among other things — and except that there are so few clubs of any caliber in this town where someone as difficult to pigeon-hole as I am can play, I'd say good riddance and no regrets. As far as I was concerned, Sawyer's only selling point was that it was there at all — a place to do what I do where such venues were all too scarce.

And then there was Louie.

He was Sawyer's one and only busboy. Blond. Buzz-cut. Maybe nineteen. Tanned the color of Kraft caramels, with a mouth as full and red and pretty as a girl's — lips that absolutely begged to be kissed. And one of the high-est, roundest, most firmly packed little keisters I've ever seen on a white boy, before or since. The beauty of Louie's buns, stuffed into a pair of faded five-oh-ones, could heal the sick, give eyesight to the blind, and make the lame take up their beds and walk. In short, ladies and germs, this was one extremely beautiful boy. And, not incidentally, quite my personal cup of tea.

22

You see, I have this thing about blonds. Snookie, in his bitchier moods, likes to fling some rather unpleasant words about — words like "fixation" and "obsession" — and describes this thing I have about blonds as (and I'm quoting here) "just one tentacle of an absolute octopus of neurosis" (unquote, and talk about calling the kettle black); but that's unfair in the way that only one's closest friends will be unfair. Not because it is entirely untrue, but because it is hardly the whole truth.

I am in no wise to be confused with those sexually exclusive types, the kind who require certain formations of body hair or eye color or height, weight, or (most commonly) length before their sexual satisfaction can be attempted; or those who can only truly enjoy erotic encounters with persons of lower social standing or class or IQ than themselves. In fact, I quite pity those poor souls of such specialized sexual menus that they are only able to make it click with black men or Oriental men or policemen or men with dirt beneath their fingernails. Not me. I like men. White ones and black ones and brown ones and yellow ones, and so on and so on and scoobie doobie doobie.

Still, I did — and do — have this thing about blonds.

23

I suppose it all started with Joel Brechtschneider back in the fourth grade.

Joel Brechtschneider was a tall, broad-shouldered, towheaded ten-year-old with sparkling blue eyes and a cute little turned-up nose with tiny brown freckles splashed across the bridge of it. And I loved him.

Joel Brechtschneider carried himself with the cocky, head-high assurance of someone totally confident of his own attractiveness. At ten years old, he was already a heartbreaker. Every girl in Cinnamon Avenue School experienced an attack of uncontrollable giggle-itis at the mention of Joel's name, both because of his status as the undisputed Cutest Boy in the School, and because it was common knowledge that Joel had appeared in several television commercials, an educational short subject on the textile industry and one full-length feature film.

Even Miss Muskat, our fourth-grade teacher, a dyed redhead with a penchant for brightly colored fishnet hose and makeup modeled after that of Dusty Springfield (perhaps the sixties' most underrated female pop vocalist — who shall finally receive her due in my book), was unable to mask her preference for Joel. He was an audiovisual monitor (handsome, athletic, *and* an A-V boy — in the fourth grade, that spelled STATUS, baby); and I'll never forget how Miss Muskat would sit in ill-concealed admiration as Joel threaded oral hygiene or Jiminy Cricket bicycle safety films through the projector. Everyone in the class acknowledged (with varying degrees of envy and admiration) that Joel had our teacher wrapped securely around his freckled finger; indeed, apart from Miss Muskat's affection, Joel might never have passed the fourth grade at all. As is so often the case with the very beautiful, Joel Brechtschneider possessed the intelligence of an end table. Still, I loved him.

Joel was everything I was not: sturdy and muscular where I was slight and frail; unfailingly athletic where I was the classic nerd-fuck on the court — any court; as consistent a "C" student as I was a consistent "A"; as fair and blond as I was Ovaltine brown. Everything I was not. Which, as any armchair analyst will tell you, is undoubtedly the reason I loved him.

Oh, come come, you might well object — ten-year-old boys simply do not fall in love with one another. With their fourth-grade teachers, surely. With Annette Funicello in rerun, perhaps. But with one another, *mais non!*

Ah, but love Joel Brechtschneider I did. And hated him.

Because, being everything I was not, Joel was everything I wished I were. Tall. Strong. Handsome. White, for chrissakes (There, Snookie, I've said it!). If constant comparison to brother David's fairer face (both fair of complexion and fair as in beautiful) was my cross to bear through childhood, then comparing myself to Joel in my mind's bathroom mirror, I truly came to abhor my flat nose and (to me) overlarge lips, envying Joel's pointed nose, nearly lipless mouth, and straight, blindingly blond hair.

Yes, this was the sixties; and yes, I had indeed heard that black was beautiful. But I never bought it for a minute. Clara's new natural hairdo and Lance's dashikis notwithstanding, I knew better. Tab Hunter was beautiful. Don (Robbie Douglas on *My Three Sons)* Grady was beautiful. Beautiful-hair-Breck girls were beautiful. Joel Brechtschneider was beautiful. Blonds had more fun. The rest of us could only hope to get by on brains and talent (with, as Gwen Verdon might say, an emphasis on the latter).

So I followed Joel Brechtschneider through the fourth grade like a heat-seeking missile. Like one long chorus of "Me and My Shadow" we were. I stuck to him like Bazooka bubble gum to the sole of your sneaker, as if through close physical proximity some small residual of those qualities I so envied in Joel might rub off onto me like Aunt Lucille's makeup when she kissed me. I did everything I could imagine to make Joel like me, to want to be my friend. I willingly traded my Hostess Twinkies for his carrot and celery sticks; I purposely dropped my guard, allowing him to copy my spelling tests. And, while Joel never actually acknowledged my active admiration, neither did he discourage it. As a result, many people mistakenly assumed we were friends. Mistakenly, because Joel Brechtschneider had no friends — only admirers and enviers.

Even as my days were occupied in adoring Joel, so were my nights filled with fantasies starring Joel. Many was the night I lay in bed, belly-down against the sheets, pajama bottoms pushed down past my knees, squirming in vague sensual pleasure as my fertile young imagination projected *The Adventures of Johnnie Ray and Joel* onto the Cinerama Dome behind my eyes. I fantasized adventures pieced somewhat haphazardly together from *The Man from U.N.C.L.E.*, Tarzan movies, and *Huckleberry Finn*, the only imperatives being danger, which demanded that Joel cling to me for safety, and swimming, which demanded nudity.

At the time, I suppose I did manage to convince myself that Joel liked me, at least a little. But, looking back on it all, I don't suppose he really did. Much more likely, he simply tolerated me for my Twinkies and whatever vague reward his ten-year-old ego might have gained from my doglike worship. For if he never called me a sissy right to my face (as some kids did: let's face it, folks, I was the one), or sang, "Ching-chong, Chinaman" at me (as some kids did, because of the rather Oriental slant of my eyes), neither did he ever attempt to rescue me or shield me (as a buddy might have done, and as it was well within his power to do) from the myriad cruelties little and big that the pretty and the strong seem to enjoy inflicting upon the plain and awkward.

I remember, once they were choosing up sides for basketball or fistball or something-or-other-ball, and Joel (as usual) was one of the team captains. And, as usual, I was the very last left after the pickings had been picked. I was odd man out, and neither captain wanted to inflict me upon his team. This happened to me so often that I was almost used to it — almost. I clenched my eyes shut and prayed, literally prayed to God with a passion I'd never known in church, that Joel would say, "Aw, c'mon, Johnnie Ray," take me onto his team, and save me further humiliation (the superior snickers of my classmates already sizzled in my ears).

But, no.

Instead, they flipped a coin. The losing captain would be forced to take me.

The look of triumph and relief that swept Joel's flawless face as he won the coin toss cut me far deeper than Ted Castleman's "Aw, shit!" upon losing the flip and gaining me. I managed to get to the end of Ted's line before the tears began searing their way down my face, so I don't suppose Joel saw me crying.

No, I couldn't honestly say Joel liked me.

Whatever feelings Joel may or may not have harbored for me, they are really much less important than my feelings for Joel. As the initial object of my prepubescent desires, Joel Brechtschneider was the front runner in the long, long line of blonds I later loved, lusted after, endured crushes of varying lengths and intensities on, ogled, whistled at, flirted with, seduced, allowed myself to be seduced by, or simply worshipped from afar, since the day Joel's family moved to New York my fifth-grade year, taking my small eleven-year-old heart away with them in Mr. Brechtschneider's '64 Ford station wagon.

Joel was almost immediately succeeded in my affections by Hans Frankhuesen, a lanky Dutch-born boy who quite unwittingly broke my heart like a lightbulb against the sidewalk, in the sixth grade, simply by being the achingly beautiful twelve-year-old he was. Hans was later dethroned by Steve Chakowski, third-chair trumpet in the John Glenn Junior High School band — in which I played first-chair flute — the proximity of whose gym locker (and the resulting proximity of whose alabaster behind) kept me in mortal terror of unbidden erections for two years running; and so on toward Louie.

Anyway, you get the point. I really dig the fair-haired boys.

I was once told by a black alto sax player named Zaz (we were in bed at the time, mind you) that my preference for white men (and blonds, the whitest of white, to boot) was the sad but understandable end result of three hundred years of white male oppression.

"You've become the all-too-willing victim of America's white-supremacist, master-race, plantation mentality," he told me.

I said, "Maybe."

But the truth of the matter is that Louie was beautiful; and the rational knowledge that I was willingly knuckling under to three hundred years of white male oppression didn't make him any less beautiful. Right or wrong, and whatever the reason, I do like blonds.

I love the sweet, buttery colors they turn in the summer. The way their eyebrows and lashes and body hair sun-bleach to near transparency. The blinding flash of tan line as their baggy boxers drop to the floor. The stunning interplay of lights and darks as my skin moves across theirs. I like that. So sue me, already.

And, lucky me, I have (in recent years) found that blonds seem to like me, too. Which, as far as I'm concerned, proves that the old myth about blonds being dumb is just a vicious lie.

Anyway, about Louie. I had been doing a slow mating dance around Louie for weeks. I made a point of saying hello to Louie upon entering Tom Sawyer's and wishing him good night before leaving. I'd brush against the boy, oh-so-accidentally, on my way to the loo. I wore my most snug-fitting sleeveless t-shirts to accentuate the biceps I'd worked so hard to build. I complimented Louie on the sweetness of his cologne, when I knew he wasn't wearing any. And although Louie never made any advances, or even anything my still-fertile imagination could construe as an advance, neither did he ever draw away when I touched him, or fail to return my smile when I lobbed one his way, or in any way discourage what anyone with eyes could see was an ongoing flirtation. Something in the way Louie's pale blue eyes lowered when I smiled in his direction told me it was worth a shot. I had decided on the way to the club behind the wheel of my raggedy old VW Beetle, this was the night. I would ask Louie home and (if all went well) fuck him within an inch of his life.

It was Friday night, as I've mentioned; the last show was over, and I was circulating. Something I did after every show. It would have pleased my notoriously well-honed sense of the dramatic if I could have simply disappeared after each performance. As the final chord hangs in the smoky nightclub air and dies away, the lights dim to black, and Johnnie Ray is gone. Excuse me while I disappear. Very Sinatra. But Sawyer's had no place to disappear to — not so much as a dressing room — and somehow, disappearing into the men's john just didn't quite cut it. So instead of disappearing, I circulated. As the audience slurped the suds at the bottoms of their beers and gasped incredulously at the sums on their checks, I slipped into a role somewhere between Leontyne Price and Auntie Mame. Working my way from table to table, introducing myself to first-timers, exchanging hugs and making kiss-kiss with the regulars — my small but neurotically loyal following. Smiling and waving like Miss Hard Cider at the Apple Blossom Parade, and tossing amusing bons mots like rose petals to the peasantry. Accepting compliments with an oh-so-modest turn of my head and a simple, sincere "Thank you so much."

I had it down to a science. I knew, almost instinctively, how much time I could afford to spend at each table so that none of my fan club would disappear into the muggy midsummer night feeling neglected. That Friday night, however, I had been stalled in midcirculation.

I was sitting at one of the front tables. Across from me sat a tall, light brown woman with a big, sloppy Afro. She had begun by commenting how unusual it was to see a black man singing rock 'n' roll, and had ended up giving an unsolicited stream-of-consciousness discourse on the history of the Negro in the rock music idiom. She looked rather like Cynthia Robinson, trumpet player for Sly and the Family Stone. She had a slight cast in her left eye. She had a voice like wet sandpaper. She was boring me to tears.

"Chuck Berry — Fats Domino — Clyde McPhatter," she listed, gesturing with the smoldering butt-end of an unfiltered Camel, "man" — she held on to the word "man" for about four counts with a fermata — "man, those cats *made* rock 'n' roll. Man, those cats *was* rock 'n' roll!"

I made a noncommittal noise and pushed myself up from the chair. This babe was throwing off my timing. I had a roomful of other people to talk to — at least to say hello to — and I had to grab the blond before he left. From the corner of my eye, I could see Louie on the opposite side of the club, clearing tables.

"Excuse me." I attempted to make a reasonably graceful exit, but the woman was having none of it. She pointed at me with what was left of her cigarette.

"Ooh mah soul!" she suddenly exclaimed.

"Beg pardon?"

"'Ooh My Soul,'" she insisted. "You know? Li'l Richard."

"Yes," I said. "Yes, of course." I was beginning to wonder if the lady was on something strong.

"Man" — she really leaned on that word — "'Tutti Frooti,' 'Reddy Teddy,' 'Rippitup'" — she was listing again.

So I thought, fuck this noise.

"Excuse me," I said with some finality, having decided to move on to the next table before she got through Little Richard's Greatest Hits in their entirety. The woman was still talking — "'Long Tall Sally,' 'Good Golly Miss Molly'" — when I turned abruptly away, bumping smack into Snookie.

Snookie Rothenberg was my pianist. He had been my pianist — also my musical director, sometimes-chauffeur, bodyguard, and de facto manager for the two years or so since I had become, in my own (usually more-or-less facetious) term — a pop vocalist to be reckoned with. Before Snookie, I had been forced to throw my act upon the mercy of a succession of glaringly mediocre (and usually under-rehearsed) house pianists. Which, believe me, shouldn't happen to a dog act.

Snookie Rothenberg was also my very best friend. We shared a relationship of such unnatural, nearly symbiotic closeness that almost everyone assumed we were lovers — the words "old married couple" had been used more than once to describe us. And we did behave like two people who'd been breathing each other's CO_2 for twenty-some-odd years, when, in fact, we'd known one another for less than three. We had pet names for each other. Snookie, when not calling me "Honey" (a word he managed to spread out over four or five syllables), usually referred to me as "J.R." (which I rather liked) or "John-John" (which I liked a bit less). But I could hardly afford to be choosy about nicknames: it was I who had dubbed Sidney Rothenberg "Snookie" in the first place

— after Snookie Lanson of the old *Your Hit Parade* show — for the simple reason that I hated the name "Sidney" and liked the name "Snookie."

Snookie and I also tended to be thinking the very same thought at the very same time, which allowed us to communicate in a peculiar mixture of grunts, shrugs, and eye rolling at times when verbal communication was inconvenient. We could speak volumes to one another across a crowded room with the raise of an eyebrow. We also shared identical tastes in almost everything — food, clothes, music, films — just about everything but men, about which we nearly always disagreed.

So why, you may well wonder, were Snookie and I — two people with so much affection for one another, two people with so very much in common — not lovers? Usually, when people asked — and they often did — I'd explain it as a classic case of two people who simply became friends too fast to ever become lovers. Which was the truth, if not the whole truth. The whole truth included the fact that, sexually speaking, Snookie Rothenberg and I lacked what in old Hollywood they used to call "chemistry."

I met Snookie in a small, loud, West Hollywood disco bar late one Saturday night, following an unsatisfying one-time showcase gig at yet another Hollywood cafe with pretensions toward art.

Now, I hate bars.

Oh, I know — everybody says that. It's the second most-used opening line in the world. Right after the hands-down favorite — "Come here often?" — comes that old standby, "Gee, doncha hate the bars?" But, honestly, I hate bars.

They're much too loud, for one thing; intelligent conversation is an utter impossibility. The only thing more inane than bar talk is bar talk bellowed over the 48-hour disco remix of "I Will Survive." Roomfuls of homosexuals simultaneously screaming, "COME HERE OFTEN?!?" at full vocal capacity.

They're also too damned dark. Being more than a bit myopic anyway and with unreliable night vision, I find it distressing that most gay bars are lit so that I am barely able to discern large shapes; except for the illumination from the occasional stray shaft of mirror-ball-reflected light darting across a face here and there, it is practically impossible to see what anyone really looks like from further than two feet away. I have personally found that

35

the sense of touch is, far and away, the most reliable in this situation. (There is, however, the occasional gentleman who will find the Braille method of getting acquainted a bit forward.)

And when they finally do decide to shed some light on the subject, it is just before closing, by which point nearly everyone is ripped to the tits and looking none the better for wear and tear; and the room is suddenly bathed in a light just slightly less flattering than a naked 40-watt bulb dangling from the ceiling of the men's room at the Last Chance Texaco, leaving you with two choices — either grab the next thing you see that doesn't make your flesh crawl and take him home with you, or go home alone again and sleep single one more night.

All things considered, I generally prefer to meet prospective romantic interests under less strained (and better lit) circumstances. Bus stops for the Santa Monica number 1 line between the beach and UCLA are a pretty good bet; also the men's department of Bullock's Westwood (both employees and customers). And, of course, any store, shop, restaurant, or street corner on Santa Monica Boulevard between Robertson and Fairfax — things can get a little scuzzy east of Fairfax.

Anyway, I was in this particular bar that particular Saturday night. The showcase had been just too, too depressing. I'd pulled a 12:30 a.m. time slot that stretched into 1:15, by which time there were four people left in the room — three of whom were drooling drunk and one of whom was still waiting to get onstage. The pianist maimed all of my charts beyond recognition — this guy couldn't have maintained a steady tempo if you beat 4/4 time upside his head with a ball-peen hammer.

I was just short of suicidal by the time I got out of there, and the only possible cure for the case of the blues I had contracted was a glass of cold white wine and a warm body. Almost any 98.6-degree form would do.

I had hardly walked into the place and returned my driver's license to my pocket before a hopeful-looking candidate sidled up to me and shouted,

"HI! BUY YOU A DRINK?" over the disco din.

"No, thanks," I yelled. My new friend was good-looking enough in a well-scrubbed college-boy sort of way, in close-cropped hair, argyle sweater, and jeans. But I had learned to be careful from whom I accepted the offer of a drink. I had encountered one too many men who thought the purchase of a beer tantamount to a marriage proposal, and who considered it odd that I was not necessarily to be had for the price of a Miller Lite.

I ordered myself a white wine, and Joe Frat scooted on up beside me, smiling an All-American Boy smile. He touched me on the shoulder and yelled something in my direction at the very moment the music reached an earth-moving crescendo; the guy's voice was no match for Sylvester's ("DANCE wid me inna DISSgo heat!"), so I didn't get a word of it. I screamed,

"WHAT?"

College Boy leaned in close to my ear.

"Do you like to get fucked with big, hard dicks?"

I was momentarily struck dumb. Did he just say what I thought he just said? I collected myself and said,

"Who among us does not?" I looked furtively about for another place to stand. Joe College leaned in again. I involuntarily leaned away.

"How'd you like to go to my place, get stoned, and fuck for about six hours?"

I just looked at the guy for a second or two, my mouth just sort of hanging open.

And then I laughed. Maybe it was nerves; maybe it was the incongruity of overtly dirty talk coming from a guy who looked as wholesome as a baked potato. But I laughed, just a giggle at first, through which I managed to say,

"Six hours? Sorry — five's my limit."

I scooped up my wine and staggered away, doubled over with laughter.

That was when I saw Snookie.

Something about the small, dark-haired man leaning somewhat precariously against one corner of the bar attracted me immediately, despite the fact that Snookie was hardly my ideal physical type. As previously mentioned, I generally like them blond and tan; I also prefer a certain amount of muscle. Snookie was — to be kind — rather scrawny, with very dark hair, and was, without a shadow of a doubt, the palest man on earth. Picture an albino with dark, curly hair, and huge, dark eyes.

Ah, but such eyes! Big and liquid, with lashes out to there. Definitely the old limpid pools syndrome. You could fall into those eyes and never be seen or heard from again. It was the eyes that got me.

So I ambled up to the pale, big-eyed stranger, sucked in a deep breath to expand my chest, crossed my arms to make my biceps bulge, and in my best butch voice said, "Hi." And after a minimum of innocuous bar talk, I said come on and he said okay. It was almost closing time — no time to dillydally.

Well, folks, then I got the guy home.

F.C. Fiasco City.

First of all, I hated kissing him. Snookie's lips were very full and very, very soft, and he had this habit of licking them right before kissing. Which made kissing him rather like smooching a bag of soggy marshmallows. Besides which, Snookie had tippled at least one snifter of Benedictine & Brandy too many (foreshadowings of countless overtippled evenings to come); among the unappealing results were a case of halitosis that could have stopped a herd of stampeding wildebeest dead in their tracks, and an incurable case of leaping impotence that rendered Snookie's smallish pale pink penis frustratingly inactive, my own heroic attempts at oral resuscitation notwithstanding.

For his part, Snookie made a halfhearted go at sucking me, but he really wasn't into it; a situation he illustrated most vividly with some off-putting coughing and retching noises. As if reading my mind, Snookie announced quite matter-of-factly that he never, but *never*, got fucked; that, indeed, he found the very notion of *l'amour Greque* entirely repulsive. To my abject disappointment, Snookie's behind, as round and creamy as two scoops of Häagen-Dazs honey-vanilla ice cream — his best feature, aside from his eyes — those lovely buns guarded the gates to a sphincter that could not have been loosened by a small nuclear warhead.

So there I sat, at 2:47 on a Sunday morning — tired and horny and frustrated, with this drunk frigid skinny white boy in my bed, apologizing repeatedly and chain-smoking Shermans. What's a boy to do?

I made coffee.

"So," I said, handing the pale young stranger a cup of Chock Full o ' Nuts, "what do you do?"

He clutched the steaming Snoopy mug full of coffee as if for dear life.

"I'm a pianist," he replied. "An accompanist, really. I accompany pop singers. What do you do?"

My ever-wavering faith in Divine Providence found renewed strength.

"I'm a singer," I said. "A pop singer."

By sunrise, I had gained both my accompanist and my very best buddy.

"We're rich," Snookie announced, showing me the small bundle of bills clenched tight in his fist. The scent of Snookie's breath told me that my very best buddy had already made healthy headway into his second or third glass of B&B. "We got twenty-seven dollars in tips."

"Thank God," I said in my early Eve Arden deadpan. "Now Mother can have that operation."

"Very funny," Snookie said. "It's the most we've made in this dump so far."

"I'll quit my day job," I said, somewhat distractedly. I was peering over Snookie's shoulder, watching Louie clearing wineglasses off a table, slipping the stems between his long tanned fingers. On him, it was a sexually suggestive act.

Snookie moved in even closer, speaking in a hissy stage whisper.

"So this is it, huh?" It wasn't really a question.

"So this is what?"

"You know," Snookie crooned, all silly-schoolgirl smile and B&B breath.

"Sure," I said. "Why not?" I slipped an arm over Snookie's shoulder and fingered his curls. I peeked over Snookie's other shoulder at Louie, who was standing with his back to me. As if feeling my eyes on him, Louie looked up, catching sight of me in the mirrored wall. I tossed him a smile. Louie smiled, blushed a little, then returned to his work.

"Just look at him, Snooks," I said, still looking past Snookie at Louie's faded denim ass wiggling back and forth as he wiped off a tabletop. "Young and blond and pretty as all hell. What choice have I, really, but to" — I whispered into Snookie's ear — "pork the living day-lights out of him? I mean, it's practically my duty."

Snookie giggled in a fashion not entirely becoming to a grown man. He read me well enough to sense that, my attempts at bravado notwithstanding, should Louie re-fuse me, I'd probably drive my car over an embankment.

"He is lovely," Snookie agreed. "And speaking of blonds" — Snookie spoke through his teeth, as he was apt to do when he'd had a few drinks and was feeling catty and conspiratorial — "didja get a load of the big one at the back table?"

"Not really," I said. "No."

I lied. I had, indeed, gotten a load. I had, of course, noticed the couple seated at the far back corner table. In a room the size of Tom Sawyer's, a room where the evening's take is in direct proportion to the number of money-spending bodies in the room, I — and, really, any nightclub performer worth his salt — could take an accu-rate nose count of an audience during the last chorus of "Mack the Knife" ("Look out, Miss Lotte LenYA! twelve, thirteen") and never miss a beat ("Look out — ol' Mackie's — BACK! twenty-five, twenty-six"). I had taken due note of the big, vaguely Nordic-looking man, and the pretty (if rather bovine) young woman with him, who had arrived late, three songs into the second set, during the intro to "Unchained Melody."

I had made a point of waiting for the two to be seated before beginning the ballad.

"You're late," I said as Anne-Marie maneuvered them to the last available table. Anne-Marie was Sawyer's surliest waitress, a twenty-year-old would-be rock star with a tendency to dress herself to look like a Patti Smith album cover. "I hope you have a note from your mother." It's an old joke, but it got a laugh — it usually does.

I noticed that, during the "I need your love, God speed your love" part, the couple leaned in close together (as did Kathleen and Martha, a pair of lesbian lovers who sat in the same front table every Friday performance, and who considered "Unchained Melody" their song); and that the big blonde woman (who reminded me of Inger Stevens in *The Farmer's Daughter)* spent the entire evening clutching her escort's arm in a rather blatant gesture of defiant (if transparently insecure) possessiveness. Without the woman, the man would have been a shoo-in candidate for a casual flirtation, at the very least. With her, he was one-half of A Couple, and therefore, strictly verboten. It has always been my policy never to mess with couples. The duo at the back table were customers, potential fans, people I would chat with sooner or later if they didn't rush off, and if I could get past Snookie.

"Honey, you're slipping," Snookie whispered wetly. "This one is D.H.C. — direct from Hunk City."

I turned and gave the guy a quick once-over. Snookie was right. The man seemed to be quite a specimen indeed. Big and powerful-looking — a thick football-player's neck protruded from his button-down shirt collar, and outsized biceps strained the material of his long sleeves. His face was mostly in shadow, but from what I was able to distinguish, it seemed a nice enough face.

43

He seemed to be adding up a credit card bill. His girlfriend still had his right arm in a grip you couldn't have loosened with a crowbar, which seemed to be inhibiting his ability to write. Attractive, yes. The guy was undoubtedly attractive. But also undoubtedly attached — physically and otherwise — to the big babe at his right. Besides, I had other, if smaller, fish to fry.

"He's cute," I said finally.

"Cute?" Snookie said, a bit too loudly. "He's gorgeous and you know it."

"All right, he's gorgeous." I decided to concede the point. "He's also, I would venture to guess, terminally straight."

"Oh, I don't know," Snookie said. "Maybe they're just friends."

"Snooks," I said, "that lady's holding his arm so tight, I'll bet he's lost all sensation in his fingers."

"Honey," Snookie crooned through his teeth, "if I had that, I wouldn't let go, either."

"Well, I'll leave him to you." I spotted Louie heading toward the men's room, and decided the time was right to make my move. "Who knows? Maybe you can steal him away. That is, if you can ever pry the lady's fingers loose. Wish me luck."

I left before Snookie's boozy little brain was able to send the words "good luck" all the way to his lips, and managed to overtake Louie as he went down the narrow hall and headed him off as he was turning toward the lavatory. I moved in close and sandwiched Louie in between my body and the wall opposite the men's room door. I corralled the boy with my arms, the palms of my hands flat against the wall.

"You about ready to split?" I looked directly into Louie's pale blue eyes. We were almost exactly the same height — Louie was maybe a fraction of an inch shorter than I.

"Uh-huh." I noticed with some pleasure that Louie's lips never seemed to meet, but were always just slightly parted. It was one of the things that made him so child-like, and, to me, so very sexy. It was one of the things that made me think of Louie as a boy, although I was no more than three years his senior.

"Think you might like to come home with me?" The very thought of taking the boy home, the forming of those words with my lips, excited me; I felt myself beginning to crowd the crotch of my black Levi's.

Louie's eyes lowered for a portion of a second, then met mine.

I leaned in even closer, sliding my hands up the wall.

"Hm?" Our noses nearly touched.

"Uh-huh." Louie's little pink tongue darted across his perpetually parted lips. "Yes," he said, with as much finality as I'd ever heard him say anything.

Shit howdy! My heart Watusi'd in my chest. I smiled. Louie saw my smile and raised me one of his own. His teeth were the small, even teeth of a little boy.

"All right, then," I said. "Don't go 'way. I'm not quite through circulatin'." Then I kissed the kid softly on the tip of his cute little Joel Brechtschneider nose.

By the time I turned back to the room proper, the couple at the far table had already gone.

After tossing rather perfunctory greetings to the few straggling fan-clubbers, I tucked Louie under my arm and into my car. Louie lived within blocks of Sawyer's, and so did not drive; he had two roommates, which precluded our trysting at his place. I drove in relative silence, with only scattered late-night traffic sounds to dent the quiet — my car's AM radio had not worked in years. I sang, "I'd like to get to know you, yes, I would" softly to myself, and held Louie's soft, warm hand between gear shiftings. Snookie sat strangely quiet in the backseat.

Upon reaching Snookie's apartment, we discovered Snooks out cold, sprawled in an uncomfortable-looking position across the car seat. Louie reacted as if we had found a newly murdered corpse in the trunk. The blond boy was wide-eyed and — to my mind — somewhat overly concerned with the state of Snookie's health. I attempted with limited success to explain that Snookie, in fact, passed out in my backseat on a semiregular basis — this was hardly a Condition Red. I lifted Snookie fireman style and carried him into his apartment and into bed.

"Are you sure he's all right?" Louie asked, his brow pleated with concern.

"My dear," I replied, "Snooks is absolutely in the pink compared to how he's going to feel in the morning."

After removing Snookie's scuffed black loafers — damned if I was going to wrestle the clothes off him — I left him to his slumbers, snoring at an inhuman decibel level, and drove Louie up to my place.

Louie was as sweet a night's sex as I'd ever enjoyed.

While Billie Holiday filled my small one-bedroom apartment with smoky blues from the stereo, we kissed (Louie's mouth tasted sweet as apricots, and his agile little tongue played delightful games of tag-you're-it with mine), and made undulating waves in my queen-size waterbed. Louie was built small and solid, but with a soft layer of baby fat that I found endearing — it gave him a voluptuous, slightly overripe sort of look, like a sun-tanned Cupid. His all-over caramel color was broken by a startling milk white streak at the crotch; the boy's butt seemed nearly phosphorescent against the deep tan. The sight of my hand against that snowy posterior delighted me no end.

Louie was hung smaller than me — which pleased me, I'm afraid — but seemed perpetually tumescent. After coming twice in my mouth, rapid-fire, blam-blam, one after the other (it was the summer of '79, after all — we all swallowed it in those days), he showed no signs of waning. I envied Louie this unflagging, teenaged potency which I, twenty-two and dead tired after a full day's work and three sets at Sawyer's, could only look back upon with nostalgia.

Louie licked and sucked me with the sloppy enthusiasm of a kid with a Fudgesicle, murmuring softly between slurps (while I recited the Pledge of Allegiance over and over to myself, lest Louie's attentions bring me over the edge too quickly); then, seconds before I would have popped my cork, he released me.

"Do you want to?" he asked, turning up his pale, perfect bottom to me.

I wanted to.

I was as careful as my advanced state of excitement would allow. Louie moaned a soft continuo as I moved inside him, caressing his smooth sides and kneading his soft little rump. The wild animal sound Louie made as he shot yet again onto my recently laundered linens pushed me over the edge, and I clutched the boy hard against me, crying out loudly enough to incite my next-door neighbor to pound a testy tattoo upon our shared wall.

Later, Louie and I lay close against one another, despite the warmth of the night; Louie's head rested on my chest. I stroked him as far as I could reach.

"You're really wonderful," he said, his breath ruffling the sparse hair between my pecs. "Onstage and off," he added.

I grazed his beardless cheek with my fingertips.

"You're pretty wonderful yourself, Son."

We lay quiet; I felt sleep beginning to cover me like an animated blanket, starting at my toes and creeping slowly up to my ankles.

"You know what?" Louie whispered.

"What?"

"You're the first black man I've ever been with."

I felt myself tense as the old insecurity monsters came galloping across me like the Four Horsemen of the Neuroses. It bugged me that Louie had said that — had made a point, however small, of my blackness; and I wasn't sure why. Maybe I was suddenly afraid Louie was slumming, or experimenting, or that maybe this was National

48

Take-a-Negro-to-Bed Week. Or that maybe, just maybe, my being black was (for whatever reason) as important to Louie as his being blond and adorable was to me. I nearly said something mean and stupid, like "So what do you want — a certificate of merit from the N-double-A-C-P?" But I didn't.

What I finally did say was,

"Zat a fact? Well, it so happens that you're the first busboy I've ever been with."

Louie giggled, then kissed me on the ear; tickling me, making me giggle too. I could feel him — amazingly — hardening again, hot against my thigh.

What more could a guy ask for? He was soft and warm. Seemingly insatiable. And he'd stay the night.

It was during the fourth grade, the same year I fell so hard for Joel Brechtschneider *(mon beau garcon sans merci)*, that I sang in public for the first time. Oh, I'd sung in front of family members (to the radio mostly), and I'd been a member in good standing of the junior choir of the First New Ship of Zion Missionary Baptist Church since the age of four (though I'd never been awarded a solo: Sister Cecile Williams, the director of the choir, thought I was a smarty-pants — she told me so, and of course I was). But this was different.

It was Christmastime, and Miss Muskat's classroom was decorated with construction paper Santas and Rudolphs, hanging side by side with metallic cardboard cutouts of menorahs. On this particular December morning, our *Music Far and Near* books lay spread upon our desks, and Miss Muskat was leading the class in Christmas carols and Hanukkah songs. "Deck the Halls" alternated with "Oh Dreidl Dreidl Dreidl" — the population of Cinnamon Avenue School (and the neighborhood in which it sat) was in a period of transition, and was at that time almost perfectly divided into the encroaching Negroes and the steadily retreating Jews.

Anyway, at one point Miss Muskat asked if anyone knew any Christmas spirituals — *Music Far and Near* was sadly deficient in them. I raised my tiny, birdlike hand and volunteered that I knew "Rise Up, Shepherds, and Follow" by heart. Along with "How Shall I Send Thee," it was one of Clara's favorites. When Miss Muskat asked if I might like to share the song with the class, I saw the opportunity to impress my classmates (Joel, of course, in particular) in a positive way, using just about the only means at my disposal. I seized this opportunity with both hands.

I stood at my place, closed my eyes, and sang (in my best Julie Andrews tones), "There's a star in the east on Christmas morn, Rise up, shepherds, and follow."

When I finished, I opened my eyes to find Miss Muskat's mouth agape, her hand atremble against her throat. And was that a tear swelling against the corner of her eye, threatening to streak her somewhat overstated mascara?

"Thank you, Johnnie Ray," she nearly whispered. "That was very nice."

In a roomful of thirty-some-odd fourth graders, you could have heard chalk dust hit the floor. Every eye in class was on me. To my pleasure, even Joel seemed impressed. I was just savoring this first tiny taste of celebrity, when I heard Teddy Castleman whisper behind me (just loud enough for me to hear),

"Even *sings* like a girl."

Louie and I slept late, and made love immediately upon waking. I flipped over on my belly, looked over my shoulder as seductively as I could first thing in the morning, and said, "Do you want to?"

Louie wanted to.

Afterward, I made scrambled eggs and coffee. Louie insisted upon washing the dishes. "Talking Book" was on the stereo and Louie was barefoot and wearing my purple "Hendrix is God" t-shirt, elbow-deep in dishwater, and I took the wildest notion to throw my arms around the boy and beg him to stay with me forever and ever and we'll never be lonely anymore.

One thing about me — I'm no good at separating love and sex. One night of even pleasant sex with a man, and damned if I can't look into his eyes and see the midnight sun. Still, if one can't fall in love, albeit briefly, with a beautiful sweet boy who does the breakfast dishes, then what's it all about, Alfie?

So I drove Louie home — already wondering if I should ask him back that night — and stopped off in the Village. And it was in the oldies section of the Tower Records in Westwood Village that I actually met Keith.

I was thumbing through the moldy oldies, as I did periodically in my never-ending search for new material. As I've mentioned before, there were a certain number of people who were coming to see me at Sawyer's every single week, sometimes both nights.

I'll never forget, Donna Summer was playing at a bone-crushing decibel level throughout the store. *Oooh, I feel love I feel love I feel love I feeeeeel love.* A song I hated with every fiber of my being. The incessant mechanical *boom boom boom* was nearly enough to send me screaming from the store. Funny thing, because now, I can't hear that goddamn song without thinking of Keith.

Anyway, I had picked up this old Rick Nelson album, and was asking myself if I really wanted to shell out $15.99 for an album I'd probably play all of once, just because the cover photo was so cool, when I noticed this big blond animal who had just entered the store, made a beeline for the oldies, and was standing to my left.

A real brick w.c., if you get my drift.

Keeping my head turned ever so slightly to the left, using the peripheral vision as much as possible — not wanting to appear too obvious — I gave the big guy a quick once-over. He was a pretty cat. A solid 8 on the Johnnie Ray Rousseau 10-scale, where Tab Hunter in *Damn Yankees* is a 9. *Pas mal du tout,* as my miscegenation-prone French forebears might have said.

He reminded me of the young Marlon Brando, circa 1954. There was something decidedly Kowalski-esque about his big-muscled body, his wide, somewhat bow-legged stance, the short honey blond hair pushed straight back off his face. Which is not to say he *looked* like Brando, exactly.

True, he did have that sloping, rather Neanderthal brow, and a nose that may, or may not have been broken

53

once or twice. And a Brando-ish sort of mouth — full, almost pouty, with the upper lip taking just the slightest precedence over the lower. It wasn't a mouth that begged to be kissed; but it seemed open to persuasion. Mostly, though, it was the guy's build that made me think of Brando. A build which, if you had to describe it in one word, that word would have to be "thick." Thick neck, thick chest, thick legs. (He was pretty thick elsewhere, too — thick-headed, among other things — but, of course, I wasn't to find that out until sometime later.) It wasn't difficult to imagine him with a hot, smoking, midfifties model Harley between his thighs. The thought caused an immediate rise in the old hunk-ometer.

The guy seemed to have started at the very beginning of the A's and was quickly and methodically picking up each album, quickly scanning the selection list and re-turning it to the bin. I could hardly help but notice the softball-sized biceps that bulged as the big guy's arm went up and down. I thought, Wow.

Now, I might as well confess here and now that I have always appreciated a man with a certain amount of solid muscle mass. I mean, I really dig the barbell boys. For me, there's no such thing as too much muscle. As a child, I never missed a Hercules movie on television. There I'd sit, not three feet from the old RCA Victor 21-inch, mouth hanging on its hinges, staring, with what can only be termed fascination, at Steve Reeves's monu-mental man-tits bouncing up and down as he walked. Buh-bump, buh-bump, buh-bump. Absolutely hypnotic. Not surprising that I'm still an absolute sucker for a pretty pair of pectorialis majorii. I'll forgive a weakish chin or a nose with a direction of its own for a really nice chest.

So, naturally, when I noticed this big blond standing there beside the oldies-but-goodies bins, not five feet away from me — and Ray Charles could have seen the cat's muscles had muscles — well, let it suffice to say that my curiosity, at least, was immediately aroused.

My senior year in high school, I was a classic 97-pound weakling. Actually, I was 96 pounds. A Charles Atlas "before" picture if ever there was one. And no great shakes as an athlete, as I've mentioned. While brother David earned every varsity letter imaginable, I set new school records in the Nerd Olympics. My total ineptitude at any and all athletic endeavors was the stuff of legend. When it came time to choose up sides for team sports, I made sure to bring a book. A brand-new softball position was created for me by some helpful classmates — Far, Far Right Field. As in, if you can recognize the batter, you're too close.

Then, my senior year, the Powers that Were in my high school deigned to augment the boys' physical education program with a weight-training class. It changed my life. The clouds of my despair parted and the golden sunshine of Hope shone through. Angel choirs sang power chords from somewhere offscreen. I felt that my prayers had finally been heard and answered; for here was a miracle no less than Max Von Sydow making Sal Mineo take up his bed and walk in *The Greatest Story Ever Told*. Because I would finally, in my last year of public school, be spared the daily degradations of team sports. And because the weight-training class was led by the most beautiful man I had ever seen — Coach Newcomb.

Dick Newcomb was a part-time ski instructor. He had a face like Buster Crabbe circa 1936, and a body like Steve Reeves in *Hercules Unchained*. A Michelangelo marble with a tan. The sight of Coach Newcomb in his uniform of white t-shirt and stretch shorts inspired me to body-building, and then some. I whacked myself raw to fantasies in which Coach's magnificence was mine to explore; in which he held me fast between his massive thighs; in which his pale blue eyes stared into mine, and he said, "You're a beautiful boy, Johnnie Ray — let no one tell you differently." Mental pictures of the straps of Coach's jock (quite discernible through the fabric of his shorts) interrupted me while I puzzled over an equation in Algebra II/Trig — and erections arrived without invitation. And in P.E., I threw myself into bench presses and barbell curls with a fervor bordering on mania.

And as if the opportunity to spend one rapturous hour per day in the same weight room with Coach — to watch him walk, to feel the occasional touch of his big, beefy hand while I strained at the leg press machine — were not enough (and it would have been), to my surprise and delight, my workouts soon began to show results. Biceps raised their dual heads where once there had been none. The embarrassing concavity of my rib cage began to fill itself in. Soon, it was no longer possible to count my ribs from fifty paces. My heart leapt within my rapidly improving chest.

And I wondered why I had never thought of it before — if I could never actually *be* athletic, then, by golly, I'd at least *look* athletic. And when Coach Newcomb slapped me on the back and said, "Seein' some real improvement there, Rousseau," it was all I could do to keep my gym shorts dry.

Once, I saw Coach emerge from his office to break up a locker room towel fight, wearing only his tiny white shorts. I covered a hair-trigger erection with my towel in the very nick of time. Coach's big, long-toed feet were bare, the chest I'd longed to view was suddenly visible to me; and he was, it seemed, even more splendid in the flesh than in my wild teenaged imaginings. After quelling the disturbance, Coach turned to me (I, of course, was in no way involved in the fracas) and said, "How's it goin', Rousseau." And he was gone.

The sight of Coach so nearly nude fueled my masturbatory fantasies through my freshman year in college.

I occasionally considered confessing my feelings to Coach. I composed letter after letter ("Oh, how I do love you! Oh, how my heart and mind are filled with you!") and burned them one by one. I imagined striding into Coach's office, closing the door behind me, and saying, "I love you. There, I've said it."

The closest I ever came to actually confessing my love to Coach Newcomb (by midsemester, I was calling it love) was to give him a Christmas card. I briefly considered actually buying him a gift, but decided that might be too much, might put the Coach off. He was one of the few people on earth who treated me like a regular guy, and I feared I might jeopardize my status by doing something he might consider unseemly. Besides, what could I give him? Socks? Monogrammed hankies? Diamonds? The moon? My throbbing sixteen-year-old heart and the small but ever-more-wiry body that housed it?

In the end, I just gave him the card. I bought one especially for him (I considered the ten-to-a-box Baby-Jesus-with-glitter-on-the-halo cards Clara bought quite inappropriate); it was large but simple, pure white with PEACE in gold Old English script. In the blank inside of the card I wrote, "Merry Christmas, Dick (oh, how I agonized over the decision to call him Dick instead of Coach). Your friend (another big decision), Johnnie Ray Rousseau."

I waited until the locker room was nearly cleared before I went to Coach's office, the card hidden in my moist armpit, beneath my Levi's jacket. My heart pulsed somewhere behind my Adam's apple as I held out the card and said, "Merry Christmas, Coach." (The inside of a Christmas card was one thing — calling him Dick right out loud was another.) Coach walked around his desk. You could have reheated leftovers in the warmth of his smile.

"Thank you, Rousseau," he said. He accepted the card, and with his other hand he squeezed my shoulder. He was so big, so very strong, and I wanted so very much to throw my arms around his impossibly narrow waist and cry out, "I love you." Instead, I managed to rasp something approximating "You're welcome," then turned and floated from the room.

He hadn't had to smile, you know. He hadn't had to get up and walk over to me and touch me. He might well have said, "Thanks, just put it on the desk," hardly looking up at all; leaving me standing there like the silly love-battered teenager I was, completely at a loss for a graceful exit.

But he didn't, God love him.

For that, for encouraging wimpy little me (intentionally and otherwise), and for giving me the one and only "A" I ever (in twelve years of school) received in P.E., I would like to take this opportunity to say,

"Good night, Coach Newcomb — wherever you are."

59

Meanwhile, back at the oldies-but-goodies section:

Feigning great interest in the "Oldies — Various Artists" collections to his far right, I walked — not too quickly — around the big guy, closer than was absolutely necessary, but not so close as to arouse undue suspicion. I figured him to be about six-one, maybe six-two — I came right up to the nape of the man's neck. Halfway around the guy, I got a noseful of his smell — clean sweat and Aramis. It was all I could do not to throw caution to the wind and bury my face in the guy's neck.

Once around to the man's left side, I picked up *Murray the K's 1962 Golden Gassers* — which I already owned — and pretended to be engrossed in the liner notes, while watching the big guy out of the corner of my eye. He was wearing basic gray sweats and black high-top basketball shoes, and a very old t-shirt, off-white and threadbare and doing an admirable job of revealing more than it hid. The guy's chest was like a white cotton shelf. His back was so broad you could show movies on it. Maybe it was the Brando resemblance, but I had an immediate fantasy of ripping that t-shirt right off that back.

Hey, Stellaaaaa!!!!

Just as my stream of thought began to flow toward the decidedly randy, the big guy turned and spoke to me.

"Excuse me."

I momentarily panicked. My heart began beating Ringo's drum solo from *Abbey Road* with the sudden irrational notion that this guy had somehow read my mind, knew what kinds of thoughts I'd been thinking about him, and was about to beat me to a smooth paste right there in the oldies-but-goodies section. I looked up into the guy's face, which was (to my great relief) pleasant, smiling, and familiar.

It was him: Mr. Far-Back-Table-in-the-Shadows himself. And might I add that he was looking perfectly edible by the light of day. He wasn't handsome exactly, what with the pronounced eyebrow ridge, somewhat irregular nose, and what could either be interpreted as a naturally high brow or a retreating hairline. Not *handsome* handsome, but sexy, you know?

"You're a singer, aren't you?" His voice was a soft, husky upper baritone. A boudoir voice if I'd ever heard one.

"Guilty."

"I saw you last night," he said. "You're very good." He smiled.

It was some kinda smile. A major smile of this or any season. A smile so bright you could read by it. So warm you could grow orchids by the glow of it. So wide you can't get around it. He was all the way handsome when he smiled.

"Thank you," I said, ever the conversationalist.

"Keith Keller," he said, extending his big right hand.

"Johnnie Ray Rousseau." I accepted his hand. His skin was soft (though I could feel the tiny hard buttons of flesh beneath his fingers — weight lifter's calluses), and

61

cool to my touch. And, corny as it sounds, as that big hand enveloped mine, a funny little quiver went through me. I don't mean zing went the strings of my heart or anything; but a very definite quiver.

I looked up into Keith Keller's smallish pale hazel eyes. (Gee whiz, as Carla Thomas once said, look at his eyes!) Was that possibly flirtation I saw sparkling in those eyes? Could that handclasp have been just a tiny bit longer in duration than was absolutely necessary? Was there something significant in the brief squeeze Keith gave my hand just before releasing it? Was it possible that Paul McCartney really *was* dead, and that silly-love-song person merely an imposter?

"You know what?" Keith said before I could ask myself any more stupid questions.

"What?"

"I'll bet you can help me."

Help you off with your pants, big fella?

Cut it out, Johnnie.

"Really?"

"I'm looking for a song. My girlfriend, Betsy, she was with me last night——"

"Oh, yes." The fat broad with the kung-fu grip. "I remember."

"Anyway, she heard this song on KRTH — y'know, the oldies station — it's called 'The Bells.' Have you heard of it?"

"Heard of it? I've been known to perform it." Actually, I hadn't done the tune in over a year, but this was no time for irrelevant details.

"You do? I don't suppose you've recorded it."

"Nope. Can't say as I have. But I can tell you who has."

"That'd be great. I'd really like to get it for Betsy." I found I experienced an involuntary abdominal spasm at every mention of this Betsy person. "She really wants it."

"Well, you've come to the right place. Come on." I led him across the store to the Rock and Pop "N" section, and pulled out Laura Nyro's *Gonna Take a Miracle*, presenting it to Keith with a little wrist flourish. "Voila."

"Thank you," he said, smiling again. A long, shallow dimple indented his left cheek. I picked up an old Van Morrison tune on my mind's radio: *I'm in heaven, I'm in heaven, I'm in heaven when you smile*.

"Now, that's not the original version," I quite unnecessarily explained. "The original is out of print. Nyro's version is the best you can do these days." I have this tendency to spout trivia when nothing else comes to mind. "Neither version, however, is as good as mine," I added.

"Really?" he said through a small chuckle. I found I could amuse him easily. I found I liked it. "I'd like to hear it."

"Well, you — you and your girlfriend, that is — you'll just have to come back to Sawyer's sometime."

"When are you there next?"

"Tonight."

"Great. I'll be there."

"You what?"

"I said I'll be there."

"You're kidding."

"Why should I be kidding? You'll do the song?"

"Sure." I'd have done a Carmen Miranda medley with fruit salad in my hair if that's what he wanted to hear.

"Then I'll be there. Okay?"

"Okay." Damn right okay.

"See you tonight, then." He offered his hand again, and I took it. I didn't really want to return it, but I could see that I was going to have to. And I got that damn quiver again. When I finally gave the big guy his hand back, it occurred to me that he didn't seem in any big hurry to take it.

Back off, Johnnie, I told myself. He's straight, Johnnie, I told myself, as I watched his wide sweatpantsed behind and impossibly broad back disappearing down the aisle. He's straight, goddammit, I told myself.

I think.

When Keith didn't show up by the second set, I pretty much gave up on him. I decided he'd been jiving me, and I resolved to get on with my life. I'd taken "The Bells" out of mothballs and shoved it into the first set without giving Snookie any good reason why; then, when the number came up, I turned back to Snooks and said never mind. He gave me a quizzical look, but eighty-sixed the song anyway.

It was a good house. The place was full nearly to the walls and the audience smiled, patted their feet, and snapped their fingers on the off beats as if choreographed ahead of time by Twyla Tharp. Louie and I had been swapping intimate smiles all evening; I was pretty sure I'd ask the kid home again. But Keith's absence threw me. I don't think the audience could tell — this was no amateur they were dealing with, after all — but Snookie could. He was sensitive as the princess and the pea when it came to my moods.

Between sets, Snookie cornered me.

"What's with you tonight, Honey?"

"I'm sure I don't know what you mean," I lied.

"All right, then don't talk to me. Who am I, anyway? Only your best friend."

"Snookie, please don't go getting Jewish on me, okay?"

"It's a man, isn't it." It wasn't a question. "Louie?"

"Snooks, I told you, Louie was better than fine." And I had told him. Now, I'm not the kiss-and-tell type, as a rule. Except, of course, with Snookie. The sound check had been a total loss until he had heard all the gory details of my previous evening. I had pointedly neglected to mention my meeting Keith Keller in the oldies section of Tower Records and my subsequent lusting for said hunk.

"Then, what?" Snookie was beginning to whine. I hated it when Snookie whined.

"I'm all right, Ma," I said with as much conviction as I could manage. I don't think he bought it, but he let it go. He was right, of course. Keith Keller's no-show was throwing me off, and I didn't like the feel of it. It was symptomatic of a silly schoolgirl crush, and I have never been so dense as to miss the basic futility of developing a crush on a man with a girlfriend. Even if the man was a four-star looker and awfully chummy to boot. I determined to wash this particular man right out of my hair, pronto. Please pass the Prell.

So, of course, when Keith finally did arrive, three songs into the second set, during the intro to "Unchained Melody," I nearly pulled a muscle in my face trying not to grin.

"Late again," I said into the mike as Anne-Marie led Keith — sans femme, I noticed — to the same far back table he had occupied the night before.

"Yeah, but this time I have a note."

I turned back to Snookie, grinning like a jack-o'-lantern.

"'Bells.'"

Snookie gave me his you-never-fooled-me-for-a-minute Jewish-mother look. Bobo twanged a bass string and rolled his eyes heavenward.

"Just play the song," I said.

And who could blame me if I sang the whole number to the far back table?

After the set, I threw aside all pretense of circulating the crowd, making a rather obvious beeline to the back table where Keith sat waiting, very much alone, his big body testing the limits of a pale pink button-down shirt.

"Glad you could make it," I said, straddling a chair and doing my level best to appear nonchalant through the growing desire to suck on Keith's lower lip. Easy, boy; down, boy.

"Sorry I was late," he said. "Small domestic problem."

"Your girlfriend? Betsy, wasn't it?" Look at me — Mr. Friendly Concern himself.

"Yeah." He combed a hand through his hair. Biceps threatened the seams of his shirt.

"Gee, I'm sorry to hear that." I hoped my nose wasn't growing noticeably.

"Thanks." He smiled a small, wry half-smile. Even that was sexy. I needed some air. "Actually, I think this relationship is on its last leg, anyway. You know how it is."

"Sure." I know how *what* is? Having a big, blonde Brunhilde of a girlfriend? Having a relationship? Having a relationship on its last leg? I knew how none of the above was. Except for an abortive two-week shack-up with Zaz, this rather kinky alto sax player (remember?), when I was nineteen, my experience with long-term, romantic relationships was nil.

"What say we change the subject, okay? Can I buy you a drink?"

Boy, where had I heard that opening before?

"Thanks, I'm not much for alcohol. I could use some food, though."

"Okay, then; could I buy you a late dinner — or an early breakfast — or something?"

"Well, I was just going over to Cafe Santa Monica for some steak and eggs." Until I said that, I was really planning to take Louie home and remove his clothing with my teeth. The steak-and-eggs idea just sprang full-grown, like Athena, from the top of my head.

"Like some company?"

I was at a loss for a tasteful way to express just how much I'd like some of his company, and probably would have said something embarrassing, had Snookie not appeared, seemingly out of the none-too-thin air, leaning over my back and extending his hand to Keith.

"Well, good evening," Snookie crooned, gushing like an opened fire hydrant. "I'm Sid Rothenberg; keyboards and musical director."

"Good evening." As Keith took Snookie's hand, I couldn't help checking to see if he held Snooks's hand as long as he held mine. I decided he hadn't.

"Snookie, this is Keith Keller," I said, looking up at Snooks with a glance that said, Back off, Buddy, or I'll break your collarbone. Snookie read me loud and clear.

"Excuse me" — Snookie took me by the arm and addressed Keith in his best Roz Russell — "might I borrow the diva for just a minute? Business, you know."

Snookie herded me toward the opposite end of the room.

"Well, well, my dear, this is definitely your week, isn't it?"

"I'm afraid I don't know what you mean," I lied.

"Oh, come on, Honey—"

"Okay, you got me. But I just don't know, Snooks."

"You don't know what?"

"I'm still not sure he isn't straight. I mean, he's got this girlfriend."

"Are you kidding? The way he looks at you?"

My heart did the splits.

"You noticed it too?"

"From across the room."

I turned and grabbed a quick glance at Keith. Our eyes met and exchanged warm greetings. He smiled. Maybe I was right. Maybe there *was* yes-yes in those pretty little hazel eyes.

"I mean, really," Snookie said, "some people do have all the luck. First little Louie and now this." He leaned in and whispered, "Call me first thing in the morning — I want the details. And your leftovers. But that's not why I stole you away. There's somebody who wants to meet you. She's a little strange" — he lowered his voice — "but be nice to her. She says she has some TV connections, and she may be of some help. So smile pretty and turn on the charm."

Snookie led me to a table where sat a small dishwater blonde woman. She could have been thirty. Or forty. She was wearing an undistinguished beige dress barely containing a set of bazooms God had obviously meant for a much larger woman. She smiled from one end of the room to the other. I hadn't noticed her during the sets — but then, my mind had been on other things.

"Johnnie Ray Rousseau," Snookie said, "this is Marsha Goldman."

"Howdaya do?" the woman greeted in a rather nasal voice laced with a New York accent. She stood, offering a tiny, manicured hand. She must have been all of four-eleven in spike heels.

"How do you do," I replied, wondering just who this little dame might fancy herself to be.

"Miss Goldman is with the Sloane Agency," Snookie explained, as if in answer.

"The third-largest entertainment PR firm in the country," Marsha injected. "Or is it fourth? Anyway, I simply adore your work, Mr. Rousseau—"

"Johnnie," I offered, hoping I hadn't been snatched from the company of the divine Mr. K just to hear some sawed-off Sue Mengers tell me she simply adored my work.

"Johnnie," Marsha intoned slowly, as if trying it on for size and deciding whether or not I should change it. "Anyway, Johnnie, I realize at this stage of your career you really have no use for a firm of the size of Sloane; however, I personally do know some rather influential people in this business" — she paused for dramatic effect — "and I'd really love to help you if I possibly can. You are a very talented young man; I'd just love to someday be able to say I helped you along. It's the manager in me. Mind if I smoke?" she asked, firing up a lavender cigarette with flowers printed around the filter end.

"Not at all," I lied. Manager, huh?

"Anyway, I suppose Sidney told you that I have some connections with the Griffin show."

Sidney? I glanced at Snookie, who gave me a "Now, be good" look in return.

71

"Well," Marsha continued, "I think it might be a very good thing for you; you'd go over big. I called a friend of mine at the show to see if he might get here for your second or third set, but, unfortunately, as is so often the case with television people, he was tied up and couldn't make it. But, not to worry: he promised he'd come to see you in the very near future, and I intend to get him here if I have to hog-tie him."

I wasn't at all sure whether or not the little lady was talking through her hat. I'd had enough professional bullshitters promise me superstardom on the rocks that I was immediately skeptical of anyone who claimed to have "connections."

"You know, Miss Goldman—"

"Marsha," she insisted.

"Marsha. You know, I'm not exactly in the market for a manager."

"Oh, I know, I know. Sidney's already told me he's managed you so far, and I'm sure he's done a fine job. But, let's face it, kids: on your own you've gotten this" — she made a gesture with her cigarette hand that took in Tom Sawyer's in all its questionable glory — "I can get you the Griffin show."

Says you, I thought.

"You're not convinced," she observed, correctly. "I understand. Why should you be? Whaddaya know from me? Look — let's just do this: you just see whether or not I can do anything for you. And if I can, then we'll talk about deals and contracts and my ten percent. Just like, you should pardon the expression, a drug deal. The first one's free. How 'bout it? Have we got a deal?"

What did I have to lose?

"Deal." I shook Marsha's tiny (if surprisingly strong) hand. "I appreciate your interest in me."

72

"You're talent, Johnnie," Marsha said, as if disclosing a secret. "I like talent. Besides, I think you and I can make some money together. I'm sorry tonight didn't work out, but you know how it is."

"Uh-huh." I certainly was getting a lot of credit for knowing how it was.

"Anyway, I have your number and Sidney has mine. We'll keep in touch. So nice to meet you, Johnnie," Marsha said, gearing up to leave. "Well, g'night all!"

"I'll walk you to your car," Snookie offered.

"Thank you, Sidney; you know a girl can't be any too careful these days..." And they were gone, a flurry of words in their wake.

I ripped into my steak and eggs with more than my wonted postperformance gusto. Keith's close physical proximity, so large and lovely across the booth from me, raised my metabolic rate like two hours of aerobics. He sipped a Sanka. We made small talk.

"You must be very excited," he said. Matter of fact, I was.

"What about?"

"About Marsha Goldman and the TV show and all."

"Oh, that. No, not really. This town is chock-full of people who fancy themselves managers; almost as many as fancy themselves performers. If I had a dime for every bozo who's sashayed up to me after a show handing me some line about 'connections in this business,' I could quit my day job. I doubt we'll ever hear from the diminutive Miss Goldman again."

"Do I detect a trace of cynicism in your voice?"

"No, not cynicism exactly. Just the working knowledge that show business is where bullshit was invented. Probably by someone a lot like Marsha Goldman."

I chomped off a bite of whole wheat toast.

"Have you always wanted to be a singer?" Keith asked.

"Oh my, yes — a singer, a dancer, a movie star, a show business institution. That sort of thing. Ever since I was so high."

"No, really."

"Yes. Really. You've heard of stage mothers — I was a stage child. I used to beg my mother to push me into show business. When they asked us in school what we wanted to be when we grew up, among all those firemen and ballerinas and nurses and astronauts, I was the only kid in the entire third grade who wanted to be a legend." He laughed. I liked it. "My first real ambition was to be a Mouseketeer. I figured, how long could Cubby O'Brien last? I used to study those shows; I'd memorize all the songs and dances. I still know them. Well, then I told my mother about it. Clara said to me, 'Boy, ain't no colored Mouseketeers.' Clara is a woman cursed with limited vision. She didn't even bother to tell me I was watching five-year-old reruns. But enough about me — for a few minutes, anyway. What about you? What did you want to be?"

"A football star," he answered, eyes lowered in a boyish gesture of embarrassment.

"So what's so outlandish? Now, I don't know from football, but you sure look like quarterback or halfback or something-back material to me."

"I was a runningback at St. Fletcher's in Minnesota."

"So, why didn't you go pro?"

"Because I was a *lousy* runningback at St. Fletcher's in Minnesota."

"No you weren't."

"Yes," he insisted, "I was. I was six feet two and two-twenty, and at St. Fletcher's that was enough. Ability was preferred but not really necessary. I spent two years wearing a groove in the bench. And my illustrious

75

football career ended at graduation." He smiled the sort of smile people tend to wear when discussing dreams bludgeoned to death with the heavy, blunt object of Reality.

I had the sudden impulse to touch Keith's cheek, oh-so-softly, with my fingertips and say something sexy but supportive, something Ann Sheridan might say, like, "Don't worry big fella — you can cross my line of scrimmage anytime." What I said was,

"You seem to have kept in good shape since college." I thought that was an appropriate remark; vaguely complimentary but much less obvious than, say, "Jiminy Christmas, are you ever a hunk."

"Thanks. I try to keep in shape."

In shape, he says. In shape. Michelangelo's *David* should be in such shape.

"I try to get to the gym three times a week," he continued. "I work out at World Gym."

"Work out with the big boys, do we? I'm impressed."

"Oh, yeah. Arnold Schwartzenegger actually spoke to me last week. He looked right at me and said, 'You finish vit dose dumbbells?' Big guy. Makes me look like a ballerina. You look like you work out some yourself."

I was so glad he'd noticed.

"Oh, nothing serious. Just twenty-five minutes of Nautilus three times a week."

"Seems to do the job," he said, smiling a dangerous smile.

I was becoming decidedly warm under the collar. I drew a ragged breath, and said,

"So — what do you, um ... do? Like for a living?"

"I'm in banking. I manage the downtown regional branch of First California. I make sure everything at the branch runs as smoothly as possible, and that all the money we start out with at nine o'clock is accounted for at five o'clock. Hardly a barrel of laughs, but it pays the bills. Exciting, huh?"

"Hey, I'm a secretary myself. I slave over a hot typewriter by day, so that I may sing my way into the hearts of hundreds at night."

"You're kidding?"

"Believe me, being a secretary is no joke."

"Wow. It's hard to believe that someone with your talent has to type for a living."

"Funny, that's what I keep saying at work."

"Well, at least you have the satisfaction of knowing you're going to be a household word someday."

"Sure," I said, "like 'spatula.' Right now, I'm just a secretary with a rather unusual nightlife. But, hey, that's showbiz. Or so they tell me."

There was a momentary lull in the conversation, during which I attacked my breakfast with renewed fervor. I could feel Keith watching in what could easily pass for fascination as I mopped up egg yolk with a corner of toast. I looked up quickly, catching him in the act of watching me. He just smiled.

What was the story on this dude, I wondered. I could swear the guy wanted me. I could practically smell it on his breath. And yet, there was Betsy, Miss Edelweiss of 1978. Could it be that she was just a front? Could it be he was pulling a fast one on her? Or maybe our fairhaired boy was a switch-hitter. Or maybe I was dead-ass wrong and he was just a friendly Joe with an affinity for truly fine pop vocals. After all (a sudden insecure inner voice decided to ask), what would this six-foot Aryan hunk want with the likes of me? What gives here, anyway?

I decided to find out.

"May I ask you a personal question?" I asked.

Keith leaned back in the booth, crossing his beefy arms.

"Ask."

"How would you describe your relationship with Betsy?"

He didn't miss a beat.

"How would you describe your relationship with the busboy at Tom Sawyer's?"

Touché.

I decided to step back a couple of paces and try another angle.

"Then I assume you know I'm gay."

"You know," he said, "I've never really liked that term — gay. I think we've rendered a perfectly good word useless."

"Don't be evasive."

"Well, you know, I usually don't like to take that kind of thing for granted. However, after your show last night, when I couldn't help but notice you kissing the busboy, your pianist, and half the audience, I rather assumed..." He shrugged.

"And it doesn't bother you — my being gay, I mean."

"Why should it bother me?"

This Keith Keller was proving himself a master of the Side Step. I was in no mood to dance.

"And are *you* gay?"

"Hm." He paused. He looked up at the ceiling like a schoolboy searching for the correct spelling of the word "neighbor." "Nope," he said finally.

"You're sure?"

"Sure."

"Then are you bisexual?"

"You have this thing about labels, don't you?"

It was rather like playing Ping-Pong with a pimento-stuffed olive.

I decided to go for a slam shot.

"Look here — are you after my black ass, or what?"

He looked not the least taken aback. One nearly invisible eyebrow lifted. The smile widened. He paused a moment before answering.

"Why, yes. Matter of fact, I am."

Oh, my ears and whiskers! He *was* after my black ass. My heart rate and breathing instantly accelerated to the point where I was afraid I might hyperventilate and faint dead away, falling facefirst into my egg-yolk-encrusted plate.

"But what about your girlfriend?" I managed to gasp.

"Oh, I don't think she's after your black ass," he replied with a little smile.

"You know what I mean." This was no time to toy with me.

"Besides," he continued, "far as I can see, you're not black at all — you're brown."

"Keith."

"Approximately the color of coffee with Coffeemate, I'd say."

"Keith!"

"Yes?" Angelic choirboy look.

I spoke as quietly and calmly as I could under the circumstances.

"You have this girlfriend."

"Oh, at least one."

"And you have not thirty seconds ago admitted to wanting my, shall we say, *derriere noir.*"

"*Oui.*"

"Then I suppose it's safe to assume that you are bisexual."

79

He shrugged.

"Let's just say that I've always enjoyed having my cake and, um, eating it, too. So to speak. Or, as James Dean once put it, 'I'm certainly not going through life with one hand tied behind my back.'"

Hm.

"You look skeptical."

That's because I *was* skeptical. Much as I hated to admit it, even to myself, I couldn't shake the nagging notion that any man who called himself a bisexual was actually just a garden variety homosexual afraid of going the whole hog. A person not entirely honest or at ease with himself or the world at large. A perennial straddler of the fence. It was a popular misconception at the time. I was young. What did I know? I kept it to myself.

"It's just that you're my first real live bisexual. I mean, I've read about them and all, but everybody I've ever known has either been straight or gay. You know — like that old song — 'Gotta Be This or That.'"

"Not me. I'm six of one and half a dozen of the other." He smiled at his own joke. "It's really very simple, Johnnie Ray. I find women beautiful. And I find men beautiful. I like sex with women, and I like it with men. I have also loved a few people in twenty-five years of life. Some of these people have been women and some of them have been men. I've never seen any reason to question it. And, until pushed up against the wall by pop singers in coffee shops, I see no good reason to call myself anything. I'm just me."

"How nice for you," I said. And, though it probably came out sounding snotty and facetious, I meant it. I have always wished I were nearer the center of the Kinsey scale (1 through 6, where 1 is totally and completely heterosexual and 6 is full-on faggot flambé. I'm about 5.7

— I masturbated with a *Playboy* centerfold in one hand once in high school). I mean, whether or not bisexuality (as Woody Allen once asserted) truly affords one twice the chances for a date on Saturday night, how could it not make life more interesting by roughly fifty percent? If nothing else, I would imagine, there is probably always something nice to look at. Still, one more thing bothered me.

"May I ask you a personal question?"

"Another one?"

"You don't have to answer it."

"Damn right I don't. Go ahead."

"Does your girlfriend know? About the men, I mean."

"Betsy? What's for her to know? We're not engaged or anything. We're not even pinned. And, as I've mentioned, we seem to be on the rocks. Besides, I don't talk to her about the other women. Why tell her about the men?" He leaned in closer. "Could we talk about something else now?"

"Like what?"

"Like the part about my being after your *derriere noir*. Like you've got the prettiest almond-shaped eyes I've ever seen. Like the constant erection I have maintained just watching you eat your toast."

He smiled a boyishly mischievous smile.

I signaled for the check.

We were scarcely in the door before we were all over each other like (as Clara might have said) white on rice. We went at one another like magnet and steel. Like winos at a bottle of Thunderbird. Like a starving man at a Fatburger.

 Oh, my word, how does one adequately describe a kiss? The taste, the feeling, the overall bodily effect.

Could I make you understand if I said that, if I live to be a thousand years old, I will never forget the taste of that kiss? That it was like tangerines — cool and juicy and just slightly sour? That Keith kissed like he'd invented it? That he kissed like Springsteen sings? That his kiss was better than some men's fucks?

Would it help if I explained that the first time Keith's big weight-lifter arms encircled and held me, and his mouth connected with mine, I trembled like someone had poured a tumbler of iced tea down my shirt; my stomach knotted so violently that I was seriously afraid I might lose my steak and eggs; and I got so hard so fast that the pain was nearly unbearable?

I could say it with song. I could have Phil and Don pop in and croon a few bars of "I never knew what I missed till I kissed ya."

Betty Everett might be persuaded to do one more chorus of "The Shoop Shoop Song" (also known as "It's in His Kiss").

Would poetry do it?

83

Say I'm weary
Say I'm sad
Say that health and wealth have missed me.
Say I'm growing mold—
But add,
Keith kissed me.

How about scripture?

"Let him kiss me with the kisses of his mouth: for thy love is better than wine."

That, believe it or not, is from the Bible. Yes, the Bible. Song of Solomon, chapter 1, verse 2. The Song of Solomon is this teeny-tiny little book just right of center in the King James version. Basically a love poem in dialogue, the Song of Solomon is decidedly short on thou shalt nots, and just chock-full of things like "his fruit was sweet to my taste" and "thy two breasts are like two young roes that are twins." As you can well imagine, the Song of Solomon is treated with criminal neglect by Sunday school teachers the world over; who, no doubt, pray daily that their students will never think to ask about that funny little book wedged between Ecclesiastes and Isaiah. "Roes" are young deer, by the way.

Considering just how racy this little book of the Bible can get, it comes as something of a surprise (to me, at least) that the Church Fathers snuck it into the Good Book at all. I like to think the old boys had a sense of humor. They figured that if they put this "kisses of his mouth" stuff right there in the Bible, then it would probably get read aloud in church sooner or later. I picture them sniggering among themselves in anticipation of some stodgy, tight-assed Southern Baptist preacher stepping to the pulpit and saying, "Hear now the Word of God," and then launching into a few verses of "thy thighs are like jewels" and "thy navel is like a round goblet that wanteth not liquor." Now, that one must really slay 'em down at the Southern Baptist Convention. Navels *and* liquor, right there in the same verse. Not to mention the breasts like roes. Hoo-boy!

But, with (again) an amazing amount of foresight, the old Church Daddies did manage to leave themselves an out. Somewhere along the way they dreamed up a truly astounding piece of jive about how the Song of Solomon was really an *allegorical* poem with Christ as the lover, and the Holy Catholic and Apostolic Church as His holy beloved.

Yeah, right.

I mean, who's gonna buy an obvious crock like that?

The Holy Catholic and Apostolic Church, that's who. Though why the Church would prefer to believe a poem about Solomon deep-tongue-kissing the Queen of Sheba (who, legend has it, was the Lola Falana of her time) is really about Jesus Christ deep-tongue-kissing the Church, is way beyond me.

Needless to say, the Song of Solomon is far and away my favorite book of the Bible. Aside from the above-quoted goodies, it also contains the line:

"I am black but comely, O daughters of Jerusalem."

I'm going to have that lettered on a t-shirt someday. My favorite, though is good old chapter 1, verse 2:

"Let him kiss me with the kisses of his mouth: for thy love is better than wine."

I don't know who wrote that line. No one does. All Biblical scholars can agree on is that it definitely wasn't Solomon. It makes me no never-mind. I may not know who wrote that line, but I know this: whoever did write that line probably thought it up shortly after dancing the old tongue tango with someone who kissed like Keith Keller.

Sweet was the wine that we drank last night
Sweet were the words you said as you
Held me tight
But what was sweeter
Than anything I know
Was when you kissed me at the
Door

Great song. "Sweet Was the Wine," by Jerry Butler and the Impressions. It's the flip side of "For Your Precious Love," which was their first chart hit, back in 1959. A dynamite single if you can get your paws on it. It always reminds me of Keith, but for an entirely different reason than does Donna Summer's "I Feel Love."

When Keith kissed me, it was sweeter than anything I know.

My arms locked around Keith's neck, and although my toes barely touched the floor, Keith held me up by heaping handfuls of my butt. I breathed in his smell and sucked his lower lip; he inventoried my teeth with his tongue. We licked each other's cheeks and chin like big cats.

Keith cupped my face in his hands, and kissed and licked my eyelids. It made me tremble — I'd never been kissed on the eyes before.

"You're beautiful," he said.

"No, you're beautiful," I said. And, Lord ha' mercy, but he *was* beautiful, his eyelids heavy-looking, lips ruddy and a little swollen from kissing.

"All right, we can both be beautiful," he said. "Let's kiss some more."

We kissed some more.

Keith reached under my shirt and massaged my back with long, big-handed strokes. I held his big head in my hands, my fingers dallied in his soft, fine hair, and I sucked his tongue as deeply into my mouth as I could. Keith spread his legs far apart to help equalize our heights, clutched me tight against him, and executed a slow, serious version of the Hully Gully without the benefit of music. Keith's crotch pressed against me, hard and distended and obviously as eager for attention as my own. We kissed until my lips hurt.

Looking back on the scene, I can only imagine we looked like two horny, hyperglandular high schoolers, standing just inside Keith's split-level townhouse condominium, sucking face like there was no tomorrow.

Keith removed his mouth from mine with an audible smacking, leaving me momentarily smooching the air.

"My gosh," he said in an understandably breathy tone of voice, "I haven't been a very good host, have I?"

"Huh?"

"I mean, I haven't shown you my place; I haven't even offered you any sort of ... um ... refreshment. Could I get you something?"

"Huh?" Keith was kneading my ass with both his hands, and I was thinking none too clearly.

"Can I, you know, fix you a drink or something?"

"Uh-uh." I pushed aside Keith's button-down collar, and kissed his Adam's apple.

"That's right, you don't drink much, do you?" He pushed my shirt up around my armpits and ran his fingertips down my chest. "How about a glass of wine?"

"No." I reached over Keith's arms and began unbuttoning his shirt. "Thank you."

"I could make some coffee," he offered. His voice had raised a full minor third in pitch.

I opened Keith's shirt to the navel, and kissed the deep, and by this time, somewhat dewy cleavage of his chest.

"No," I whispered between kisses. "Nothing for me." Kiss. Kiss. "Thank you."

"In that case," he said, "what do you say we go upstairs and rumple the sheets?"

"Shit howdy, Cowboy," I whispered into the V of his clavicle, "I thought you'd never ask."

He was the very stuff of which my warmest, wettest dreams were made; my blond fetish incarnate; my every Steve Reeves muscle fantasy made flesh.

There was just so very much of Keith, height and width and solid muscular thicknesses, that I felt nearly overwhelmed by it all. Oh, I'd been with men with muscles before. A dancer. A gymnast. One guy who did a hundred push-ups a night and had tits of death and not much else. A couple of small-scale bodybuilders like myself. But nothing like this. Keith Keller was simply more man, more actual bone and sinew and skin, more look and touch and smell and taste than I had ever held overflowing armfuls of before in my young life. And standing next to Keith's massive oaken four-poster, relieving Keith's shoulders of his shirt, I found that — like the proverbial kid in the candy store — I wanted all of him, all at once.

My hands were everywhere they could reach; kneading the great hard skeins of muscle that padded Keith's shoulders, palming his sides; playing Lionel Hampton xylophone glissandi with my fingertips up and down the twin rows of ripples that were Keith's belly; hefting his incredible tits.

Keith bent to kiss my neck, and I submerged my nose in his hair, which was soft and sweet-smelling, as if he shampooed with honey. He touched me tenderly, carefully, as if afraid of hurting me, of breaking me accidentally, like a china teacup. And the fact that he could indeed have broken me, if so inclined, seemed almost palpable, even through the gentleness. I was sure I could actually feel the strength Keith held in check, like the vibrations of an electric hair clipper against your face. It excited me. And when the strength broke through the softness, and he snatched me suddenly into his arms, taking my head between his hands (hands strong enough to crush my head into a gray goulash had he wanted to), and kissed me, nice and easy — and then nice and rough — it excited me the more.

Keith shoved me down on the bed and undressed me as if I were a little boy, his little boy; pulling off my penny loafers and socks, yanking my pants off from the cuffs, rubbing me up and down with his big, soft paws.

"You're beautiful, Babe," he said, plucking at my nipples, tickling my balls, and generally making me crazy.

I sprang up and reached for Keith's belt. I wanted his pants off; his crotch lumped and bulged like an ill-wrapped birthday present, and my fingers ached to unwrap it. The contents promised to be some toy, and I wanted to play. I wrestled Keith's belt loose and yanked his zipper open. His dick sprang out like a jack-in-the-box — pop! goes the weasel.

It was just like the rest of him — big and thick and juicy-looking — I could scarcely wrap my hand around it. This in no wise diminished my desire to wrap my face around it. Au contraire.

It veered just slightly to the right. It looked like the perfect food — delicious and nutritious, high-protein and low-fat, so good and so good for you. Health food, really. And so much more appetizing than tofu.

I made a lunge for it, but Keith caught me by the shoulders and tossed me backward again.

"Oh, no you don't," he said. "Me first."

He quickly shucked his pants down and climbed onto the bed, and onto me. Now, if you've never had 200-some-odd pounds of solid blond on top of you, it's difficult to express the feeling. Warm. Safe. Maybe even loved. (The sense of warmth and safety and the sense of love are often, and understandably, mistaken for one and the same.) True, having that much man on your chest can make breathing a bit difficult; but once Keith was on top of me, I decided I never wanted him off.

He wrapped himself around me and kissed my face, rubbed his rough, beard-stubbly cheeks against mine, dry-humped me slow and easy. I grabbed his big head and kissed him as hard as I could, lest he forget it was a man he was with that night. I turned his head to the side and sucked his earlobe. When he made a noise somewhere between a sigh and a moan, I knew I'd hit on something. I nipped and tongued in and around his ear, licked him behind the ear, and he cried out loud.

"Like that, do ya?" I whispered.

Taking me by surprise, he pinned my shoulders to the bed with his hands and looked down at me with a nasty smile.

"Yeah," he said. "I like that."

He kissed a meandering path down my chest and belly, finally crouching between my thighs. He buried his face in my crotch, snuffling me like a puppy.

"God, you smell good," he said; his words were somewhat muffled, as he was facedown in my groin.

He waged an all-out attack on my lower half, nuzzling and licking, slurping and nibbling, all the while skillfully avoiding my somewhat overexcited penis, which was by this point swollen past the point of discomfort, twitching and spitting, and, frankly, I would not have been surprised if it had found voice and simply said, "Hey, Keith, over here!"

When Keith did finally take old Snarfle in hand, my old boy threatened to shoot the works right off the bat. I sucked in a couple of deep breaths and began reciting my times tables silently to myself. I'd gotten as far as two-times-two-is-tootie-two, when Keith slurped me right down his throat. I moaned a long descending octave. I was in the hands — so to speak — of an expert.

I was excited to near delirium already, so I knew this wouldn't take long. I tried reciting the Gettysburg Address, but it somehow came out sounding just like the Song of Solomon. After entirely too short a time, I felt myself about to blow. For some reason, it occurred to me, just as I was coming, that maybe I should inform Keith. I mean, maybe he didn't swallow it.

"Excuse me," I managed to gasp, "but I'm coming."

And I did. And it was, as some of my funkier kinfolk might say, a mutha. A real live screaming, thrashing, toe-curling sonofabitch orgasm, through which Keith continued sucking me until I thought my hair might straighten. I slapped at Keith's shoulder, screaming unintelligibles.

Keith just grinned, licking his lips like a cartoon kitty-cat.

My turn.

I crawled the length and breadth of Keith's big bod, licking and kissing armpit and nipple, sucking and slurping earlobes and toes, nuzzling balls and tickling asshole, and generally lapping Keith up like a six-foot sundae, slowly, oh so slowly spiraling down toward his dick.

As Perry Como used to sing, hot diggity dog!

It was bigger than a breadstick. It was hotter than July. It was pinker than a plastic flamingo on a San Fernando Valley lawn. It demanded attention like the neon sign over a Las Vegas porno mart. It looked like fun.

I went for it like it was the last dick on the planet. I nuzzled it, butted it back and forth with my face, felt the heat of it, breathed in the sweet, yeasty smell of it. I took long licks up and down the length of it, nibbled the fat vein along the underside of it, flicked my tongue buzz-saw fashion on the hot spot behind the mushroom-cap head of it.

Gobbling as much of my fat friend into my mouth as I could, holding the considerable overflow with both hands, I suctioned and slurped and slobbered around Keith's wienie like a Hoover canister model vacuum, bobbing up and down, up and down until, a scant few minutes later, Keith cried out a deep, throaty noise, and I felt the heat and tasted the taste of Keith's sperm, a flavor like almonds and buttermilk and chlorinated pool water.

I siphoned the sticky stuff from Keith's rubber-headed nozzle until he forcibly pulled my face from his crotch, dislodging the hypersensitive noggin from my mouth with a loud, popping PLOOIP! not unlike the opening of a three-dollar bottle of champagne.

Keith shot up, gasping for breath, his well-worked-over penis as red as an August sunburn, and still hard.

"Jeeeeziz, little boy! What're you tryin' to do? Kill me?"

I smiled, licking a dripping string of spooie from my lips.

I didn't answer. I simply smiled. But had I been in a more talkative mood, I might well have quoted the Divine Joni M. and said,

"Oh, I could drink a case of you, Darlin'."

We lay toasty warm, and a little bit woozy, in the big four-poster, my back to Keith's chest, my butt against his finally soft crotch, his big arms around me making me feel like I never wanted to be anywhere else but there, in Keith's bed, in his arms. Had I the energy, I might easily have proposed marriage, at the very least.

"Mr. Keller?"

"Hmph?"

"Do you suppose I could stay the night?"

"Just try to get away."

He hugged me tight against him, growling like Roy Orbison.

I awoke still wrapped in the sweet warmth of Keith's arms. I could hear the sound of rain on the roof, one of those freakish summer showers peculiar to L.A. Four bars of every rain song I knew went through my head. "Rhythm of the Rain" by the Cascades. "Walkin' in the Rain" by the Ronettes. "Pennies from Heaven" by Bing Crosby. I moved back against Keith's body — this could easily get to be habit-forming — and fell back to sleep.

It rained off and on all that morning and half the afternoon, and I spent it all with Keith. His kiss was as fresh and sweet first thing in the morning as it had been the night before, and when I awoke again, we picked up where we'd left off.

By the time I found myself flat on my back, toes to the breeze, with Keith between my thighs doing a slow Watusi against my belly, I had a pretty good idea what was on the big boy's mind even before his right middle finger found its way to my asshole, introducing itself and beginning to get acquainted. Long before he actually whispered into my ear,

"I'd really like to fuck you."

Now, the idea of having my kidneys relocated by Keith's big Nordic schwanzstucker was more than intriguing, in the abstract. But, rather like the thought of being gang-banged by West Hollywood in its entirety, it seemed the kind of thing that might make much better fantasy than reality. The facts of the matter were that my nether region had never before been approached by a tool of the proportions of Keith's; and the length and girth of said wanger held the promise of some discomfort, at the very least. Permanent internal damage was not out of the question.

Keith, no doubt, read my reticence on my face — he could probably feel it on his finger.

"Hey, Babe." He took my face in his hands. "I won't hurt you. I'd never hurt you," he said. "I promise."

And I wanted to believe him.

"I want to be inside you," he said. "I want to be one with you."

Now, let's face it: very few men could read that line and make it play. Keith did, somehow. Maybe it was the finger trailing up and down the cleft of my behind; I don't know. At any rate, he kissed me — a soft, sweet little baby-kiss — and my fate was sealed. I've already told you the sort of effect Mr. Keller's kiss had on me, so it should come as no surprise that, when Keith kissed me, then looked down at me with the imploring eyes of a small boy begging Mom for a nickel for the ice cream man and said, "Please?" — it was all over. I was his as surely as if he'd picked me off the notions counter at Woolworth's and laid down cash for me.

Keith suddenly jumped out of bed and rummaged through the nightstand drawer. He snorted a little "hmph" and slammed the drawer shut. He headed to the bathroom, his hard dick preceding him, waving like a divining rod. I could hear him opening and shutting drawers and cabinets one after another; then he left the bathroom with a frown creasing his brow.

"Right back," he said, exiting the bedroom. I heard a rapid *bumbumbumbumbum* of Keith's feet against the carpeted stairs and, after a minute or two, the more widely spaced *boom — boom — boom* of him taking the stairs at least two at a time. Back in the bedroom, Keith was just a bit winded, but still erect; in his hand he held a one-pound tub of whipped butter.

Brando again.

"Sorry," he said. "It was all I could find." He approached the bed slowly, as if afraid I might object to being sodomized with a high-cholesterol dairy product. "It's unsalted," he announced, sounding so much like a television commercial and looking so much like the centerfold of a boymeat magazine that I just had to laugh.

He climbed back into bed, where he proceeded to send me to the ceiling, nipping the inside of my thighs with his lips, tonguing the underside of my dick, and slowly working first one, then another, and finally another finger up into me. I bucked up and down like the mechanical horse in front of a grocery store, pushing myself up into Keith's face and pogo-sticking on his hot buttered fingers.

By the time he pulled his fingers out and handed me the plastic tub that I might (oh, so literally) butter him up, I was ready to attempt just about anything he might think up. I generously buttered (as Betty Crocker might say) Keith's dong and buttered his balls just for fun. Shiny with the grease, Keith's wacker was an awesome sight indeed; I said a brief silent prayer as I wiped my hands on a towel and lay back against the pillow.

"Now just relax, Babe." Keith grasped me by the backs of the knees and raised my legs high. I did my level best to relax. I used all the relaxation exercises I could remember from sensitivity group. I breathed deeply and slowly. In. Out. In. And out. I imagined myself on a big cloud, floating, floating. I silently talked the tension from my body, piece by piece:

The tension is now leaving my neck. Breathe, breathe. The tension is now leaving my shoulders. Breathe. My back ... my lower back ... my buttocks ... my—

Just before the tension was scheduled to leave my sphincter, Keith began entry. Slowly. Gently. With all the tenderness and care possible.

It hurt like a sonofabitch.

It felt like the fist of a two-year-old boy. I nearly ate my own fist trying to muffle the scream.

"OhmygodBabeI'msorry!" Keith cried, pulling back.

"Nonononononon!" I said through clenched teeth and fingers. "Just ... give me a minute ... to get ... used to it."

I breathed. I floated. I did my best to talk my asshole into relaxing itself around the big, redheaded intruder.

I thought about yawning, big, wide yawns. About the Holland Tunnel. About the Grand Canyon. And slowly, the pain began to subside. My eyes still shut tight, I whispered,

"Okay. Go slow."

"No," Keith said. "You do it."

I reached out and took Keith by the hips. I ran my hands up and down his big flanks, and slowly pulled him to me.

Did I mention that Keith's kiss was better than some men's fucks? Well, Keith's fucks were (as Al Jarreau used to sing) better than anything.

We showered together; scrubbed each other's back, hugged each other with slippery arms, and shared soapy kisses, then patted each other dry. As I was pulling on the Levi's I'd worn the night before, Keith tossed a shirt to me: a football jersey from St. Fletcher's, number 19. Old and soft and nearly big enough for two people my size. It was full of Keith's smell, and I buried my face in the fabric before slipping the shirt over my head. It fit like a muumuu.

"It looks great on you," Keith said. "Keep it."

As if I'd ever planned to give it back.

We made breakfast, managing to bump into one another at every turn, even though his kitchen was three times the size of mine. I fried about half a pound of bacon — "I'm a bacon freak," claimed Keith — and Keith whipped up a batch of the best pancakes I'd ever tasted. He polished off eleven of them.

There was little conversation as we ate. We were both hungry, and besides, just as I was thinking up something snappy to say, Keith would smile one of those smiles, or wiggle his toes up my pants leg, and rendered me a blithering idiot.

Later, I sat tucked beneath Keith's arm as we watched Cocteau's *Beauty and the Beast* on the Betamax. After which, we made love again on the TV room couch, and then again in the bed. I lay close to Keith in bed, feeling sated and contented, if a bit friction burned.

Keith picked up the small digital clock on the nightstand.

"Ah, shit!"

"What is it?"

"I'm sorry, Johnnie Ray, I'm going to have to ask you to leave."

"Oh."

"Somebody — Betsy — Betsy's coming over. She'll be here in less than an hour." He paused a second. I was speechless. "I'm sorry." He reached out for me, but I slid quickly out of the bed.

"No I'm sorry I've really overstayed my welcome anyway I don't know why you didn't boot me out long ago—" I was yanking my clothes on and talking a mile a minute, trying to outrun the tears.

Keith jumped out after me.

"Johnnie Ray." He caught me up in his arms and hugged me hard. I made myself as stiff and unyielding as I could. "Johnnie Ray" — he tilted my face up toward his — "I don't want you to go; you know I don't. But I have to see Betsy. I have to talk to her. It's important — especially now."

"Forget it. It's none of my business and besides—"

"Hush." He set a fingertip against my lips. "May I see you again? May I call you this week?"

I managed a smile.

"You better."

103

 By the time he walked me to my car, it had stopped raining; a warm mist floated through the air.

"I've had—" what could I say? — "I've had such a nice time."

"Me too. I'll call you. Soon. But call me if you want to, okay?"

"Okay."

"Bye." Keith leaned toward me, then snapped back. He looked up and down the deserted street. Then he kissed me, real fast.

"Bye."

He stood on the sidewalk, so damned sexy in his shorts and half shirt, waving. I somehow managed to turn the corner before the tears came.

The phone was ringing like crazy (Could it be him?). I could hear it through the door, and I turned the locks as fast as I could (Him? What, already? Not fifteen minutes after kissing you good-bye? Grow up!) and flung open the door (Why not? Maybe just trying the number. Maybe just making sure I got home in one piece. Maybe just to say hello how are you Honey I love you or — something.) and raced to the phone. (Oh God, it must be him!)

"Hello?"

"John-John." But it's not him, and then I die.

"Oh, hi, Snooks."

"Johnnie Ray Rousseau, where in Heaven's name have you been? I swear, Johnnie Ray, as God is my witness, you *will* get an answering machine if I have to buy it and install it myself. I've just been calling and *calling*. You would *not* be*lieve* the morning I have had today. I've spent the entire morning on the phone with Marsha Goldman, a JAP if there ever was one, but a good JAP to have in your corner, let me tell you. You're not going to believe this. Are you sitting down? Between last night and this morning, Marsha's gotten us booked at the Blue Dahlia. Can you believe it? Here we've been trying to crack that room for months, Marsha Goldman

105

makes one phone call and we're in. Can you stand it?

"They want you to come in this Wednesday, and then, if they like you we'll take over Wednesday nights, and then if we do well they could move you to a weekend night. Oh, and I think we should get Maxie to run the lighting board. It'll cost us a few bucks, but I think we should try to look as good as we possibly can, don't you? God, I can't wait, can you? Bye-bye, Sawyer's! And that's not even all.

"Marsha told me she absolutely *hates* your head-shot — she saw it out front at Sawyer's — and she thinks you should have a new one taken right away. So, she says, she's going to set up an appointment with this photographer friend of hers. And you'll never guess who li'l ol' Marsha's photographer friend is — Rudy Wilson. Yes, *the* Rudy Wilson, as in Barbra's last album cover and Bette's last album cover and that *Rolling Stone* cover of Travolta. I mean, Rudy Wilson doesn't even point his camera at anybody who's not famous, but Marsha says he'll do you just as a personal favor to her. Could you die?

"Can you believe it? Here I'll bet you thought she was just another big talker, and look what she's done already, in less than twelve hours. Honey, if this little lady says she can get you the Griffin show, well, I bet you can just take that right to the bank, whattaya wanna bet?

"What's the matter, Honey? You haven't said a mumblin' word. Is something wrong?"

"Goddammit, Snookie — I'm in love!"

"When I say I'm in love,
you best believe I'm in LUV-el-you-vee!"
—The Shangri-las

I was a goner. That's all she wrote. Th-th-th-
th-th-th-th-th-th-th-that's all, Folks! Johnnie
Ray was in LUV-el-you-vee.

Now I'm not the kind of guy who falls in love all the time. Like Snookie, for instance, who, were he to be perfectly honest, would have to admit that he falls madly, but hopelessly, in love once a month, like a menses. True, I do tend to fall in *lust* two or three times a day; and, as I've mentioned, I am prone to temporary spasms of galloping romanticism following just about any satisfactory sexual experience; and I've already admitted to humming a few bars of "Chapel of Love" while Louie washed the breakfast dishes on that sunshiny Saturday morning I formally met one Mr. Keith Keller. But, as to falling in love, I had up to that point, in what I can only snickeringly refer to as my adult life, fallen in love, but really head-over-teacup faw-down-go-BOOM in love, exactly once before, when — no; I think I'll save that story. Anyway, I'd been in love, and I knew good and well what it felt like. Like an itchin' in my heart. Like a heat wave.

Like I can't do nothin' but love, Babe, eight days a week. Like nothing else.

And this was eye-tee, it.

I explained this to Snookie over my third breakfast in less than fifteen hours, shortly after three o'clock that afternoon. Snooks and I were sprawled over our usual corner booth at Tippy's. Snooks was making short work of a spaghetti chili size with a side of raw sliced onions, alternating bites with gulps of black coffee and long drags on a Benson & Hedges Light. I was having the usual — three eggs over medium, bacon very crisp, whole wheat toast — and doing my level best to avoid Snookie's cigarette smoke, which was following me like a homing missile.

"It's the real thing, Snooks. I can feel it in my heart. In my bones. In my anus. And *please*, could you blow that cancer elsewhere?"

"I'm sorry — it seems to like you." Snookie waved at the dense cloud of smoke encircling his head and slurped at a string of pasta with audible gusto. "God, I'm hungry. I haven't eaten a bite since yesterday. Where is Mary? I could stand a warm-up on the old coffee cup."

Snookie and I loved Tippy's. It was our place. We'd been sitting at that same corner booth at least once a week since time began — if someone happened to be borrowing it when we arrived, we'd wait. As I said, we loved Tippy's. Because the food was good, as long as you stuck mainly to the breakfast menu and avoided the tuna salad like the Black Death. Because it was a quick block-and-a-half walk from either of our apartments. Because it was open twenty-four hours, and it gave one an almost spiritual sense of security to know that there was always a fresh pot of coffee on the hot plate just waiting for you, anytime, day or night.

Most of all, though, we loved Tippy's waitresses. Tippy's was one of the last strongholds of *real* waitresses between the San Fernando Valley and the Pacific Ocean. It was indescribably refreshing to be served by a waitress who really was a waitress — not some actress slash dancer slash model *posing* as a waitress while waiting for her agent to call. One grows so weary of dealing with the parade of helium-headed foofoo girls passing themselves off as waitresses all over Hollywood, Westwood, Beverly Hills, and the West Side; girls who are so busy memorizing a scene from *The Rainmaker* for their acting workshop they can't remember a simple breakfast order; girls who will leave you to grow a long gray beard waiting for a refill on your coffee because, after pouring your first cup, they'll go out and have their nails done or maybe to a cattle call for a community theater production of *The Music Man* in Torrance.

Tippy's waitresses were *waitresses*, by golly. "The Girls," as we liked to call them, were career waitresses — lifers — and generally as intellectually simple as they were physically plain. Big Mary, who was, even as Snookie spoke, filling his coffee cup, was a huge, unkempt Guernsey cow of a woman, with pockmarked skin and fingernails seemingly gnawed to the quick, but with a disposition as warm and sweet as Snookie's coffee — he took four sugars.

"Thanks, Mary," Snookie said, smiling up her.

"How you boys doin' today?" Mary asked, refilling my cup to the brim, without looking and without spilling a drop. Big Mary was from Houston originally, and everything she said sounded like a song by Tammy Wynette.

"Just fine," Snookie answered for us. "You look particularly lovely today," he said with a look of mock seduction in his great brown eyes.

109

Mary smiled her beige, uneven smile.

"Git own outa here." She slapped Snookie a playful smack on the shoulder before lumbering away, giggling girlishly to herself.

"I don't know what to do, Snooks. I haven't felt like this in years. I want to move in with him. Tonight. I want to bear his children and breast-feed them. I want to carve 'Johnnie loves Keith' into the trunk of the very next tree I can find; in fact, a telephone pole will do. I want to write his name over and over and over." And indeed I was, even as I spoke, absently dipping my right index finger into the egg yolks on my plate and attempting to write Keith's name on the tabletop. I caught myself in the middle of a rather sloppy sticky yellow "E" and quickly popped my fingertip into my mouth and sucked it clean. "Oh, Snookie, I am wreckage, a total loss, DOA. I mean, dig it: this guy just happens to be about the most beautiful thing I've ever set eyes upon. Like, did you ever see a dream walking? Like, everything I longed for as a child except stardom, of course. So naturally, one fine Saturday night he breezes into Sawyer's with his woman of the week and decides he wants me as a refreshing change of pace, takes me home and fucks me senseless and makes me feel more magically delicious than a box of Lucky Charms. And I fall in love. Splat."

"You're right," Snookie deadpanned, "your life is definitely over."

"You don't understand, Snooks. I didn't want to fall in *love*, for crying out loud. Not with a 200-pound former football jock with a girlfriend. I just wanted to fuck a real live fantasy for once in my life. Quick and painless."

"So what's so bad about falling in love? There are more serious diseases to contract than that."

110

"Oh, no, Snookie; you couldn't be more wrong. Falling in love is the nation's number-one crippler of young adults. And I, Johnnie Ray Rousseau, am this year's poster child." I absently crushed an isosceles triangle of toast into fine crumbs. "I just don't have time to be in love, Snookie. I've got a bone-crushing day job and what I'm trying to pass off as a show business career, and frankly, my dear, there just isn't enough of me to go around. Besides which" — I stared past Snookie's right earlobe into space, talking at least as much to myself as to Snooks — "besides which, if he doesn't love me too, I'll probably take poison. In the immortal words of Carly Simon, 'I haven't got time for the pain.'"

I awoke Monday morning from a sleep filled to bursting with vividly nasty, Technicolor blue movie dreams starring Keith Keller, Ricky Nelson circa 1962, a large white horse, and Johnnie Ray Rousseau as the Beaver. My wake-to-music radio alarm clock went off in the middle of Connie Francis singing, "Stupid Cupid, stop pickin' on me." I sported a history-making hard-on and had no time to answer its urgent call. I found it necessary to recite the Preamble to the Constitution in its near entirety just to get soft enough to pee.

I had showered, shaved, and dressed in my Boy Secretary drag — button-down shirt and tie, but no jacket — and was pouring the onion-and-bell-pepper polka-dotted batter for my morning omelette into the pan, when there was a knock at the door.

"Who the hell?" I opened the door to reveal the undisputed, hands-down winner of the Johnnie Ray Rousseau Wet Dream Oscar, looking bankish but beautiful in a charcoal gray three-piece and a decidedly unfiduciary smile.

"Good morning," he said. "I was in the neighborhood and I—"

I had Keith in my apartment, back up against the door, my arms around his neck, and his lips locked in the labial counterpart of a full nelson before he could complete his sentence. Our position had not changed substantially by the time I caught the unmistakable odor of an onion-and-bell-pepper omelette burning to a crisp.

I chipped my disastrous first attempt at breakfast from the bottom of the pan, and cooked another omelette, of which I ate half; feeding the other half to my gray-suited darling, one bite for him, one for me. I was chewing and preparing to swallow a "one for me," when Keith reached out and traced my jawline with his right index finger, stalling me in midmastication. He looked into my eyes, the whole of apple-cheeked, snow-peaked Scandinavia shining in his own (those hazel eyes which leaned decidedly toward blue that blue Monday), and said,

"Wild Thing, I think I love you."

I was forty-five minutes late for work.

I was at the time spending five days a week impersonating a secretary at the law firm of Cohen, Nelson, Bieberman and Schwartz. (Yeah, I know. Pretty ballsy of me going on about actresses posing as waitresses, when here I was, a pop vocalist to be reckoned with, impersonating a secretary. I never claimed to be fair.) Cohen, Nelson, Bieberman and Schwartz was four partners and one (not-so-incidentally female) associate, subleasing half the seventeenth floor of a savings and loan building in Century City. Down in the depths on the seventeenth floor.

I lived for the day when I could bid the law firm of Cohen, Nelson, Bieberman and Schwartz farewell forever, but, at that point, my nightclub earnings were barely enough to keep me in Afro Sheen. L.A.'s an expensive town, and a boy's gotta eat.

I shared secretarial chores for Cohen Nelson's five lawyers with Sylvia Scott, a thirtyish, artificially redheaded party animal in tight-fitting skirt-and-jacket ensembles and life-threatening spike-heeled shoes. Sylvia had the face of a girl who, in another place and time, could have been cast as second-lead comic relief in Betty Grable movies, and a slight speech peculiarity which made her sibilances amusingly similar to those of Abigail ("Dear Abby") Van Buren, or your aunt Rose a half hour or so after midnight on New Year's Eve. I couldn't help smiling every time I overheard Sylvia pick up her phone line and say, "Shylvia Shcott shpeaking."

Sylvia was also the proud owner of a bosom that would give Jane Russell pause, and a smile as bright as a movie premiere at Grauman's Chinese, and, in my opinion, more than her fair share of boyfriends. Hardly a day went by that did not see a sizable FTD delivery for Sylvia Scott. Her office looked like a funeral parlor.

Sylvia was just easing a dozen long-stemmed sterling silver rosebuds into a vase as I arrived, smiling a smile you couldn't have slapped off my face. On Sylvia's desk, all nine of her telephone lines were blinking.

"Howdy, stranger," she said. "Glad you could make it."

"Hi, beautiful — sorry I'm late." I kissed Syl on the cheek. She was an okay gal, and I found it more trouble than it was worth to attempt to dislike her, despite her remarkable knack for dodging, ignoring, and generally avoiding work. She never seemed to be busy, and yet her desktop was always immaculate. You could eat off her typewriter. While my desk had the perennial appearance of a small war-torn country. "Only one dozen," I said, sniffing a lavender bud. "You're slipping."

Sylvia cocked her head to one side, handed me a rosebud and her patented Woman's Intuition Look.

"Well, you look like *you've* had some weekend."

"What do you mean?" I tried and tried to stop grinning, but nothing doing.

"Honey, the last time I saw somebody glowin' like that, she was pregnant. Now, what's up?" She dropped her voice to *sotto voce*. "It's a man, isn't it?"

"I'm sure I don't know what you're talking about." I beat a hasty retreat to my office lest I burst into a shower of girlie giggles.

"Liar liar pants on fire!" Sylvia called.

I had scarcely landed in my chair and begun answering some of the telephone lines Sylvia had chosen to neglect, and marveling at how my In basket had magically given birth to a five-inch stack of paper over the weekend, before Bernie Bieberman burst through my door. Bernie was my least favorite of the Cohen Nelson partners, a short, balding, hyperkinetic transplanted New Yorker with Dexedrine for blood and a manner as abrasive as Old Dutch Cleanser.

"Johnnie Ray, I need this right away, it's a triple A priority!" he said, thrusting a handful of yellow legal pages into my face.

"Good morning, Bernie," I said, contemplating murder.

This was, as I've mentioned, the summer of '79. It was earlier that year, January I think, when a young San Diego girl named Brenda Spencer made national headlines by opening gunfire on her high school, killing two people and wounding others. When asked why she did it, Brenda was quoted as saying, "I don't like Mondays."

Keith joined me for breakfast again on Tuesday morning — this time with fresh croissants from Paris Pastries on Westwood Boulevard. "I was just passing by," he said. When he came back on Wednesday, I decided this was a tradition I could easily come to enjoy. I was by this time the indisputable Fastest Omelette in the West, and the postbreakfast smooch festivals I celebrated with Keith sent me to the office grinning what Sylvia described as my "Cheshire-cat-that-ate-the-canary grin" from one side of Century City to the other.

Johnnie Ray and the Boize debuted at the Blue Dahlia Wednesday evening. The Blue Dahlia was a bar–disco–showroom complex located on a neon-flashing strip of Ventura Boulevard in Sherman Oaks dedicated to furthering the Great American Heterosexual Pickup. Its facilities included three (count them — three) bars, one with an aquarium big enough to house Orky the Killer Whale and family; two TV lounges full of marshmallow-soft modular furniture bolted to the floor in what at the time were termed conversational groupings; two dance floors (one "disco" and one "new wave," both of which, despite their genre distinctions, always seemed to be playing "Shame" by Evelyn "Champagne" King); and the showroom.

The Blue Dahlia's men's restroom was wallpapered in matte black with metallic gold silhouettes of couples coupling in every imaginable position (and one or two I hadn't imagined, but did make a mental note to attempt at some later date). I can't vouch for the ladies' room — but one shudders to think.

The Blue Dahlia was frequented by a representative cross section of L.A.'s Caucasian middle-class singles — executive secretaries and bookstore clerks, cabdrivers and aspiring actors who waited on tables part-time, real estate securities lawyers and gofers at Paramount trying to sell that screenplay, the former high-school sex bombs and the girls always described as having a great personality, the captain of the football team and the captain of the chess team, the buxom and the bookish, the stumpy and the statuesque, the hunky and the humble, the best of them and the rest of them, the long and the short of them — they all came to the Blue Dahlia, glossy synthetics on their bodies, and on their faces the unmistakable look of those who have been kicked in the butt by love. Severely and repeatedly. Whenever I began to believe that the gay bar scene had cornered the market on loneliness, I needed only to push open the blue leather upholstered door of the Blue Dahlia to be reminded that loneliness knows no affectional preference.

Snookie and I had been in to check out the Dahlia's showroom a couple of times before. The general run of bands showcased there tended to feature at least two synthesizers and a bargain-basement Pat Benatar impersonator as lead vocalist. Preceding us that Wednesday evening was the best of the lot, a band fronted by a young woman billed only as "Randi." Randi was less a Pat Benatar impersonator than a one-woman Janis Joplin tribute. She wore a sequined tube top and a pair of electric blue spandex pants that one could only imagine sported, on one severely straining inside seam, that most dangerously misleading of garment tags — "one size fits all." Randi's hair looked as if she'd combed it with a Cuisinart. Despite looking like a psychedelic blueberry, the woman was, as Clara might put it, a stone singer. She had a voice like a cement truck with a killer case of the blues. She moved like Medea on methadone withdrawal. She was wonderful. And she and her band were being moved to Friday nights.

Snookie and I watched Randi with the sort of professional respect we made it a point never to waste on the mediocre. I noticed, with some concern, that roughly one-third of the audience was paying Randi even the slightest attention. The other two-thirds were watching one another out of the far corners of their eyes, licking their lips in furtive agitation — hardly a performer's ideal audience, but what else could one expect in a room where the most pressing interest was not pop music, but poontang?

As Randi closed her set with "When a Man Loves a Woman," tearing through the song like the last diva on earth singing the last blues song, me and the Boize were preparing to take the stage. Marsha Goldman had Tom Porcelli (the portly Mafioso type who managed the place) backed into a corner, and was obviously talking his ear off — figuratively, of course: Marsha couldn't reach Porcelli's ear — about heaven only knew what. Mr. Moto was absently drumming "In-A-Gadda-Da-Vida" on the tabletop with his fingers. Bobo was gently, but firmly, discouraging one pretty Quiana-swathed young lady after another, drawing as much attention as possible to his left ring finger. Steve was not to be found, and was undoubtedly in the men's room, almost certainly combing his hair for the fifth time since our arrival, and probably studying the wallpaper for pointers. Snookie was soaking up a Courvoisier much too quickly for my comfort. And I was quietly chewing a divot out of my lower lip.

As her band began striking their setup, Randi did a modified Jayne Mansfield jiggle over to our table, smiling a big, wide smile that lit up her face like Christmas Eve night.

"Hi, I'm Randi." She extended a pudgy little-girl hand. Her fingernails were painted to match her pants.

120

Her speaking voice was like Louis Armstrong whispering the secret of life.

"Johnnie Ray. Rousseau. You're good."

"Thanks." Her smile widened. "Nervous?"

Vigorous nod.

"Don't be. They gon' love y'all. Marsha says you're great, and she knows her shit." Somebody called Randi's name from across the room.

"Whoops. Gotta go."

"Oh." Snookie was visibly bummed. "I'd rather hoped you could stick around and hear us."

"Don' worry. Ah'ma be back in time to hear y'all. I jus' gotta go ina back fah minit; friend o' mine got some toot fuh me." She patted Snooks on the cheek like a Jewish grandmother. "See ya later. Sing pretty now."

"Randi!" called the impatient voice.

"Ah'm comin', shit!" And she jiggled away, tossing us a finger-wave bye-bye over her left shoulder.

"Snookie," I whispered, "what's some toot?"

Bobo hissed a spitty snicker.

"Jesus!" said Mr. Moto, rolling his almond eyes.

"It means cocaine, Honey," Snookie explained with motherish patience.

"Oh."

"Oh," my ever-loyal sometime band parroted back.

If you'd stopped me as I stepped off the barely raised platform that was the Blue Dahlia's stage and asked me, I could not have honestly said that the set had gone well. In my small opinion, the set sucked. Sucked out loud. It was as if the audience and I were in two separate movies. Parallel universes or something. It was like singing to the tenants of the Movieland Wax Museum. If one-third of the audience had been listening to Randi, Johnnie Ray and the Boize seemed to be going for a perfect score — nobody, but NObody was listening to us — with the visible exception of Marsha Goldman and Tom Porcelli (from a far corner of the room) and Randi (smiling a cocained smile from a ringside table).

We tried everything we knew. Top 40 hits. Oldies but goodies. Witty Bette Midler-ish patter between songs. Embarrassing rock concert cliches like clapping my hands over my head and saying, "Come on, everybody, put yo' hands togethah!" Nothing seemed to do the job.

We finished the 25-minute set (it seemed more like twenty-five years) to scattered applause — mostly from Marsha and Randi.

"Oh, Snookie..." I leaned against Snookie's shoulder, a broken man. We were certainly never going to get hired after a reception like this. And even if we were, did we want to be?

"I know, Honey."

Marsha made her high-heeled way toward us, Porcelli lumbering up behind her. Marsha was smiling like they were going to make it illegal in the morning.

"Johnnie! Sidney!" she called as she elbowed a path across the room.

"What's she so fuckin' smiley about?" Snookie said. "We just died a thousand deaths up here."

"Drugs," I said. "The woman is obviously on hard drugs."

"Well!" Marsha said as if it were a complete thought.

"Well?" Snookie repeated.

"Well, you're in," she said with a little flip of her cigarette-wielding hand.

"In what?" I said.

"In the Blue Dahlia on Wednesday nights," Porcelli announced. Porcelli's voice and accent was a Sid Caesar parody of a gangster.

"You're not serious," I said.

"Of course he's serious." Marsha slapped me a playful but sharp slap on the arm. "You'll start a week from tonight."

Snookie and I exchanged looks.

"I don't know if you noticed or not," I said, "but the audience didn't know we were alive."

"Sure they did," Porcelli said. "They just don't always take the time to applaud."

"Or look up," Snookie said under his breath.

"They liked you." Porcelli made an expansive gesture. "Trust me."

"What do they do when they *hate* a band around here?" Snookie asked. "Get out the tar and feathers?"

"Form a lynch mob?" I added.

"Give 'em twenty-four hours to get outa town?" Steve quipped over his shoulder as he snapped his guitar case shut.

"Cute, boys," Marsha said in a tone meant to convey something to the effect of, If you boys blow this paying gig with your lame attempts at drawing-room comedy, I will give you *such* a pinch. "Very cute, indeed. Now if you're finished playing *Saturday Night Live*, we'll go back to the office and talk to Mr. Porcelli here about your pay; and, incidentally, my ten percent thereof."

As Marsha herded Porcelli, Snookie, and me toward the backstage offices, I nudged Snookie with my elbow. Pointing at Marsha's low-set back, I mouthed the word "manager." Snookie mimed, "I know."

We shrugged in unison.

Porcelli's only complaint dash suggestion concerning our set was that it contained too much in the way of oldies, ballads, and — as Porcelli so succinctly put it — "weird stuff." He asked that we work up some more Top 40 material — "Put in some Bee Gees," he said; I fought back my gag reflex.

Now, let it not be supposed that I am some sort of pop music elitist. Au contraire, I have always appreciated the sheer juvenile silliness of American Top 40 pop. One of my all-time favorite records is "I Will Follow Him" by Little Peggy March. It has long been my belief that when the late, great Lester Bangs (perhaps the greatest rock music critic ever, though I'm open to discussion, and definitely worth a chapter in my book) called rock and roll "a lot of raving shit," he meant it as a compliment. I should point out, however, that (a) I hated the Bee Gees like the Montagues hated the Capulets; (b) I had always programmed my own act, with assistance from Snookie and conditional power of veto from the Boize, and the thought that some overfleshed nightclub owner with garlic breath should tell me what I should and should not sing really made my asshole pucker; and (c) Tom Porcelli requested that Johnnie Ray and the Boize "work up some more Top 40 material" during the summer of '79, the selfsame summer that saw Rod Stewart's "Da Ya Think I'm Sexy" dominating the Top 40. Need I say more?

It became immediately apparent that the Blue Dahlia was unlikely to become the artistic apex of my career. The job did, however, promise to pay well. It made Tom Sawyer's look like a charity gig. And Marsha Goldman, self-styled artistic manager and very possibly the Fastest Mouth West of the Mississippi, was mine all mine for a mere ten percent right off the top of our gross earnings, at the Blue Dahlia and from any other gigs I might manage to get, through her or not, until the termination of our business relationship.

Our contract with Marsha was a three-way handshake between Marsha, Snookie, and myself (Snooks and I were a team — the Boize were hired help). Even as I clasped that diminutive hand in my own, I had a creeping hunch that going into a business relationship with Marsha Goldman was comparable to wheeling and dealing with Rumplestiltskin, using one's firstborn child as collateral. But the thought of exchanging amusing anecdotes with Merv on his nationally syndicated talk show was a strong lure indeed; thus, had there been a dotted line handy, I likely would have signed upon it.

I didn't see Keith on Thursday, although I and my omelette pan were more than primed for his arrival. He called me on the phone.

"Hi, Babe."

"Hi. Why aren't you here?" I was becoming quite possessive indeed.

"'Cause I'm already at work. I'm going to be here early for the next week or so."

"Oh, *merde*." The past three mornings had added whole new dimensions to my concept of breakfast, and I'd already come to expect it.

126

"I know. Can I see you tonight?"

"I've got rehearsal tonight until about dawn."

"And of course, Sawyer's tomorrow night."

"Of course."

"See you after closing tomorrow night then?"

"I'm likely to be half past dead by then."

"I'll take that chance, thanks."

"All right, then. Can't say I didn't give you fair warning."

"My place?"

"Sure, Sailor."

"Have a nice day."

"You, too," I said, feeling my own day had already been, if not entirely ruined, at least badly bruised.

"Hey," Keith almost whispered.

"Hey what?"

"Love you, Babe." And he hung up.

Now, I never did believe that hearts actually skipped beats, outside of extreme physical exertion compounded by a previous history of cardiovascular irregularities; I always felt the phrase "my heart skipped a beat" was just another one of those overwrought, overused, clichéd love-song metaphors like "your love has given me wings" or "the story in your eyes" or "he hit me and it felt like a kiss."

How wrong I was.

When Keith Keller said, "Love you, Babe," my heart skipped a beat. Or, more accurately, it syncopated a beat, it accented the off beat. The rhythm section in the center of my chest dropped its wonted straight-ahead, hup-two-three-four Sousa march beat and adopted a rhythm something like the old Bo Diddly riff:

CHUNK

a-chunk-CHUNK

I was up till two a.m. that night working with Snookie. We hiked over to Licorice Pizza and bought a fistful of current 45s — they're cheaper than sheet music — and spent the whole night long listening to hit after hit after hit; we finally set aside ten or twelve possible additions to our repertoire for the Blue Dahlia. Snookie pulled chord structures out of the air and plunked them out on his out-of-tune Yamaha spinet. And I, ear smack up against the one working speaker, discerned obscure, muffled, mumbled, or otherwise unintelligible song lyrics, writing them down on page after page of a green steno pad when I could figure them out, making them up ad lib when I couldn't.

Finally, around one, Snookie's upstairs neighbor began stomping on his floor, his usual signal that enough was enough already, and Snooks and I adjourned to Tippy's for a late-night bite.

I collapsed into bed about an hour later, weary to my very bone marrow, knowing I was going to hate myself in the morning.

I hated myself in the morning.

I overslept by half an hour. I felt tired and achy and mean, and my eyes felt as if the sandman had left dunes in them. I'm the kind of person who can survive on a few hours' sleep for one or two nights in a row. I hadn't slept more than five hours a night in over a week, and it was beginning to take its toll. I was a zombie, the undead. I stubbed the living daylights out of my right big toe feeling my way along the walls to the bathroom. I cut myself twice shaving — with an electric. I had no time to eat; I gulped down three raw eggs and two time-released megavitamin capsules, washed it all down with half a glass of slightly sour low-fat milk, and called it breakfast.

When I got to Santa Monica Boulevard, it looked like a parking lot. Still life with automobiles. And I said,

"Uh-oh. This is gonna be some day."

When I finally got to work, some twenty-five minutes late, I found that the law firm of Cohen, Nelson, Bieberman and Schwartz had declared National Drive-a-Male-Secretary-to-the-Very-Edge-of-Suicide Day. My old buddy Sylvia was out sick with an unspecified ailment that (given Syl's history) I could only suspect amounted to an overwhelming desire to spend the day at the beach.

Sylvia, who worked an average of one Friday per month, seemed to have personally instituted the four-day work week, and had neglected to inform the labor board or the law firm of Cohen, Nelson, Bieberman and Schwartz. This left yours truly to handle all the work for all five (count 'em, folks — five) lawyers.

I was on my feet half the day, up and down the halls like Jesse Owens, running errands, distributing mail, making and pouring enough coffee to sink the *Bismarck*. The other half of the day was spent typing my little fingers to bloody nubs. Letters, memoranda, and legal documents danced through my typewriter in an endless conga line of letterheads. Telephone calls overlapped each other like the hits on a Top 40 radio station. I never managed to take lunch. When, sometime around two in the afternoon, Bernie Bieberman managed to find me behind an Everest of paperwork, answering nine telephone lines with one hand and typing a seven-page inter-office communication with the other, and when he actually found the unmitigated balls to ask, "Johnnie Ray, are you busy?" I drew a long, deep breath ("Slowly I turn ... step by step ... inch by inch...") and quietly suggested that Bernie consider the permanent cerebral damage that might be incurred from a merciless bludgeoning with an IBM Selectric II self-correcting type-writer. He retreated quickly.

By the end of the day, our boy was dead. We're talking doornail material. Paul McCartney striding barefoot across the *Abbey Road* album could not have been more dead. In fact, legend has it that, if you play "Boogie Wonderland" by Earth Wind and Fire backwards at 33 ^{1}/$_3$, you can hear me saying, "Jesus Christ, am I ever beat!"

I crawled into my apartment, hunger and fatigue fighting it out for control of my body. Fatigue won by a

TKO, and I crumpled into bed for a few precious minutes of rest before going to Sawyer's and attempting to pass off one sorry piece of human wreckage as an entertainer.

I felt only slightly better a scant two hours (and no dinner) later, sitting at a back table at Sawyer's, clutching a cup of coffee and wishing only that I could shoot it directly into my bloodstream. Snookie massaged my shoulders with his strong, long-fingered hands. As I was nearly numb with fatigue, I did not actually feel it, but it was a nice gesture.

"Oh, Snooks," I moaned, "just shoot me. Shoot me now. They shoot horses, don't they? Jane Fonda told me, they really do shoot horses."

"Now don't worry, Honey," Snookie said, "I could wheel you onstage in a deep coma, with eye-vees in every orifice, and you'd still give a performance. You'll get through it."

I got through it.

I staggered up to the mic stand, grabbed onto it for dear life, and went on automatic pilot for three full sets. I haven't any idea what I sang that night, or if I was even passably good. But I got through it.

I made no attempt to circulate after the show. I'm not sure I even said good night to Snookie. I sleepwalked to my car, fell behind the wheel, and somehow made it to Keith's.

Keith greeted me at the door with his big arms full of hugs and his lips fairly dripping with kisses. I yawned hello and collapsed into Keith's arms, wanting nothing so much as to fall asleep against Keith's chest.

Keith's earth-tone modular sofa was singing Circe's solo, and I answered the call, making a beeline to the couch, plopping onto it, and kicking the loafers off my poor, tired feet.

"I bought a nice Chardonnay," Keith said, seemingly oblivious to the fact that I was about to be declared legally dead. "I'll get it. Be right back," he said, heading for the kitchen. "Don't go 'way."

In lieu of a reply, my mouth flew open in a yawn I could barely cover with both hands; and I settled back into the sofa cushions. I closed my eyes, and yawned again, making no attempt to cover it.

He couldn't have been gone more than a minute or two.

I awoke to the smell of frying bacon, a scent which had the rather Proustian effect of sending me back in time and space to Clara's kitchen. Clara cooked breakfast exactly once a week, on Saturday mornings. The rest of the week David and I were left to our own devices. Still, those Saturday-morning breakfasts of bacon and eggs, or pancakes and Log Cabin syrup, were among the high watermarks of what was otherwise a dreary childhood at best. Eyes still unopened, I snuggled under the blankets, wrapped in warm, fuzzy memories of familial love and hot hominy grits with melting butter.

Slowly, it dawned upon me where I was. I reached out and felt the uninhabited side of the bed — it was still warm. Keith had obviously carried me to bed. I was more than a bit sorry I hadn't been awake for that one. I buried my face in Keith's pillow, and enjoyed the smell of his hair. I stretched out across the bed, covering as much of it as I could. I had awakened in Keith Keller's bed, and I liked it. Liked it a lot.

I climbed out of bed with some reluctance, pulled on my jeans, and followed the breakfast odors downstairs.

Keith stood in the kitchen, backlit into silhouette by the Saturday-morning sunshine streaming through the

133

window, in a gray UCLA t-shirt, a pair of once-white gym shorts, and no shoes. He was shoving scrambled eggs around a frying pan. My mouth watered; whether from the breakfast scents in the morning air or the sight of my sunlit love, who could tell? Keith smiled in my direction.

"'Morning, June," he said.

"Hello, Ward," I cooed in my best Barbara Billingsley. "Where are the boys?"

Keith set down the fork he was holding and swept me into his arms in a flourish of mock dramatics.

"I gave them each a quarter and sent them to the movies."

He kissed me a long Hollywood kiss.

"Hope you're hungry," Keith whispered in mock seduction.

"By some coincidence, I'm starved."

"Then I hope you like scrambled eggs," he said. "If you don't, just lie to me," he said, turning the eggs out onto plates. "There's only so much a man's ego can withstand."

I leaned against Keith's back and kissed the nape of his neck.

"Hey, I'm real sorry about last night," I said. "I'd had such an impossible day, and I was *so* tired. Certainly no reflection on the company."

"Well, that's good to know. I was beginning to harbor serious doubts about my sex appeal."

"Believe me, Mr. Keller: your sex appeal is very much intact."

"God, what a relief," he said, pantomiming wiping sweat from his brow. "Sit. Eat," Keith said, carrying the plates to the table. "There are children starving in Europe."

"India."

"Wherever," he said, taking a seat across from me.

"Make no mistake," I said, digging into a healthy helping of eggs, "Keith Keller gives good breakfast."

"Thank you," Keith smiled. "You're encouraged to kiss the cook."

Our smiles met over the table at a midpoint between our faces, shook hands, and walked off arm in arm.

"Anyway," Keith said, "I did learn a valuable lesson from this experience."

"Really, now? And what might that be?"

"If I ever hope to spend any time with you in a waking state, it will probably have to be during daylight hours. And, by the by, what are you doing today?"

"You mean you actually want to spend the day with me after the rollicking good time I showed you last night?"

"Of course. Do you think I'd slave over a hot stove for just any old Friday-night trick? So, how about it? Today? Huh? Can we, huh?"

"No, I'm afraid not. I've got to drive out to Laguna Beach this afternoon. Me and Snookie are doing a wedding down there in the morning, and tonight we're going to see some friend of Snooks in some show or other. I'm all yours for the next, oh, two or three hours, though. That is," I said in a breathy Rita Hayworth vamp voice, "if you want me."

"Oh, well," he said. "If that's all I can get. Eat up fast and get your *derriere noir* upstairs and back into bed pronto."

"You nasty boy."

"Too true. Want some coffee?"

"Love some."

Keith went to the kitchen to pour the coffee, and I watched his lovely caboose pull away.

"How do you take it?"

"A lotta milk, no sugar. You know," I said, accepting a cup and tickling the back of Keith's hand in the bargain, "you're going to make somebody a good little husband someday."

"That's what I'm hoping," Keith replied, a meaningful look in his eyes that I didn't have the chance to question, as we were interrupted by the ring of the telephone.

"Hello?" Keith answered. A quizzical look crossed his face. "Yes, he is." He held the receiver toward me. "It's for you."

It was my turn to look puzzled. Who knew I was here? There was only one person alive with the gall to track me down to Keith's place.

"Hello, Snookie, and this better be good."

"Oh, Honey, I'm so sorry to call you there, but I had to get in touch with you, and you weren't at home, so I figured if you were half the man I think you are, you had to be with him, and he was in the book, and I'm really sorry. You weren't like right in the middle of anything, were you?"

"Not yet, but make it quick, okay?"

"Okay. Quickly. Marsha just called. Rudy Wilson had a cancellation today."

"You're kidding."

"No. He was supposed to shoot some glamour-puss this afternoon — Marsha wouldn't tell me who, and would I just *love* to know — well, it seems her boyfriend beat her up, gave her a shiner that Max Factor couldn't begin to cover, so she had to cancel."

"Oh, shit! Why today? Why the hell'd he have to hit her today?"

"Oh-ho. Planning to spend the morning with Tall Blond and Adorable, were we?"

"In a word, yes."

"Johnnie Ray, believe me, I know what you're going through, but you need this photo shoot, you've got to have a really good head shot, and this is Rudy Wilson, for chrissakes."

Sigh.

"What time?"

"High noon."

"Great shit in the morning — it's ten-thirty now. I'm going to have to hurry."

"All right then, hurry. Pick you up, your place, eleven-thirty."

"Okay, dammit."

"Bye. Dammit."

Click.

I returned to the table, where Keith was absently chewing on a piece of toast.

"Why do I get the feeling I no longer have you for the next, oh, two or three hours?"

I plopped down into my chair.

"Goddamn it, I've got this photo shoot with Rudy Wilson."

"*The* Rudy Wilson?"

"The very one. He seems to be a friend of Marsha's, and he agreed to do a session with me whenever he had some free time. He had a cancellation today, and he's offered to fit me in. I really have to do this. You've seen my head shot — it's about two years old; Snookie took it in his apartment. No frills, just one-two-three, smile, and say cheese. And this is *the* Rudy Wilson, after all."

"So I won't see you again until next week."

"I know."

"Well, when do you have to go?"

"'Bout an hour."

Keith raised one eyebrow and the corresponding corner of his mouth in a nasty little half-smile.

"'Bout an hour," he said. "That should be just long enough."

"Long enough for what? One hopes."

He just smiled.

The Rudy Wilson himself met us at the door of his Hollywood mansion. He was a surprisingly small elfin creature, balding and barefoot, wearing a pair of jeans he must have owned since high school, and a "So Many Men, So Little Time" t-shirt. He kissed Snookie and me on both cheeks; he and Marsha kissed and embraced and called each other Dahling like dear old friends.

"Mahsha, Dahling," Rudy nearly sang, "you didn't tell me he was so beautiful." Meaning me — I tried not to smile. "Such cheekbones." He scurried along the marble floor, and we followed as best we could.

Mr. Wilson was obviously doing quite well for himself, thank you very much. The house was done in high tech; but very high tech — bare black marble floors, chrome and glass furniture everywhere, a general air as warm and homey as an empty Frigidaire. Not my particular cup of tea — I'm an Art Deco man, myself — but it was striking and obviously cost mucho.

"My deahs," Rudy called over his shoulder, "I've just finished a shoot, and the place is a mess! You know rock stars."

"Oh, of course," I said, tongue firmly planted in cheek.

."Rock stars?" Snookie said. "Who? What rock stars?"

Rudy's studio was a veritable mob scene of makeup people, lighting people, friends, and assorted hangers-on — obviously left over from the rock star shoot — with everyone milling about while Debbie Harry tested the distortion threshhold of some artfully hidden stereo speakers. Various potables, smokables, and mirrors were passed freely around, and Snookie quickly got into the swing of things, circulating the room, drinking wine, and sampling anything that crossed his path. Marsha chatted animatedly with the various exotic Hollywood types, many of whom she seemed to know personally.

A tall, reed-thin blond boy handed me a glass of wine I didn't really want — I sipped it anyway — while another pretty young man, in David Bowie's old hair, a white silk caftan, and entirely too much makeup, applied a light base of Max Factor Light Egyptian to my face. The dozen or so silver bracelets on the boy's right wrist played softly in my ear.

"You know, they created this makeup for Lena Horne," the boy said in a voice he'd borrowed from Marilyn Monroe.

"Yes, I did know."

Pause. Brush-brush.

"You have beautiful skin," he said.

"Thank you."

Brush. Apply.

"Would you like me to suck you off?"

"I beg your pardon?"

"I said, would you like me to—"

"I — uh. What? Here?"

Now I like a good bee-jay as much as the next fella, and this was hardly my very first offer; but there was something about being so brazenly propositioned by this willowy little number in the white dress that caught me quite off guard.

"Whatsa matter, Honey?" he said, tickling my throat with his makeup brush. "Cat got your tongue?"

I hadn't yet managed a coherent reply before Rudy called, "Ready!"

It took me a while to get relaxed. I looked like a wooden Indian, and I knew it.

As a general rule, I have a bit of trouble with cameras pointed in my direction. Just another bothersome little holdover from my childhood. I did not photograph well as a youngster. I still cringe at the sight of snapshots of David and me. Standing next to my ever-lovely brother, in the backyard, or on Main Street in Disneyland beneath my mouse ears, I look like so much compost.

"David is so photogenic," they'd say, careful not to mention me, and I'd want to be dead. When I was about seven years old, I went through all of Clara's photo albums and tore myself out of each and every group picture. Lance whipped me with his thinnest belt until welts raised like bas-relief on the backs of my legs.

I tried another approach. I became the invisible child.

When Lance unleashed the Brownie at family barbeques, I locked myself in the bathroom. Or hid my face behind my hands (no amount of "Johnnie Ray, move your hands" from Clara would stop me). Or slipped behind Aunt Lucille's picture hat. Except for school pictures, there is scarcely a snapshot in existence of me between the ages of seven and seventeen.

So there I stood in *the* Rudy Wilson's studio. I couldn't very well lock myself in the john. Aunt Lucille was nowhere to be found.

141

"Relax, Dahling," Rudy coaxed as I struck one stiff, phony-looking pose after another. "Relax."

Finally, Snookie yelled,

"Dammit, Honey, would you just please fuckin' relax — we haven't got all day, and you're wasting this man's time!"

Well, that snapped me out of it right away, let me tell you. I stuck a genuine Clara Jane Rousseau attitude — hands on hips, lean forward, head cocked to one side — and said,

"Well, how'd you just like to kiss my big black ass, okay?"

"Beautiful," Rudy cried over the constant *click-whirrrr* of his camera. "Not exactly what I had in mind, but at least you're relaxed."

I smiled at Snookie. The little sonofagun really knew me like a book.

Rudy darted about, clicking his camera rapid-fire, clucking orders to the people shoving around the huge, hot lights and reflectors and the wind machine that billowed my shirt, if not my hair: I dug the way Rudy called everyone "Dahling" or "Deah" or "Sweethaht," just as I had always imagined a hip, happening Hollywood photographer would talk. And I played High Fashion Model to the max. I was the cover of *GQ*. I was the cover of *Rolling Stone*. I was Suzy Parker and Twiggy and Ebony Fashion Fair. I sucked in my cheeks and shook my completely immobile hair. When Rudy actually said, "Lick your lips, Dahling," I did.

When he was finished, Rudy kissed me full on the mouth.

"My deah," he said, "if you don't get a picture out of that, my name ain't *the* Rudy Wilson."

We didn't pull into Laguna until nearly six. Snookie insisted upon driving, and, as the photo shoot had been a solid ball, and I could still pick up Keith's smell on my fingertips, I was in no mood to argue, despite the fact that I hated Snookie's car with all my heart and soul. It was a late-model AMC Pacer; all window, a fishbowl on wheels — on a hot day, there was no escaping the heat. And it was a very hot day. Besides, Snooks lived in that car. There were McDonald's Quarter Pounder wrappers in the backseat that would have required carbon dating; the ashtrays were in a perpetual state of overflow. But it was a good deal roomier than my Vee-dub, and the radio worked — a definite plus for a long jaunt — so I said what the hey.

The car overheated four times on the way, and by the time we reached the Beach, we were as hot and gritty as the white lines on the road. We pulled into a Denny's for dinner, and rubbed off a few layers of freeway from our faces in the men's room.

Two friends of Snookie's were putting us up for the night. Just where these two guys fit into Snookie's life was a fact Snooks chose to evade, although I managed to gather something about his having met one of them in a sauna somewhere. At any rate, one of these fellas was appearing in a local summer stock production of *West Side Story*. Two tickets for this production awaited us in a tiny white envelope with Snookie's name on it at the box office of the nearby junior college. James would be meeting us at the theater before the show; James's lover, Brian — who was playing A-rab in the show — would meet us after.

I disliked James on sight. I very seldom pass judgment on a person at a glance, but when I do, that judgment is carved into stone tablets, unchanging and eternal. James was tall and blond and good-looking in a cleft-chinned, long-toothed, obvious sort of way. He was wearing a scoop-front tank top and a pair of Levi's that had obviously been sandpapered at the crotch. His skin had the tough, grainy appearance peculiar to genuine rawhide wallets and to the faces of those who consider suntanning an art form. There was no doubt in my mind that this man combed lemon juice into his hair on a habitual basis.

When he shook my hand, I knew we'd never be bosom chums. For me, a man's handshake must be firm and sure. Shaking hands with James was like grabbing a handful of yesterday's Caesar salad.

Snookie, on the other hand, seemed to think James was the very cat's ass. He gushed over James well past the point of disgust. Had there been an Adirondack Little League baseball bat handy, I would surely have broken at least one of Snookie's kneecaps, just to stop him from giggling.

Our seats were in the front row. And as every stage-door Johnny knows, front-row seats in almost any pro-scenium arch theater in America means one of two things: the back of your neck aches for a week to ten days following the performance, or you spend two hours and forty minutes watching shoes. I never, but never, sit front row. Snookie knew this only too well, and as we scooted sideways over a rowful of feet toward our seats, he shot me a look imploring me not to say anything snotty about looking straight up all evening long. A monument to self-control, I said nothing. Snooks maneuvered himself next to James, while I was seated next to a woman roughly the size of a '66 Chevy Impala, and her baby.

West Side Story has never been one of my favorite stage shows, mostly because I love the movie so much. Who could hope to compete with Natalie Wood's face and Marnie Nixon's voice? Not to mention Rita Moreno's legs, George Chakiris in tight purple pants, and the original Jerome Robbins choreography. No semiprofessional stage production could hope to compete with that. Still, people keep mounting one production of the show after another, and I seem to get shanghaied into going to at least half of them. I've seen Maria played by a black girl and Anita by a blonde. I've seen countless Caucasians in brownface (Max Factor Light Egyptian, perhaps) playing Puerto Ricans. I've seen Officer Krupke played by a woman. And, I swear to God, Snookie once took me to a rat-infested run-down flimsy excuse for a theater in Hollywood where *West Side Story* was done in punk rock drag, with the Jets as skinheads and the Sharks in safety pin chic. When Maria walked onstage in a purple Mohawk, I walked out in a huff.

This production was much more traditional. Right off the rack. A B-plus term project for *West Side Story* 101. The orchestra was abbreviated — the string parts mimicked by a Prophet 20 synthesizer — but, except for the occasional disagreement on some of Lenny Bernstein's more ambitiously syncopated passages, it was okay. Maria was pretty and witty and gay, if a bit shrill. Tony was also pretty and witty and (unless my boofoo geiger

145

counter was on the serious fritz) also quite gay. He had one of those warbling nasal tenor voices that made my back teeth ache. The last note of "Maria" demanded a bullet to bite on. The Sharks' Puerto Rican accents owed much to Ricky Ricardo.

Both gangs were composed of just the sort of three-dance-classes-a-week-at-Roland-Dupree's, theater-major-dance-minor-at-Cal-State types I'd come to expect of stock productions of this and every musical written since before Cohan ever saw the flag. All of them cute as cocker spaniel puppies with their high, perfect little dancers' butts and baskets bulgy with dance belts; all of them dancing as if the floor had little numbered footprints painted on it; all of them queer as a three-dollar bottle of cologne.

During the "When You're a Jet" number, one of the Jets (the boys without the café au lait paint jobs and the Frito Bandito accents) caught my eye. It wasn't just that he was the best dancer in the bunch (which he was), or that he was blond (which didn't hurt), or even that he was as pretty as a three-no-trump bridge hand. It was all that. I elbowed Snookie.

"Snooks," I whispered, "wouldja just look at that."

"That's Brian," he said. "We're spending the night with him."

"How nice," I said.

The *West Side Story* cast party was held at James and Brian's immediately following last curtain call. As cast parties go, it was first cousin to every other cast party I'd ever attended. Lots of beer and cheep wine, pizzas delivered cold, lots of loud music, and couples grinding in every possible corner of the house. What set this particular fete apart from any one I'd attended in high school was that, by my own count, only three couples included both a boy and a girl.

146

Snookie had taken a fancy to the tall, dark, and handsome number who had played Tony in the show. His name was Rex. Honest. Straight-straight nose, entirely too many teeth; a voice like a Bach trumpet and a lisp you could shower in.

"Now, I don't even want you *looking* at Rex," Snookie warned me on the way from the theater to the party. "He'll take one look at that smile of yours and those damned biceps of yours and I won't have a prayer. Besides, you've got yours at home."

"Don't worry about me: I think the man is quite insipid myself. I gladly leave this one to you."

"Well, just see that you do."

So, when Rex made his fashionably late diva's entrance, and made a beeline across the crowded living room to where Snooks and I stood, smiling like there was no tomorrow, I said,

"Excuse me, but I do believe I smell my soufflé burning," and I fairly sprinted into the kitchen.

Brian was at the sink, rinsing glasses. He was even more adorable offstage. Every inch of five feet three, he looked rather like Beany from the old Beany and Cecil cartoons: snub-nosed and freckled and cuddly-looking as the old teddy bear your mom took away when you were five. He looked up and smiled.

"Hi. I'm Brian."

"I know. I'm Johnnie Ray, and you were very good in the show."

"Really?" He stopped in midrinse. "Did you really think so?"

"Yes, I do. You were one of the best things in the show." It was nice not to have to lie. I'd have trouble telling any performer he was good if he wasn't, no matter how cute he might look in a pair of sawed-off Levi's and his lover's too-big shirt, dishwater dampening the front of his short yellow-gold hair. "In fact, I thought you should have been Riff."

"So did I. That little bitch was suckin' off the director, I swear. What'd jew say your name was?"

"Johnnie Ray."

"Johnnie Ray," he repeated. "What's your sign?"

"Capricorn," I admitted, trying not to laugh. What's your sign? I mean, really.

"You're kidding? Me, too. When's your birthday?"

"Christmas Day."

"You're kidding? Mine, too. Jesus Christ, we're sisters!" And he jumped up on tiptoe, threw his arms around my neck (his hands dripping warm wet spots down the back of my shirt), and kissed my cheek.

"Well, well, what have we here?" Rex sashayed into the kitchen. "I'm sure James would just love to see this. Where the hell's the wine, anyway?"

"Over there, bitch," Brian said, one hand still resting against my belly. "And you know damn well that was perfectly innocent. Johnnie Ray and I have the same birthday. We're cosmic sisters."

"I'll bet." Rex poured himself a tall glass of dago red.

"Where is James, anyway?" Brian asked.

"Last I saw him he was rubbing up against half the chorus."

"Twat."

I peered around the kitchen door and spied James against a wall exchanging tongue sushi with one of the Sharks (Chico, I think — it was hard to tell with their makeup off). Chico's hand was well beneath the waistband of James's gym shorts.

I turned to look at Brian's face. It had the look of a car windshield just hit by a BB gun.

"I hate it when he does that," Brian whispered.

I put my arm around Brian's shoulders; he didn't pull away.

The last of the guests who weren't planning to stay the night finally stumbled out around three-thirty or four. Rex was staying. In what I'm sure he considered a major coup, Snookie booked himself into the second bedroom with Rex. Another cast member — Baby John, I believe — spread a few blankets for himself on the living room sofa, and I unfurled a sleeping bag on the floor nearby. I didn't mind. If I'm tired enough — and that night I was really beat — I could sleep standing up in the cheap seats at Dodger Stadium during the seventh-inning stretch. Despite the juicy sex sounds streaming from under the doors of both bedrooms, I'd probably been stretched out on the floor for five or six minutes before dropping off to sleep.

I awoke suddenly from some vaguely nasty dream of Keith, opened my eyes, and looked up into little Brian's not-so-little crotch. I was momentarily startled, both from the expected temporary sense of what the Germans call *Gevurfenheit*, thrownness, that clichéd "where am I" feeling of waking up suddenly in a strange place, and because I had no idea how long Brian had been standing over me. My dick was so hard it hurt; whether from the mental residue of my dirty dream or from the sight of Brian's genitals dangling over my face like the perfect present on the Christmas tree, who could say?

"Are you asleep?" Brian asked, dropping to a cross-legged seated position on the floor next to my head.

"No. Not anymore." I propped myself up on my elbow. "What's up?" Besides the obvious, of course.

Brian cocked his head toward the first bedroom. I was pretty sure I recognized Snookie's voice among the sounds of carnal pleasure emanating from the room, attesting to some rather wild goings-on behind door number one.

"Not into mob scenes?" I said.

"Uh-uh."

"Me neither. One at a time, *s'il vous plaît.*"

We sat quiet for a moment, during which I couldn't resist reaching out and touching Brian. He was, after all, so close, so seemingly vulnerable, and so very naked. I ran my finger over the instep of one of his tiny feet, strummed his teensy toes like ukelele strings.

"You're so small," I thought aloud.

"Thank you," Brian said.

"I'm sorry. That wasn't a value judgment or anything. I just..." I considered mentioning that Brian's full-size genitalia were all the more striking set as they were against his three-quarter-size body, but decided to drop it.

There was another momentary silence; Brian reached over and fingered my hair. When the quiet was pierced through with a particularly piercing howl from the bedroom, Brian quickly jerked his hand back to his lap.

"James loves me," Brian said all of a sudden. "Whatever else he may do, James truly loves me." Brian's voice had raised in volume a bit; I glanced over to the couch where slept Baby John. He didn't stir.

My erection had finally subsided, allowing me to sit up and face Brian without embarrassment.

"Of course he loves you," I said, more out of a spasm of cosmic sisterly comfort than out of any real conviction concerning James's alleged love for his diminutive roommate.

"We're going to get married," Brian said.

"Married? How do you mean?"

150

"I mean married. In the church."

My first impulse was laughter. As that seemed quite inappropriate to Brian's tone of voice and facial expression, I held it in check.

"Married," I repeated. "Might one be so bold as to inquire why?"

"I'm from Tennessee originally. Chickasaw County. I was raised up in the Baptist Church. And where I come from, when two people love each other, they get married."

I looked into Brian's eyes as well as I could in the semidark. The boy seemed dead serious about this marriage thing.

Now, I was raised in the Baptist Church myself. I briefly considered pointing out to little Bri that, to my knowledge at least, the Church was not in the practice of marrying male couples; but thought better of it, and said nothing.

"We'll get married," Brian said with some finality. "It's only a matter of time."

I was hard pressed for a comeback for that. Brian relieved me of the responsibility.

"You know something," he said, "I've never been attracted to a black man before." He reached over and stroked a soft, slow little road down my chest. I watched in silence as his childlike hand moved down my front, leaving a prickly sensation trail in its wake. He'd really caught me looking the other way with that one.

"You have a very nice body," he said, tracing a particularly prominent vein in my right biceps with his finger. "You have beautiful genitals," he whispered, cupping my balls with one little-boy hand, not quite encircling my cock with the other. No one was more surprised than I when Brian spit into his hand and began stroking me. I took hold of Brian's plump, pretty dick, and we jerked each other off like a couple of nasty schoolboys.

I came quickly ("I'm comin', Beany-boy!"), clapping a hand over my mouth for fear of waking Baby John. Funny thing, but as I blew my wad all over my own belly and Brian's fingers, the face I saw behind my tightly clenched eyelids was Keith's. Brian shot nearly up to his face, biting down on his lower lip and clenching his sticky little fists.

We wiped each other off with wet paper towels in the kitchen, smiling and giggling, touching and kissing.

"Would you hold me, please," Brian said. "Just please hold me."

And hold him I did. I sat on the kitchen floor, back against the cool enamel of the stove, and held the little boy-man close all night. Brian smoked cigarette after cigarette, and we talked and talked. About love. And sex. And marriage. And the childhood horror of having the same birthday as Jesus Christ. Until we could see the sun rise over the kitchen windowsill.

I awoke shortly after nine o'clock, after less than three hours sleep. I had a wedding to sing at eleven. Snookie was already up, sitting in the kitchen in his boxers, sipping coffee with James and Rex, looking well rested, well fucked, and (to my groggy little mind) just a bit smug.

I stumbled into the kitchen, half-blind and quite naked, following the coffee smell.

"Well," James crooned, "what have we here?"

"Mmnf," I said.

"Hope we didn't keep you awake last night," said James.

I nearly said something real bitchy, like "Oh, no problem — the sounds of your boyfriend jerking on my dork drowned you out." But I just let it go.

"Actually," Rex said, "I wanted to ask you in, but Sid here said you really needed your sleep."

"Dear Snooks," I rasped. Snookie smiled sheepishly, unsure if I was being sarcastic or not. I meant it. I regretted it not at all that I had not been the fourth wheel of their little joy wagon.

"Coffee?" James offered.

"Oh, God, yes."

I quickly downed three cups of black coffee and two strawberry Pop Tarts; showered, shaved, and dressed in my one and only suit (a gray single-breasted Calvin Klein). Snookie exchanged deep tongue kisses and telephone numbers with both James and Rex at the door, and said hey let's get together sometime. James said hey stop by anytime.

Brian was still asleep when we piled into Snookie's Pacer and putted away. I would have liked to have said good-bye to the kid, and wished him luck.

I wonder if they ever got married.

The wedding was a beautiful, if an odd, experience. But then, Otis and Marlena were a beautiful, if odd, couple. They'd come up to me after the second set one night at Sawyer's, a man with his arm around his woman friend's heaving shoulders, the woman weeping like a two-year-old who's just dropped her double-dip rocky road ice cream cone kersplat on the hot summer sidewalk.

These two were easily the plainest couple I'd ever laid eyes upon. Plain as dirt. Plain as the nose on your face. Two-cents plain. Not ugly, mind you, I mean not turn-you-to-stone butt ugly, but plain. He, short and plump and doughy as a cold popover; she, all stringy off-blonde hair and tiny close-set eyes magnified to ridiculous proportions by a pair of what used to be called granny glasses (the nosepiece of which was held together with a wound-up wad of Scotch tape). They were probably no more than a couple of years older than I, but they had a look of perpetual middle age: they looked about forty-two; they had probably looked forty-two at birth, and in ten years they'd still look forty-two. I loved them immediately.

"Hi, there," said the man, extending a pudgy hand, furry nearly to the nails. "My name's Otis, and this" —

he indicated the walking tear duct under his left arm — "is Marlena."

"Hi," Marlena half sobbed. Sniff. Hiccup. "Hi."

"Hi," I said somewhat tentatively. "Is something the matter?"

"Oh, no." Otis made an overlarge cartoonish gesture with both arms. His shirt was sweat-soaked from his armpits halfway to his waist. "It's just that we'd like you to sing at our wedding."

"Oh, really?" I smiled. I love weddings. Here comes the bride, all dressed in white, goin' to the chapel of love. Gimme that white lace and orange blossoms every time. No matter how tired and cynical I may become, every time I hear those do-you's and I-do's, damned if I don't have to blink back a tear, and damned if I don't believe in the whole crock all over again. Love. Marriage. Forever till eter-nah-tee. The whole schmeer.

"Well," I said, "if I'm free the day of your wedding, I'd be honored."

Marlena sobbed a thank-you.

"Did I do that?" I asked, indicating the still-sobbing Marlena.

Otis nodded.

"She started right in the middle of 'Earth Angel,' and she hasn't stopped since."

"Really?" The idea that I'd moved this ordinary Plain Jane of a woman to tears was pleasing indeed. As a man who still bursts into uncontrollable tears every time I hear "So Much in Love" by the Tymes, I could appreciate any woman moved to hysterical tears by song, especially mine.

"In fact," Otis continued, "that's what we want you to sing at the wedding."

"What's what you want me to sing at the wedding?"

"'Earth Angel.'"

"You're kidding."

"Nope," he insisted. "It's our song."

Marlena, who had by this time finally managed to find the OFF switch on her optical sprinkler system, stopped her sobbing, sniffled, and nodded her agreement.

"Oh," I said. How odd, I thought. In my relatively brief career as a semiprofessional pop vocalist, I'd done at least my fair share of weddings. Weddings are the pop musician's bread (if not butter). They are, by and large, the most excruciating kind of gig a musician can play, but they usually pay well, so I did them. Every chance I got. I'd sung the Ave Maria from the choir loft at St. Monica's; I'd sung *Fiddler on the Roof* medleys at the *tres juif* Hillcrest Country Club in Beverly Hills. I'd sung "We've Only Just Begun" and "For All We Know" so many times they should have made me an honorary Carpenter. But never had I been asked to sing anything as off the left wall as "Earth Angel."

"Seriously?" I had not discounted the possibility that this guy was pulling my leg. I mean, we did "Earth Angel" as a full-on doo-wop number, four-part harmony and the whole deal. Sha Na Na material. Where were these two planning to get married? On a New Jersey street corner?

"Of course," said the finally dry-eyed Marlena, her first completely intelligible words so far.

"Well," I said, "'Earth Angel' you want, 'Earth Angel' you shall have."

"Oh, thank you." Marlena suddenly hurled herself at me in a potentially whiplash-inducing embrace around my neck.

"Just a coupla things I oughta tell you," Otis said.

And I thought, Uh-oh. Here it comes. I disengaged Marlena from around my neck.

"The wedding's going to be in Laguna Beach," Otis said.

"Is *that* all." I shrugged. Although I'd never actually been to Laguna Beach, I was relatively sure I could cope with it.

"And," Otis continued, lifting the westernmost half of his one long, bushy eyebrow, "I'm afraid we can't afford to pay you very much."

"Well, how much is not very much, exactly?"

"Two hundred dollars?"

Now, there's only so much two hundred dollars could get you in this ever-changing world in which we live in, even as far back as the summer of '79. One thing two hundred dollars would definitely *not* get you was any five-piece combo known to man. There wasn't so much as a Canoga Park garage band (median age of members being fifteen and a half) that would haul down to Laguna for two hundred lousy bucks.

What Otis and Marlena got for two hundred pazoo-zahs was me, Snookie, and the American Popular Song in what in many states of the Union could pass for its entirety. The hatchback of Snookie's Pacer carried to Laguna Snookie's entire pop sheet music collection — the entire contents of his piano bench and a small filing cabinet, the top shelf of his bedroom closet, and then some. That collection in hand, and my own astounding memory for song lyrics in mind, we were ready for just about anything.

The wedding, held in the living room of the rambling Frank Lloyd Wright-ish Laguna Beach home of Marlena's parents, easily fell into the just-about-anything category. For one thing, Otis was Jewish and Marlena, Irish Catholic, which afforded all the latter-day Abie's Irish Rose-isms one could ask for, and then some. The couple were married under the chuppa, Otis looking like Petrushka the Dancing Bear in his powder blue polyester tuxedo, Marlena as close to pretty as she was likely to ever get in a white satin dress with puffy Snow White sleeves. A clergyman of unclear denomination read from the Torah, the Douay Bible, and Kahlil Gibran, after which I stood in the elbow of the rented baby grand piano and sang "Earth Angel." Snookie had done a simple, decidedly un-Penguin arrangement, so it was likely that many of the older guests (squirming in their uncomfortable Abby Rents folding metal chairs) found it indistinguishable from "We've Only Just Begun." After the song, Otis broke a glass with his heel, and half the guests yelled mazel tov, while the rest crossed themselves.

The reception was held in the downstairs rumpus room. Snookie pounded more sound out of a small, not-quite-in-tune upright than I would have thought possible, and there was dancing. We played dance band, Snookie taking two or three choruses, me taking a vocal chorus (look at me — I'm Marion Hutton), and then Snookie taking the last chorus and out. I must have sung eight or nine choruses of "Bei Mir Bist Du Schoen" — every time we'd finish, the Jewish delegation would yell, "Vun more time." We fielded requests from people our age who asked for "My Sharona" and who were laughingly surprised when we did it, and from roly-poly middle-aged ladies with Betty Boop voices, who gigglingly requested Al Jolson hits and were pleasantly shocked when I — a 22-year-old shvartz — knew them. I rummaged through the stacks of sheet music while Snookie played instrumentals. We did "Smoke Gets in Your

Eyes" and "There's a Kind of Hush," and "Earth Angel" again. We did "Great Balls of Fire," "Whole Lotta Shakin' Goin' On," and "Sea Cruise" as an impromptu medley, and we twisted the afternoon away.

While Snookie played a fox trot and I looked through the charts for "I've Got the World on a String," Otis, his clip-on butterfly bow tie dangling from his collar, touched me on the shoulder.

"You don't have to do this if you don't want to," he said.

"Oh?" I'd come all the way to Laguna for two hundred clams to sing in somebody's rumpus room. What could he possibly think might be beneath me?

"Aunt Lena wants to sing," Otis said.

I glanced at Snookie, who'd been listening while he played, and I knew he felt the same way I did.

"This is your wedding, Dude. You want Aunt Lena to sing..." I shrugged.

Otis led a tiny, bent woman in white to the piano. She was all of four and a half feet tall, with a little hump in her back. Her lacy white dress gave her an achingly sad Miss Havisham look — the only other woman in white was the bride herself. Aunt Lena's hands were gnarled into utter uselessness by arthritis — she no doubt required help dressing — but her eyes were the sparkling clear dark eyes of a young girl.

"'Sunrise, Sunset,'" Otis said.

Snookie didn't need the chart for this one. There hasn't been a Jewish (or even a half-Jewish) wedding since 1964 that didn't include "Sunrise, Sunset."

The old lady hooked her tiny arm around Otis's and held him fiercely to her side as she half sang, half whispered, "Is this the little boy I carried?" You could have heard a pin drop onto the indoor-outdoor carpeted floor

160

as Aunt Lena rasped her way through the first verse. This tiny relic of a woman, obviously the matriarch of Otis's family, even hushed the Irish faction, who held their champagne-loosened tongues out of respect for the old lady's years.

"When did he grow to be so tall?" she sang, barely whispering the line; then turned her face to Otis's sleeve and cried barely audible sobs, her tears beading up and rolling off the plasticene fabric of Otis's suit.

Otis held the old tante in his arms, and I took up the song, gesturing the guests to sing along. By the time we finished, there wasn't a dry eye in the house. Least of all mine.

It was nearly ten by the time I got home. I found a note Scotch-taped to my door. I recognized the handwriting immediately; even if I hadn't, it was written on "From the desk of Keith Keller" stationery. It read:

Roberta Flack
"Blue Lights in the Basement"
side one
band one
Love, Keith

My heart did that Bo Diddly thing again. I knew very well what song the note referred to, and I hoped I was right about what the man meant by it. I dropped my overnight case and suit bag to the floor and double-timed it to the stereo. I flipped to the "F's," pulled out the album in question, and plopped it onto the turntable. And as Roberta sang, "Why don't you move in with me?" I punched Keith's phone number in rhythm with the Fender Rhodes piano in the background. He answered on the second ring.

"Ya mean it?" I said.

"I mean it," he said.

Monday morning, Keith joined me for a hurried breakfast of coffee and the strawberry croissants he brought. We ate quickly and adjourned to the bedroom to celebrate our upcoming cohabitation. I stretched out on the waterbed and Keith invented nasty new arcade games with my joystick. I watched, delighted, as he greased me up with Vaseline and slowly lowered himself, straddling my hips, coming to rest on my pelvis.

I had never imagined that the big guy might like to be fucked. I was sitting back on the big cloud number nine, watching Keith execute a slow set of deep squats on my wienie. He was as beautiful as anything I had ever seen, kneeling over me, head back, lips parted and somewhat swollen, sucking in short breaths through his teeth like someone learning to smoke dope. I plucked at Keith's puckered, distended nipples, traced the deep clefts where his hard waist merged with his pelvis; my fingers followed a prominent blue-green vein running like a ragged road from his navel, over the porcelain white skin where his tan ended, down to his groin. I jerked him off with both hands.

Afterwards, Keith lay in my arms, warm and sticky wet and smelling of fuck, his big head on my chest, the weight of him nearly painful. I stroked his big, damp back, stubbing my fingertips now and then on one of the moles that peppered his back and shoulders.

"I love you, Johnnie," he said.

"I love you, Keith."

We lay there for a while, knowing we couldn't afford the luxury much longer; that we'd soon have to shower the love-funk from our skin, dress, and get to work. A disturbing thought fell into my mind like a stray eyelash into your eye.

"What about Betsy?" I wondered — silently, I'd thought, until Keith raised up on his elbows.

"What?"

"Betsy," I repeated, not entirely sure this was a subject I should have broached right then. "What about Betsy? You loved her."

"Oh, Babe," he said. "I did love her once. And in my way, I guess I'll always love her. But it's been over between us for a long time. I think she knew it, too. But she just didn't want to let go." He rolled off me and lay on his back looking up at the ceiling. "And I didn't want to hurt her if there was no need to. I wasn't in love with her, but I wasn't in love with anyone else." He moved onto his side and touched my belly. "Until I met you, my dark beauty, there was just no need to hurt her."

I clutched Keith to me as tightly as I could. My love for him, and the knowledge of his love for me, made me overflow with gladness like a shook-up beer overflows with foam; even as the probability that our love would someday, sooner or later, also end tapped me on the shoulder like a pesky neighbor.

"I wish I could tell you it's forever," Keith said, as if picking up my thoughts like the smell of my skin. "All I can tell you is I love you, Babe."

"I know," I said. "We've got to go to work."

Snookie was uncharacteristically skeptical of the move.

"Are you sure this is what you want?" We were back at his place after work on Monday, bopping out new charts for the Blue Dahlia.

"Sure, I'm sure. The man of my every jerk-off fantasy has asked me to move in with him. And you ask if I'm sure this is what I want."

"Well, Honey, you must admit this is all rather sudden. I mean, you've only known the man two weeks. I'm the first to admit he's the S.S. *Dreamboat*, but what do you really know about him?"

"He loves me, Snooks." I straddled the piano bench whereon Snookie sat and hugged him close from behind. "And I love him. I knew I loved him that very first night. What else is there to know?"

"What else?" Snookie pulled free of my embrace and turned to face me. "Honey, you know I'm as much in favor of the old *l'amour toujours* as anybody on the planet, so I hate to have to be the one to point out that you were the gal who, one short week ago, didn't have time to fall in love, and suddenly you're taking up housekeeping with this hunk banker with a past history of some confusion in the sexual preference department."

165

"Meaning?"

"Meaning" — Snookie jabbed his half-smoked cigarette into an overflowing ashtray and lit a fresh one — "meaning you might stop talking like the Ronette's greatest hits for a minute and just consider a few things."

"Such as?"

"Such as, what ever happened to that girlfriend of his — Brunhilde or whatever her name is."

"Betsy."

"Yeah, what about Betsy? How do you know he won't go running back to her week after next?"

"Snookseleh, Snookseleh, Snookseleh," I said. "It's over between Keith and Betsy. He told me so himself."

"And you believed him?"

"Of course. True, he was lying on top of me at the time."

"Oh, fine."

"It's over between them," I said. "Over and over and over again."

"All right then, we'll give him the benefit of the doubt."

"We?"

"But how do you know you can live with this man? You've lived alone for a long time now; you've gotten pretty well used to having your own space. Besides, what if he's got some really disgusting habits? Like he leaves his filthy underwear with the visible skid marks laying around the house?"

"Like you?" I gestured toward a small pile of decaying laundry that had taken up what seemed to be permanent residence in one corner of the living room.

"Beside the point," he said quickly. "Entirely beside the point."

"Oh? And what, pray tell, *is* the point?" There was something sticking at Snookie's craw, and I had a hunch it had nothing to do with whether or not Keith Keller was a slob. "Well? Go ahead, spit it out. I can take it."

"All right. What if he wants you to stop singing?"

"What?"

"Let's face it, Honey — your schedule is tight and getting tighter by the minute. You're not gonna be home one helluvalot. And this could be the year your career really takes off. What if this banker person likes having you around so much that he wants you around all the time, every minute? What then?"

I chuckled the loose, carefree laugh of someone lobotomized by love.

"Snooks, Keith is not going to ask me to stop singing. I'm a singer. A singer sings. Keith knows that."

"Yeah?"

"Yeah. Are you sure that's what's eating you?"

"Of course." Snooks avoided my eyes. "What else?"

"Like maybe the possibility that Keith Keller might come between us?"

"I'm sure I don't know what you're talking about."

"That's my line, Sidney Isaac Rothenberg, and look me in the eye." I turned his face toward me. "Isn't it possible that maybe, just maybe, you've been thinking that if I move in with Keith, then we won't be Lucy and Ethel anymore?"

Snookie looked at me for a long moment. I caught just the smallest early–Judy Garland tremor around his lower lip.

"Maybe," he said.

"Oh, Snooks." I gathered my buddy in my arms and we held each other close. I blinked back a tear; Snookie sniffed wetly. "You know you'll always be my Ethel Mertz."

Snookie hiccupped and sniffed again. He said,

"I thought *you* were Ethel."

And so it was that I gave notice to the landlord of my small, furnished, one-bedroom apartment, and moved myself and my few belongings into the two-bedroom, two-and-one-half-bath townhouse condominium of one Keith Keller, Assistant Vice President and Branch Manager of First California Bank. And was quite happy.

For a time.

The move was easy for me, physically and emotionally. I owned very little in the way of furniture, as my apartment was a "furnished"; only my waterbed (a constant breach of rental agreement), which was drained, dismantled, and retired to the far corner of a walk-in closet in favor of Keith's massive four-poster, was truly mine. My compact stereo (no match for Keith's carefully coordinated ensemble of components) was banished to the closet in the company of my bed. My clothes, boxes of books, and several large, unwieldly crates containing my prized record collection, made up the bulk of the load I brought with me exactly one week from the night Keith (with some musical assistance from Roberta Flack) asked me to share his home.

After moving my belongings in, Keith and I dined at Pancho Villa, toasting each other with margaritas and seafood enchiladas as the ocean slapped at the bottom of the window whereby we sat. We adjourned to what had that very day become *our* bed, where we celebrated again.

Later, we went dancing out in West Hollywood. Keith, much to my surprise, proved (for a 200-pound white dude of Norwegian and German blood) to be a damned good dancer. How did he dance? Close. Very, very close.

We did all sixteen dances. We exchanged patently suggestive pelvic movements and nasty smiles as song merged almost imperceptibly into song. I was used to wearing out two or three dance partners a night — I liked finding someone who could keep up with me.

They played Bette Midler's "Boogie Woogie Bugle Boy," and Keith taught me the jitterbug — or tried to. I was used to dancing pretty much free-form, but I smiled gamely and counted to myself (one, step-step, back, step-step), while Keith turned and spun me like Ginger Rogers. I smiled wide, proud to be with my big, sexy lover, knowing my fellow dancers must be wondering what I could have done to land the most beautiful man in the place.

Keith took me into his arms, and I wrapped myself around his big, slippery back, our humid skins slipping and sliding against each other. We danced close and slow, swaying softly as a tightly packed floorful of dancers shook and shimmied, and some disco band (whose name I shall likely never remember, but whose voices I'll never forget) sang, "I'm a man, yes I am." Keith squeezed me so tight it nearly hurt as I sang into his ear, "And I can't help but love you so."

Later, I was leaning against the cool black wall, part of the long, long lineup of young men that stretched against both sides of the dance floor, thumbs hooked into belt loops, weight tossed onto one sneakered foot, my own version of the basic West Hollywood pseudo–James Dean cool-young-dude look on my face. Keith was at the bar fetching drinks. "Heart of Glass" began to play and even more dancers squeezed onto the already jammed-up dance floor. A long tall dude the color of a Hershey's semisweet bar strode over to where I stood. He had cheekbones clear up to his temples and the whitest smile

I had ever seen. He was shirtless, and as long-muscled as a greyhound, every ripple in his chest and stomach accentuated by the party lights and a sheen of sweat. His Levi's hung precariously low on his slim hips, inviting the eyes downward toward a bulge that was, to say the least, impressive. I thought, Wow.

The guy pointed a long index finger at my chest and said,

"Dance?"

"No," I said. "Thanks."

He stepped closer. There was a sweet, musky smell coming off the guy that I liked.

"You alone?" he asked.

I shook my head no.

"Too bad," he said. "Washa name?"

"Johnnie Ray."

"William." He pronounced it "Wee-yum." William held out his hand; his grip was hot and sweaty and strong. "You're gorgeous, Johnnie Ray."

"So are you, William." I retrieved my hand. "So are you."

I smiled. There's nothing in this earthly life I like more than being complimented, especially by beautiful men.

"You sure you're not alone?" he asked.

"I'm sure," I said. "Dammit."

"Oh, well." William shrugged. "Later." And he walked away, his high-set ass shifting in time with the music.

"Who was that?" Keith was back with an orange juice for me and a club soda with lime for himself.

"Just a guy," I said. "Asked me to dance."

"What did you say?"

"I said no, obviously."

"Did you get his phone number?"

"What would I want with his phone number?"

"Never mind," he said.

We didn't stay out much longer. Keith was pointedly quiet all the way home. And when we got there, we didn't make love again as I'd hoped we would. Keith kissed me a rather mechanical good-night, turned his back, and went to sleep.

I lay awake for what seemed like hours.

William seemed to have been quite forgotten by morning. Keith wrapped himself around my back like a big warm coat, held me close, and kissed the back of my neck until I shivered. The previous evening's discovery of Keith's surprising and, to me, wholly irrational jealousy — and of the granite silence that was his reaction — disturbed me, but not much. Nobody's perfect, after all, and I was beginning to wonder when Keith might begin to show himself to be an imperfect being like myself — heaven knows, I was beginning to wonder if he was. Besides which, I was flattered that I could elicit such a response in someone whose very insteps I worshipped. The concern I had harbored that my love for Keith easily overbalanced his for me on the Libra of our love was smoothed over.

Keith mumbled something into the nape of my neck.

"What?"

"I'm sorry, Babe," he said. "About last night. It's just that I..." He sucked in an audible breath. "God, I love you, Babe. It kills me to think of you with another man."

"Then don't think about it," I said. "I'm with you."

I turned around to face him, and we smooched our lips off until Keith had to get ready for work.

I didn't get up until after Keith had kissed me good-bye and gone off to make the world safe for T-bills. I was taking the day off — I figured Sylvia owed me one.

I called Clara.

"Hi, Baby," she said in that soft, sleepy voice of hers. I told Clara I was madly in love and obscenely happy, and had just moved in with the man of my dreams. Clara said, "That's nice, Baby."

Clara is, without doubt, the mellowest woman alive. She just doesn't get excited. If I told her I'd just been elected pope, she'd say, "That's nice, Baby."

"When you comin' to see me?" she asked.

"Soon, Ma."

"Make sure I'm still breathin'," she added. Jewish guilt. All mothers are Jewish mothers.

"Soon, Ma."

"You can bring your friend if you wanna."

"Thanks, Ma. Bye, Ma."

"Bye, Baby."

I took a long, steaming shower and didn't bother to shave. I had opened the bathroom door wide to help clear the steam as I dried myself off, and I could swear I heard a noise downstairs. I wrapped a towel around my waist and grabbed the first object I could find with any potential as a missile — a can of Foamy shaving cream.

I met my intruder at the foot of the stairs. It was a short, squat, middle-aged, walnut brown woman in a uniform the color of a Pepto Bismol spill. She had the sort of remarkably unlined skin that many black women somehow retain into their eighties, so I could only imagine she was somewhere between fifty and death. She was wearing knee-high nylons and heavy-looking orthopedic shoes on her feet, and a $19.95 Dynel acrylic curly salt-and-pepper wig on her head. She was at least as startled as I, and we both screamed; she dropped an immense overstuffed handbag to the floor, and I dropped the can of shaving cream onto my foot, which made me scream a James Brown please-please-please scream, grab my injured foot, and do the one-legged flamingo dance.

She planted both fists into her considerable pink polyester hips in a gesture that reminded me of my aunt Ruth.

"Who are you?" she demanded in a voice midway between that of Pearl Bailey and a California Highway Patrolman sure he can smell marijuana in your car upholstery. "What chu doin' here in Mistah Keith's place half-nekkid?"

"I'm Johnnie Ray," I said. "I live here, and I'm standing here half-nekkid because I'm just out of the shower. I trust you're the cleaning woman. Keith didn't tell me he had a cleaning woman." And here I'd thought the boy was just compulsively tidy.

"Where Mistah Keith at?" she asked, fists still firmly against hips and glaring at me in a manner that let me know she saw right through my little charade and knew me for what any fool could see I was — a burglar who takes showers before taking the silver service and the rare coin collection.

"Keith has gone to work," I said, dredging up as much condescension as I could, clad only in a bath towel, with water droplets dangling like pearl earrings from my lobes. "My name is Johnnie Ray, and I live here. And what might your name be, if I might be so bold?"

She smiled, showing a gold front tooth with a five-pointed star cut out of the gold. She shifted her weight onto one foot.

"Well, well," she said, her tone at least half mocking, "you must be a college boy. You sure *sound* like a college boy. They teach y'all to talk down tuh yuh elders in college, boy? Where Miz Betsy?"

I was becoming more than a bit fed up with this woman's Hattie McDaniel routine.

"Miz Betsy don't live heah no mo'," I said with enough sarcasm to kill the snails in the truck garden. "I lives heah now. Dig?"

She stopped for a moment, probably to consider the possible truth, and then the impact of my claim. She looked at me like I was a moth under a magnifying glass, frowned, and scratched her head through the wig. I could almost see the thought cross her mind like a horse-fly in front of the television screen. She looked at me askance.

"You live here?" she asked as if she'd shot me up with sodium pentothal and was watching the needle on the lie detector.

"Yes," I said, somehow keeping the words "you stupid old bag" from my lips.

Her face took on an inscrutable look; she was about to play her trump card, to ask the trick question that would expose me for the liar she knew I was.

"Where you sleep?"

I smiled. The old bitch had this coming.

"Upstairs," I said with a showy matter-of-factness. "With Keith."

The stricken look that swept the lady's face told me I had achieved the desired effect. This fine upstanding God-fearing Christian woman was about to scrub three toilets in a bona fide den of iniquity, and was talking to a towel-clad sinner against God and the Holy Spirit.

"Lawd ha' mercy today!" she cried.

"Don't forget the baseboards," I called as I bounded upstairs.

176

"Did you meet Lena Mae this morning?" Keith asked at dinner that evening. I'd fixed fried chicken (Clara's recipe, and without question the best fried chicken you've ever put in your mouth), and Keith was going at it like it was the last chicken on earth.

"Oh, yes," I said. And I can only conjecture that there was something in the tone of my voice or the set of my jaw that made Keith choose not to pursue the subject, because after tossing a quizzical glance across the table at me, he allowed the matter to drop, like peas off his fork. And it never came up again.

"Good meal, Babe," Keith said in a husky, sated voice, attempting with vigorous napkin strokes to clear a path in the grease that glistened on his face from ear to ear.

"Finger-lickin' good?" I said in my Scarlett O'Hara voice.

"Oh, indeed." Keith took my left hand (sticky with grease and liberally breaded with crunchy chicken crust), brought it to his lips, and began sucking my fingers clean. He made growling beast noises down in his throat, and tickled my palm with the tip of his tongue. I giggled like a little boy on the upswing of a seesaw.

Neglecting to fold our napkins properly, we made love beneath the dining room table.

All in all, those first several weeks I spent with Keith were among — no, scratch that — they absolutely *were* the very finest, most excellent several weeks I had ever in my life spent. I was, for a short time, as close as I had ever come to having (quite literally) everything I had ever really wanted, to obtaining, owning, grasping in my trembling arms my very Heart's Desire. I felt that, even if I didn't exactly hold success firmly by its long and slippery tail, if it was not quite within the grasp of my ever-stretching fingertips, then certainly the appearance of Marsha Goldman had brought me close enough to see the bloodshot whites of its beady little eyes.

Lifewise, lovewise, love-lifewise, I was officially in seventh heaven. Seven-and-a-halfth. I found myself in the almost unimaginably enviable position of not only having fallen in love so hard that the bruise on my tailbone had yet to fully heal; but of having the Man of My Dreams fall seemingly as hard for me as I had for him. Keith Keller had sauntered, quite by chance, into my life and answered the musical question "Lover man, oh where can you be?" with the musical answer "Turn around, look at me"; and in doing so, he had made yours truly the most deliriously happy singing male secretary in the whole of Los Angeles and vicinity.

The whole thing seemed to be working out so well, at first. I felt I had the three most important aspects of my life — job, career, and home, not necessarily in order of importance — well in hand, and I juggled them like an expert; with seeming effortlessness, with a confident smile on my face, very seldom dropping a ball; and when one did hit the stage floor, I retrieved it gracefully and worked it back into the air with style and flair. Which is not to say that my act was as easy as it looked — juggling never is. Still, for those first few magic weeks, at least, I seemed to be pulling it off. I was going for it all — marriage, career, the works — and, by golly, it looked as if I might jolly well *have* it all.

The Boize and I were working harder than ever, what with weekends at Tom Sawyer's and Wednesday nights at the Blue Dahlia, keeping ever on the lookout for Marsha Goldman's phantom friend with "connections" at the Griffin show. Not that I exactly had my heart set on doing the show — my knee-jerk skepticism kept me from completely swallowing anything Marsha or anyone like her had to say. Still, I thought, it would be nice.

Marsha's dangling of a national television appearance before my face like a solid gold carrot had the undesirable effect of making me feel my career as it stood was standing in a deep rut. Sawyer's had, by this time, become as routine as a 27-year-old marriage. Not unpleasant, mind you, hardly that. It's just that there were no surprises left. The same loyal, altogether predictable bunch of neurotics showed up every Friday and Saturday night, like clockwork — Keith would come one night a week, usually Saturday, sit at the back corner table, and lend his own inimitable brand of moral support — and I went through my paces, more or less by rote, depending on my mood, the kind of day I'd had to endure at work, the phase of the moon, that sort of thing.

The act had for some time been taking on the earmarks of a small cult event, like *Rocky Horror* or *I Love Lucy* reruns. Attempts to add new material were as often as not met with cool audience response, and vocal requests for old favorites. The act became static, and I became bored.

Oh, sometimes that feeling of family could be warm and comfortable as your old long-haired Persian cat. Like the night a killer head cold rendered my throat as pink and raw as a veal cutlet in the butcher's window. By the end of the last set, my voice was down to a ragged whisper. I was closing with "Golden Slumbers," and when I opened my mouth to sing, only a toneless rasp emerged.

"Why don't y'all sing this one tonight," I said. And they did. And it was, to borrow a somewhat hackneyed expression, heartwarming. Mostly, though, Tom Sawyer's was looking more and more like a dead end every minute, and the fact that we were taking home more money for one night at the Dahlia than for two at Sawyer's didn't make it look any better.

Which is not to say that working the Blue Dahlia was a picnic in the country. Oh, no. The Dahlia, for its part, had only its financial aspects to recommend it. There is nothing more frustrating, I decided during one particularly uninspired set at the Dahlia, than trying to entertain a roomful of people who are trying to score. Besides which, Marsha Goldman (very much in attendance those first several nights at the Dahlia) informed us after our second night there of Porcelli's request that we include more Top 40 material. We reluctantly, painfully, as if at gunpoint, added "What a Fool Believes" and (cringe) "I

Will Survive" (Porcelli asked for it by name) to the repertoire. I feared I was in danger of becoming the lead vocalist for a genuine Top 40 band, a fate I considered comparable to being locked into the stocks in the village square to be looked upon with scorn and pelted with offal by passersby.

Faced with audiences who considered me living Muzak, and a club owner who should have hired a deejay and a stack of 45s, I quickly grew to abhor the Blue Dahlia with a passion I generally reserve for the liver-and-onions dinner at Tippy's. I hated it. Snookie hated it. The band hated it, and let me know they hated it at every possible opportunity. Only two considerations kept Johnnie Ray and the Boize working at the Blue Dahlia — money (Bobo and Hicks took to singing the O'Jays' "moneymoneymoney mon-ey" chorus upon entering the club), and Marsha's oft-repeated belief that the Blue Dahlia constituted a major career move for me.

"Johnnie," she'd say, in that fingernails-on-a-blackboard voice of hers, "who's gonna see you in a dive like Sawyer's? Nobody, that's who." She had a point. "I would never bring my friend from the show *there*. You can be *seen* here."

"On the subject of the show, Marsha," I'd begin.

"I'm working on it," she'd say.

"She's working on it," the Boize would chime in, a Greek chorus in blue jeans.

One Friday night, two, maybe three weeks after I moved in with Keith, I breezed into Sawyer's as usual, to find Louie was gone.

"He quit," Anne-Marie told me, absently picking at her rapidly chipping black nail polish. "Just up and quit."

I hadn't paid Louie much attention since falling for Keith; hadn't, of course, slept with the boy since that first night. We'd shared a very sweet moment, he and I; a moment I'd scarcely given a moment's thought. And now he was gone. And I found I missed him, more than I ever would have guessed.

I didn't even know his last name.

Living with Keith was, in some ways, not substantially different than dating Keith. We didn't see much more of each other than before I had moved in. The main difference was that nobody had to drive home with his socks in his pocket.

Certain key aspects of our life together slipped easily into the Valley of Routine — Keith was Mr. Routine himself. Just for instance: he was used to waking up every day, Monday through Friday, at 6:45; making himself a two-strips-of-bacon-and-one-egg sandwich for breakfast (sometimes Betsy made them); washing down a One-A-Day with orange juice; and going to work. Now, he made two sandwiches (sometimes I made them) and he awoke at 6:30, which gave us fifteen extra minutes for cuddling, nuzzling, smooching, and (often) running late.

On the other hand, those first several weeks with Keith were like a live-in courtship. He sent flowers to my office with a card that read, "Wild thing, I think I love you." (Sylvia instinctively dove for them, assuming the dozen red rosebuds were for her. She sucked in her cheeks, lifted one penciled eyebrow, and said, "Well, well, well" when she read my name on the card.) I cooked Keith's favorite knackwurst and sauerkraut (from his mother's recipe) wearing only a "Kiss the Cook!" apron.

We started out making banana splits one evening, and ended up doing some very silly things with a couple of bananas and a can of Reddi-Whip. We wrote each other frightfully bad poetry. We grinned at one another for no good reason, the way young lovers do.

Although we lived beneath the same ceilings, we knew one another hardly at all. Every day together was a field trip of discovery, an ongoing study of this strange new flesh we'd found, counting out our similarities and plumbing the depths of our differences.

Our differences, if not quite grossly outnumbering our similarities, certainly showed themselves more readily. That we were attempting to merge two wildly divergent temperaments and lifestyles was almost as immediately apparent as the fact that Keith was large and fair and I small and dark. I was a pop singer. He was a banker. Period.

Keith liked to have dinner at seven o'clock. Not 6:45. Not 7:10. Seven. And I was used to having dinner on the run, as often as not tossing a cup of milk, a couple of eggs, some wheat germ, an aging banana, and anything else in the refrigerator that looked interesting into the blender, slurping it down, and calling it haute cuisine. The day Keith knocked himself out making Bavarian chicken with basil and potato pancakes, and I ran in just long enough to kiss him hello and good-bye, grab some sheet music, and split for a rehearsal I had neglected to inform Keith of, I realized something had to be done.

Keith was also used to being in bed, with intent to sleep, by ten o'clock; I worked past midnight three nights a week, and was used to staying up late even when I wasn't working: checking out new clubs, looking over other singers, or just hanging out with Snookie over cup after cup of coffee at Tippy's. Which meant that Keith was often fast asleep by the time I crept home, finally ready to call it a night.

We both gave a little, as one must in the name of love. I did my best to schedule rehearsals so they conflicted with dinner as seldom as possible, and kept my extracurricular night-owling to a minimum. And Keith never complained or pressured me about my late nights — well, hardly ever. And when I'd tiptoe into the bedroom where Keith lay sleeping in (to me) unnatural silence, I'd kiss my slumbering lover good night on a hot flushed cheek or nape of neck or exposed shoulder; crawl into bed and feel Keith reach for me in his sleep, pulling me close to his hot, sweat-dampened body; climbing up out of the deep well of sleep just far enough to kiss the back of my neck and whisper, "Love you, Babe."

I realize now, looking back on it all, that Keith's putting up with what for him must have seemed my wild, neo-Bohemian lifestyle for as long as he did was a major concession for him. Keith was by nature the king of the homebodies. It was, in fact, only by a wild fluke that Keith had been at Sawyer's at all that steamy July Friday night I first set my mother's slightly slanted eyes on him. He had only gone out at all because Betsy had whined and pouted and stamped her little foot until he relented. (God bless that little foot, wheresoe'r it may sleep tonight.) Left to his own devices, Keith preferred to stay home on Friday evenings — every evening, if the whole truth be told, but on Fridays especially.

"I'm a banker," Keith explained to me one Saturday afternoon, as we lolled in bed among mounds of disheveled linens, both of us sticky and pungent after lovemaking. "And in banking, Fridays are hell on wheels. It's payday. Everybody and his pet dachshund wants to yank money out for the weekend. If you've ever started your workday at 8:30 in the morning, spent half the day taking verbal abuse from the sort of lowlife you wouldn't sit next to on a bus, only to find yourself still in the office at 7:30 that evening because your head teller is two-thousand-some-odd dollars out of balance, then you know what I'm talking about. By the end of the day on Friday, I am beat. Beat."

I could see that. And, in principle, it made sense. But the facts of the matter were that I worked hard for a living, too; and that Keith's career day ended at five, as mine was just beginning. But that was the difference between us. I loved the nightlife. I liked to boogie. Keith's idea of a festive Friday night was a cold Budweiser, some dinner (nothing too complicated), maybe a movie on cable, make some love, go to sleep. By ten.

Which is not to say we never went out. We did.

We went to the movies. We shared a passionate love for films, and we indulged it together as often as my schedule permitted. I'll never forget the Sunday afternoon we saw *Since You Went Away* at the Vagabond in Hollywood. You know that great scene where Jennifer Jones runs alongside the train that's taking Robert Walker away to make the world safe for you-know-what, weeping and waving and calling good-bye. Well, I cried like a baby, just like I do every time I see that scene. And, to my surprise, I heard a wet little sniff from the seat next to mine, and found my former running back from St. Fletcher's in Minnesota, swabbing tears from his cheeks with a monogrammed hanky. I realized then that I could never truly love a man who didn't cry at movies.

We went to concerts, too. Keith and I shared a passionate love for music. So we loved different kinds of music. So what? We learned to share.

186

Keith reintroduced me to Mozart, with whom I had been quite out of touch since I gave up my flute lessons in the ninth grade. Mozart and I had never been on the best of terms. I somehow made it through a recital of old Wolfie's sonatinas, the same way I got through the classical concerts Clara felt maternally obliged to drag me to as a child. I closed my eyes and pictured Baryshnikov dancing to the music, clad only in a dance belt (as a child, I had imagined Edward Vilella). Much better was a UCLA Opera Workshop production of *The Magic Flute*. I had seen the opera on a field trip in the fifth grade, and remembered a surprising amount of it. During the Queen of the Night's big aria (and quite a coloratura nightmare it is), I turned to Keith (who sat wearing his nicest dark blue suit and a look of artistic rapture), and said,

"It's got a good beat, you can dance to it, I give it a 65."

He didn't laugh aloud (we were watching an opera, after all — in fact, as I recall, he elbowed me rather hard), but I'm sure he was amused.

And I did try, really I did. I smiled through my pain when Keith decided to fill the living room with Mahler, whom I found pompous and morose by turns; I did not run screaming from the house when Keith took a notion to listen to (and sing along with) the *Ring* cycle in its entirety over a series of evenings, even though I cannot but hear the "Ride of the Valkyries" without checking the sky for choppers (I'd seen *Apocalypse Now* three times), and even though I found Wagner in general overly grandiose and just too, too Teutonic. Similarly, when I took it into my head to enjoy the entire David Bowie collection in one afternoon, Keith looked as if his teeth were being drilled without the benefit of anesthesia. We finally struck a bargain that if I would not inflict

Bowie upon Keith, he would not inflict Wagner upon me.

We worked out together, Keith and I; just about three times per week, alternating between his gym (World Gym, home of the future Mr. Olympias — a place I felt much more comfortable staring into than standing in, as the size of most of its inhabitants made even my well-muscled lover seem perfectly Lilliputian) and mine (a somewhat trendy Nautilus establishment, full of tanned, streamlined people in matching leotard-and-leg-warmer outfits, where I felt quite at home, though Keith stood out like a linebacker in the corps de ballet). I was used to working out solo (easy enough to do with Nautilus machines — I mean, it's not as if you're going to drop one onto your face), and the buddy system took some getting used to.

Still, I quickly grew to enjoy my workouts with Keith. To my mind, Keith was never so beautiful as when he was lifting. Well, almost never. The sight of him between sets, waiting for a fifty-pound plate or something, his muscles pink and pumped, his threadbare tank top falling down over one shoulder and exposing a big brown nipple, made my blood rush straight downward and caused a serious overcrowding problem in my jockstrap. He looked so juicy, it was often all I could do not to take a bite out of him right there by the squat rack.

Keith was an aggressive workout partner, pushing me well past the point I would push myself; coaxing, cajoling, teasing that last skin-bursting repetition out of me, oblivious to the impending possibility of my throwing up. Within two or three weeks, I was beginning to outgrow my shirts.

We drove out to Lancaster to see Clara.

"I can see where you got your looks," Keith said while Clara was out of earshot. "Your mother's a knockout." And she was. I was, as always, just slightly amazed that this tiny lady with the fashion-model cheekbones, perennially girlish figure, and unlined face was indeed my mother. In a pair of Calvin Klein's, dirty pink fuzzy bedroom slippers, and a t-shirt with the word "Foxy" in glittery script across the bosom, Clara could easily have passed for a college girl.

"He's a hunk," Clara said of Keith in a stage whisper I'm sure he could hear.

"Hands off," I said, "this one's mine."

While Clara gave me the body count — which was what I called Clara's bringing me up to date on the illnesses, accidents, marriages, births, and (especially) deaths among her family and circle of friends ("You remember your aunt Roxie in San Diego?" "No." "Well, she dead."), she plied Keith with enough jambalaya and collard greens to feed the state of Louisiana in its entirety ("That all you gonna eat? Big boy like you?").

We spent a hazy gray Sunday afternoon at the L.A. Museum of Art, walking until our legs gave out. We picnicked on the sparsely grassed lawn, sitting cross-legged on our blanket while a Mexican family played touch football much too close for my comfort. In a rare spasm of domesticity, I had packed a lovely lunch; and had forgotten to include a single utensil. But we adapted. I spread Gulden's Brown Mustard onto ham-on-ryes with my fingers; Keith slurped my homemade potato salad from those same fingers, and never asked for a spoon. We stared stupidly into each other's eyes, the way young lovers do.

In the gift shop, Keith bought me a huge, glossy coffee table volume on the treasures of Tutankhamen.

"It's beautiful," I said. And it was. "But why?" Keith thumped his fingertip on the book's cover, a close-up of the face on the boy king's mummy case.

"Because he looks like you," Keith said.

And, lo and behold, there was a resemblance.

That was when Keith started calling me "K.T." For King Tut, you know.

Of all the things I remember about the time I spent with Keith, what I remember best and most fondly is the sex. Both because making love with Keith was to sex what Clara's crab-and-okra gumbo is to food (hot, sticky, and impossibly delicious); and because, as I recall, Keith and I spent relatively little time together not making love. During those first few magic weeks when I'd have bet my bottom dollar on us to win, Keith and I made love often and wonderfully well. We couldn't keep our hands off each other. We made love like a condemned man eats his last meal. We were junkies and love was our jones. And each fix made us itch for the next one.

And we're talking double-live, gonzo sex here. True, at this point in my young life I was hardly Xaviera Hollander in terms of sexual experience. Still, I'd been around the block enough times to know good sex from bad sex from incredible, earth-shifting transcendent sex. Until Keith, I had always assumed that most sex was good sex. Louie, for instance, was good sex. Four out of five casual pickups are going to be good sex; that skin-tingling adrenaline pump that comes of finding a thick slice of new meat in your arms for the first (and probably only) time, coupled — so to speak — with the fantastic voyage of exploration as you discover uncharted muscular and dermatological territory (oh, for the hills and valleys, the peaks and gullies of the male physique), are usually enough to keep your excitement level easily within the "good sex" category.

Bad sex is considerably rarer. I mean, you can practically always chalk sex up in the "pretty good, nothing to write home about" column of your score sheet if you have experienced orgasm. But there is bad sex out there waiting for you, if you happen to be unlucky enough to stumble onto its flaccid little lap. Zaz, the sax man with whom I had briefly shared a sordid one-bedroom in Venice when I was nineteen — now, that was bad sex. I mean, the man was BAAAAAAD sex.

I met Zaz (whose real name was Alphonso del Vaughn Washington, but who the hell wants to be called a thing like that?) at a little hole-in-the-wall nightclub in Hollywood, owned by two huge, vicious women named Debbie. It was a Monday-night showcase (Monday is showcase night all over show business), and I had pulled my usual 12:47 a.m. time slot. Immediately preceding me was a big, nappy, utterly unkempt young man who played one long, quite unlistenable alto sax solo (a cappella and seemingly improvised) for over twenty-five minutes (about fifteen minutes more than was allotted each performer, and about twenty-five minutes too long, period). When the audience began to boo and jeer, he simply turned his back. He might have gone on until sunrise or worse, had not the larger of the Debbies lumbered up to the stage, snatched the saxophone from the man's mouth (drawing blood from his lower lip), and all but carried him off the stage.

I proceeded somewhat tentatively with my set. (This was during what I have since termed my "French Dirge

Period." I woke up one morning and decided I was Edith Piaf. I was doing entire sets of dramatic ballads — "If You Go Away," "Come In from the Rain," that sort of thing.) After which the sax player came up to me as I was about to leave, stood much too close to me, and said, "I bet you only do it with white boys."

I found this an unusual but effective opening line, especially considering I had indeed only slept with white boys. It wasn't policy or anything — I hadn't slept with all that many of anything — I'd simply never been asked to bed by a black man (and at this point in my life, I never initiated). While I flipped through my mental file cards for a snappy response, he said, "Shame to waste your pretty self on white boys." He smiled. His teeth were the color of your grandfather's World War I doughboy uniform.

To this day, I have no idea why I went home with Zaz. Maybe it was the lateness of the hour, my weary and weakened state; maybe he caught me just far enough off guard. Maybe I felt just the tiniest bit guilty that I had indeed never slept with a black man, and somehow thought of Zaz as a kind of dues paying. But go I did. I followed Zaz into his tiny, filthy pigeon coop of a one-bedroom loft apartment, and slipped between the piss-stained, sour-smelling sheets of his frameless bed. And he was BAAAAAD sex.

Zaz wasn't much for preliminaries, which was fortunate, since kissing Zaz was like licking the lid of the garbage pail behind La Wanda's Bar-B-Q Shack. He smelled rather like the corner where you keep the cat box. After only the shallowest attempts at what used to be termed "foreplay," Zaz jumped on top of me, rubbing his dick against my belly in that unreasonable facsimile of fucking once known among the previous generation of preppies as the "Princeton Rub." After a very short while, Zaz made a sound like one of those little round boxes that mimic a kitten's "mew" when you turn it over, and spewed his orgasm all over my belly.

After which, he rolled over into a noisy case of sleep, leaving me wet and sticky and quite unsatisfied.

It probably comes as some surprise to you that I lived with this man for the better part of two weeks, during which I discovered that his pet sex act was for me to beat him off with a handful of olive oil. But that's a whole 'nother story. The point is that I had, at the time I lived with Keith, had my share of good sex, and easily my fair share of bad sex (one per lifetime is quite enough, thank you). And sex with Keith Keller was — as one famous bon vivant and notorious homosexual might have put it — the top.

Bette Midler used to say that bad sex was just two people who didn't fit together. That being the case, I can only imagine that Keith and I fit together like Cinderella's tootsie and that famous Waterford wedgie.

We were stark raving cuckoo about each other's body. Keith, during a quick breather in a mouth marathon of kissing, would whisper (in a voice similar to the one Jennifer Jones used in *The Song of Bernadette* to describe her vision of the Holy Mother in the village refuse dump), "God, you have the best lips." Or I'd be standing at the stove, turning bacon strips, and he'd walk up behind me, grab a couple of handfuls of my behind, and say, "God, you have the best ass. Why can't a woman have an ass like this?"

For my part, I loved every square inch of Keith Keller; and I make that statement confident that during the time I lived with Keith, I managed to eyeball, finger, nuzzle, and tongue him in his absolute entirety at least once over. I loved Keith (both with my heart and with most other parts of my anatomy) from the half-dollar-size callus that formed on the ball of each of his big, high-arched feet to the spot at the crown of his head where his baby-fine hair was thinning like it was the crowd at a movie house and some schmuck had just yelled, "Fire."

I loved Keith's Mr. America biceps and his incredibly bowed legs (standing with his feet together, he looked like the Arc de Triomphe, and he'd never even been on a horse). I loved his nipples, each as ruddy and tender-looking as a little wound, and as sensitive as the tenor in a small-town opera company. I loved the birthmark on the right side of his pelvis, pinkish brown and shaped like the state of North Dakota, staining Keith's untanned skin like a gravy spill on Clara's white linen tablecloth. I loved the smooth, breathy sound of Keith's voice and the sour-dough bread smell of his crotch.

I loved Keith's dick to the point of religion. I made up names for it like a primitive tribe might name its god over and over. The hooded stranger. The redheaded cyclops of love. Snyrdle. I found adorable the little blue-green vein that traversed the dorsal side of Keith's great dork like an erratic highway on a tubular map of New Mexico. I marveled at the way the big thing swerved decidedly to the right (like much of the American voting populace during the summer of '79, as the Carter administration could be heard gasping its last) as it grew hard at the sight of me.

I developed a relationship with Keith's penis as an entity quite separate from Keith himself. I petted, fondled, and kissed it like a newborn puppy. Played with it like the Wham-O Toy Company's latest answer to the hula hoop. Devoured it like America devoured Big Macs — it was indeed a meal in itself. Opened my back door and invited it in gladly, like your next-door neighbor come to return that five bucks he borrowed last spring.

Keith liked to talk during lovemaking. Me, I'm a moaner, a groaner, a hummer (as if well versed in the tune to the Song of Solomon, but weak on the words). Keith was a talker, a cheerleader at the Super Bowl of Love even as he played the game. He called me "Lover" while we loved. There are nights, even now, when I am able to keep myself warm by wrapping tight around me memories of Keith, his big legs over my shoulders, his face a Renaissance rendering of a saint in rapture (Sebastian sans arrows, or, rather, pierced by just one), his slightly parted lips whispering a love litany: "Oh yes, Lover, oh please, Lover, it feels so good, Lover."

There are nights, too, when I'll wake up, very much alone, very much erect, from a dream I have instantly lost without a trace upon waking; and smell Keith's smell in my bed, feel the touch of his fingers on my skin. And it makes me shiver.

If anyone had tried to convince me that a man, any man (especially a man who, before meeting me, had never even heard of Bo Diddley), could leave that sticky a trail of footprints across the kitchen floor of anyone's mind, let alone my own, I would have thought them somewhat overconcerned with sex, at least.

But Keith Keller left me so marked. God damn him, and every other banker that ever lived.

Anyway, the Relationship (Snookie tended to refer to my relationship with Keith with a capital "R") rolled along as smoothly as a Chevy with four new shock absorbers, with only the very occasional pothole to jar the ride. Oh, now and then Keith would become impatient with my late hours, or I'd do something I knew would piss him off even as I was doing it just because I bloody well wanted to do it, like hang out after hours with Snookie and maybe Randi and some other homeless musicians. And the next time I saw Keith, I'd know he was angry. I'd find him sitting bolt upright in his favorite blue velveteen wing chair, nearly obliterated from view by that day's *Wall Street Journal*, silent with a deep, resonant silence it probably took him years to perfect.

I can only imagine that, as a boy, Keith was probably something of a pouter. There was something of a pout in the silence he habitually adopted when angry. He didn't actually poke out his lower lip like Shirley Temple or hold his breath until he turned blue or anything really melodramatic. Still, anytime I found Keith communicating with me in a series of grunts from behind the Dow Jones Industrials, I knew I'd blown it somehow, and I knew I had two alternatives. I could wait it out, act like nothing was wrong, and wait for the storm to blow over. Or I could try to vamp him out of it; tiptoe downstairs in, say, just my jockstrap, gently remove the *Journal* from his tense little fingers, perch astraddle his lap, and say (in my best sex-kitten whisper),

"Whatever it is, I'm sorry." A couple of slow, circular pelvic motions. Maybe a little kiss on the forehead. "Let's not fight, okay?" By which time, the big guy should be reduced to something the consistency of rice pudding. His fingers are toying with my straps. His lips are kissing my nipples hello.

"Goddamn it, K.T.," he'd say, "why can't I stay mad at you?"

Strangely enough, it was not my brilliant career that began tossing the occasional sugar cube into the gasoline tank of our love affair. It was Keith's somewhat overzealous possessiveness and jealousy concerning me, in conjunction with the fact that I was (and am) by nature something of a bush-league exhibitionist, and a full-blown, semiprofessional-status flirt.

Snookie, in the spirit of telling me the Whole Stinking Truth as only your closest and dearest will tell you (only trying to help, of course), has been known to point out that my tendency to make "If you've got it, flaunt it" into the eleventh commandment only evinces a deeply imbedded insecurity concerning my sexual attractiveness.

So what else is new?

I took Psych I in college (I got a B-plus), and even if I hadn't, it wouldn't take Dr. Joyce Brothers to figure this one out.

I mean, it's the oldest plot in the book: *The Ugly Duckling* as that old queer Hans Christian never told it.

Once upon a time, there was a little colored gay boy (a young queen, a princess as it were) named Johnnie

Ray. He is a plain child. He is an awkward adolescent. He throws a baseball like a girl. He is the last in his gym class to sprout pubic hair.

But suddenly, at the ripe old age of fifteen, Puberty showed its pimply face at Johnnie's bedroom window, and the boy — who, it turned out, was merely a classic late bloomer — bloomed.

And when I did finally begin to, well, bloom; when my face began growing into my teeth; when my Chinaman's eyes became a rather exotic facial asset; when, moreover, I discovered the pleasing results obtainable through weight training (Thanks again, Coach) and the geometric nightmare that was my physique began to form a more harmonious whole; when, in short, little Johnnie Ray achieved his escape from the Land of the Ugly Ducklings, clutching in his hot little fist a one-way ticket to Swan City, I suppose I should, in all fairness, have lived happily ever after.

Except for a couple of little things that Hans never mentioned — like the fact that, after spending one's entire life as an ugly duckling, swan status can take some getting used to.

I, for one, found that, once relatives (who had formerly commented that the best thing about my looks was that I was smart) suddenly began pointing out what a "nice-lookin' young man" Johnnie was growing into; once I began to notice that girls were looking at me, but really *looking* at me; I found that being recognized as a Physically Attractive Person quickly became the most important thing in my life.

It was then that I, a mild-mannered high school senior with a 3.8 grade point average, shed the Clark Kent glasses of my soul and emerged as (Look! Up in the sky! It's a bird! It's a plane! It's—) SUPERFLIRT!!

I flirted with everything that moved. Boys. Girls. Clara's friends. David's friends. I winked suggestively at moving vehicles and fire hydrants just for practice. Both because being good-looking was (as Sly Stone might have said) a whole new thang for me, and I was quite heady with it all; and because of something else Hans kept from me: that even after growing from ugly duckling to full-on swan, I would look into the mirror and find staring back at me — as often as not — a skinny, big-headed, slanty-eyed boy. The old ugly duckling.

Not even to mention the small but stubbornly adhesive chip I'd been wearing on my shoulder since the day, during the second semester of my senior year in high school, when I first saw the Classified section of the *Advocate*, and first read the words, "No fats, fems, or blacks, please."

I'm afraid I took it quite personally.

And I'll tell you, I didn't get over that one for a long while. No, I take that back — I'm still not over that one. This new knowledge that some, perhaps most, white gay men considered black men sexually unsuitable added fuel to the fires of my overall sense of physical inferiority (coals to Newcastle, indeed).

So when a white man exhibited sexual interest in me, not only was it a swan's personal victory over an ugly duckling past; it was, to my mind, a peculiar sort of victory against racism. It was proving Them wrong — all the stupid, small-minded Them who would actually commit the words "no blacks, please" to print. Wrong wrong wrong.

Of course, it wasn't nearly enough for one white man to want me. By cracky, I wanted them *all* to want me. I didn't actually want to fuck each and every one of them individually — far from it. No, most of the time it was the flirtation itself that really mattered — at the first sign that a man wanted me, I'd simply smile a rather self-satisfied little smile to myself, notch my gun handle, and move on.

And (I shudder to admit this — I'd hate for you to think I was a seriously neurotic person) whenever I did take a white man to bed — even Louie; yes, I'm afraid, even Keith — there was no escaping the nasty little voice way, way back in my head, yelling, "No blacks, huh? No blacks, my ass!" The prettier, the blonder, the more Aryan the man, the bigger (if no more permanent) the sense of victory at the sight of the man's fair head bobbing between my thighs. I suppose I truly am, as Snookie often tells me, a sick, sick woman.

Which brings us back to the summer of '79, when, strolling along the Santa Monica Pier with Keith, I unbuttoned my shirt completely, allowing my shirttails to blow like little white flags in the ocean breezes, allowing those same breezes to tickle my tummy and cool my moist armpits, and allowing anyone who might enjoy doing so to view the clear-cut delineations of my abdominal muscles and what was becoming a very nice chest.

"Button your shirt, K.T.," Keith said in the sort of voice people generally reserve for use while rubbing the puppy's nose in what he did on the new white rug.

"Why?" I raised my arms behind my head; I noticed a couple of older queen types in expensive haircuts and white patent-leather shoes licking their chops as we passed.

"Just button your goddamn shirt, K.T.!" The dog has done it again on the same rug, and we're considering having it put to sleep. Keith wouldn't even look at me.

I stopped dead in my tracks, fighting back tears, fighting back the urge to tear the big guy a brand-new asshole, clutching the two sides of my shirt to myself. Keith walked on alone for a few yards, then stopped. Turned and walked back to where I stood, absolutely atremble with hurt and rage. He took me by the shoulders.

"I'm sorry, K.T.," he whispered. I blinked tears and sniffed snot. "I just don't want my main squeeze walking around the goddamn pier with everything hanging out like some cheap little hustler on Santa Monica Boulevard."

I attempted to speak but sort of choked instead. Anyway, what could I have said? "Gee, I'm sorry, but you see I'm just awfully neurotic"? Keith took me into his arms right there on the pier, and I wept an archipelago of wet spots onto his shirt; and we walked off, Keith's arm around my shoulders, mine about his waist, my shirt buttoned to the throat.

Then there was the time we were in the Pleasure Chest (the A&P of sexual paraphernalia — "Studded leather harnesses and feather boas with sequins? Try aisle 10.") buying a tub of what is politely termed "personal lubricant" — neither butter nor the high-priced spread Crisco, Vaseline nor Jergens hand lotion proved suitable to our uses — and I had stopped at the expansive greeting-card rack. It was by this time mid-August, and so hot you could poach an egg on the small of a skateboarding beachboy's back, and I was, that particular Sunday afternoon, somewhat scantily clad in a white tank top, a pair of infinitesimal gym shorts (on a clear day you could see all the way to Catalina, if you catch my drift), and high-top tennies — my Peter Berlin fuckable-young-boy getup.

Well, there I stood (chest out, stomach in, rear bringing up the rear), when an older gentleman (polite term — less polite terms include "old toad") wearing one of Truman Capote's old suits and twelve or thirteen pounds of silver-and-turquoise conch jewelry, sidled up beside me, stood just a little too close (this town wasn't big enough for me and his cologne), and executed a perfect imitation of Jayne Mansfield's squeal from *The Girl Can't Help It*.

"Why, you pretty thing!" the man crowed. The voice was like Julie Andrews recorded at 45 and played at 33⅓.

I turned, widened my eyes.

"Who, me?"

"Now, stop it," the man said, slapping me on the arm, his hand lingering for a moment and then sliding down my biceps. He smiled the earth-tone smile of a heavy smoker. He was handsome, straight nosed, and cleft chinned, with eyes as blue as the pattern on a Corningware casserole; he had surely been a knockout as a young man. He was now close enough to fifty to see the gray hairs up its nostrils, a good twenty-five pounds overweight, and the blusher unskillfully applied to his cheeks accentuated, rather than masked, the dirty tricks that Time (the bitch) was playing on his once-beautiful face. "You're a lovely boy and you know it. I just wanted to thank you for sharing it with us all."

"Please," I said, lowering my eyes in Lillian Gish modesty, "you're embarrassing me."

"My arse," he said with a bad-boy grin.

I smiled. This man had seen this game before. Might have helped design the court.

"You do have a lovely body," he said. "I'd like to do something with you sometime."

"Oh?" I'm sure my eyebrows raised. My, my, this one was nothing if not direct.

"That's not what I meant, Duckie," he said. He pursed his lips. "Although that would be nice, as well. You don't know who I am?"

"No," I had to admit. "Should I?"

"Well!" he snatched a card from the rack. It was a photograph of the Perfect Tanned California Blond Boy (from the back, it might have been Louie) on tiptoe, hands behind his head. I'd have known the style anywhere.

"You're Matthew Richards?" I had been admiring (and jerking off to) Matthew Richards's work for years; Matthew's Boys (along with the best of Roy Dean and Rip Colt) had been the standard for male physique photography for even longer than that.

"You betcha."

"And you want to photograph me? Li'l ol' me?"

"Why, yes."

"Gosh." I very seldom use the word "gosh." This, however, was the very living end. I had obviously become one major swan here. If there was anything I wanted to be more than I wanted to be a singing star, I wanted to be a sexpot. And here was Matthew Richards, a veritable Vargas of the male nude, offering to make yours truly into just that — a sure-as-shit, backlit, airbrushed j.o. fantasy.

"So what do you think?"

"No," I said. "But thank you. I really mean that." I touched the man's leathery cheek. "You've made my day; possibly my week."

"But, why, Darling? Surely you're not going to plead modesty. Not in that outfit."

"Oh, no," I admitted. "It's just that — well, frankly, my boyfriend would *kill* me."

At which point, Keith descended the stairs, the little black paper bag with his purchase in hand.

"Ready to go, K.T.?"

"Okay, Daddy-o."

Richards made a head gesture in Keith's direction.

"Boyfriend?"

"The very one."

He gave Keith a lingering once-over, then a twice-over.

"How nice for you both," he said.

"K.T.?" Keith raised a menacing eyebrow.

"Gotta go." I extended my hand to Richards, who clasped it in his cushioned palm. "Thanks again. Very nice to meet you."

"My pleasure. Ta, Ducks."

In the car:

"Who was that?"

"Matthew Richards. Well-known photographer of the male nude. He wanted to shoot me. As it were."

"K.T.," Keith said through an exasperated sigh.

"K.T. what?"

"K.T.," another exasperated sigh, "it was a come-on, pure and simple. You like to think you're so hip and with-it, and you don't even know a common, garden-variety come-on when you're slapped across the chops with it."

"And why, may I ask, is it so terribly far-fetched that the man might have wanted to take my picture?"

"Johnnie Ray, you're cute. Okay? You're a beautiful kid. But sometimes I really wish you could stop kissing mirrors and playing sex kitten long enough to see how foolish you look sometimes."

"Foolish?"

"Foolish, K.T., as in, like a goddamn fool. I mean, really, walking around like that, dressed like some little street hustler, some old queen hands you a line and suddenly you're Marilyn fuckin' Monroe lying all over the red satin. Don't you believe you're beautiful? Don't

I tell you enough that you're lovely? Don't you believe me? Jesus Christ, Babe, I just wish I was enough for you."

"Of course you're enough for me, it just—"

"Bullshit. I'm not enough — nobody's enough. I don't think there's enough people on earth to tell you you're cute enough times so you'll be satisfied and just fuckin' leave it alone."

It was one of those extremely rare instances when I was totally at a loss for words. The big guy had my number down to the last digit. I bit my lip and dared the tears to come. I felt like kicking a hole through the floor of the car.

"Well, fuck you," I finally said, a desperate reply if there ever was one.

"Such a way with words," Keith said.

Needless to say, the silence was deafening at the old homestead that night. We didn't speak. We didn't make eye contact. We didn't make love. When Keith marched up to bed (at about a quarter after nine) he didn't even kiss me good night. Which was wise, as I probably would have bitten his lips off. I was consumed with the sort of rage I feel only when someone has managed to hit one of my major neuroses right on the head. I do hate for anyone to be so completely right about me.

But I cooled off, gradually, and accepted, grudgingly, that Keith was right. I wasn't just a flirt; I was a desperate flirt. And I resolved to do better. To go on the wagon, as it were. Had I known of a Flirts Anonymous, I would surely have joined up. I did my level best to keep my shirt on and my eyes to myself, and generally managed to keep my nose clean.

And then Sly called.

It was a warm August Sunday afternoon, and Keith and I were in bed (Sunday afternoons in bed were something of a tradition by this point), well fucked and smiling, what little there was in the way of cool breezes tickling our naked skin. I was very nearly asleep, so when the telephone rang, I jumped halfway out of bed in a single bound. My hello was woozy and a little perturbed. When a familiar husky voice said, "Baby Bear?" I nearly fainted dead away.

"Papa Bear?" I said. Out of the corner of my eye, I could swear I saw the muscles of Keith's shoulders tense.

I had met Sylvester Stewart my sophomore year at the Big U. I was in the chorus of the Opera Workshop's production of *Aufstaedt und Fall der Staat Mahagonny* (Brecht and Weill, you know). It was easily the most horrendous production of a Kurt Weill opera ever mounted, but that's a side issue. Stage-managing this disaster was a six-foot, fortyish teddy bear of a man; as burly and barrel-chested a Daddy as ever was. He was about as male as male could be; strictly T.O. — Testosterone Overload. He was almost totally bald, and sported a blue-black five o'clock shadow by noon. Tufts of dense black hair played peekaboo over the collars of his polo shirts. He'd sweat great wet swatches down and across his back and chest at the very mention of physical exertion. He turned me on.

And while I took pleasurable notice when he smiled at me or winked at me or slapped at my ass while I waited in the wings for an entrance, I considered none of these acts conclusive — he seemed pretty chummy with the entire cast. The first move, if any, would have to be his.

I was alone backstage one evening while the company was taking five, brushing up on my time step just for the hell of it, (STAMP hop shufFLE ball-CHANGE, STAMP hop shufFLE ball-CHANGE) when all at once he was standing there, leaning against the wall, a bushy black eyebrow rising on his endless forehead. He said,

"Hi."

STAMP. Hop-hop. Trip trip. Stumble. Aw, fuck it.

"Hello."

"Johnnie Ray, right?"

"Uh-huh."

"Sylvester Stewart." He held out a huge, hirsute paw of a hand, which I allowed to encircle mine about one point five times.

"Really?"

"Really, what?"

"Sylvester Stewart," I said.

"What about it?"

"You know," I said in my wonted aw-c'mon-everybody-knows-this attitude, "you have the same name as the leader of Sly and the Family Stone."

"Whose family?" he said.

"Skip it," I said.

"All right," he said, moving in close enough for me to smell the Dentyne he was chewing. "I was wondering if you had any dinner plans for tonight."

"Actually," I said, my breath ruffling Sylvester Stewart's chest hair, "I thought I might have it with you."

And have it with him I did. We tore a roast chicken at the Old World, shared a carafe of the house chablis (despite my being barely nineteen years old), and were in Sly's split-level brick-front Westwood apartment, and in Sly's bed before you could say hot fun in the summertime. Sly wore a permanent fur coat — only his palms, the soles of his big feet, and his shiny bald pate were fur-free. It would have required a lesser imagination than my own to dub him "Papa Bear." He loved me sweetly and gently, and I slept all night in his fuzzy arms.

During the two months or so during and following the production of *Mahagonny*, Sly treated me to dinner at Ma Maison (where we saw Dyan Cannon spill shrimp cocktail across the front of a cream-colored Bob Mackie original). He escorted me to a Leontyne Price recital and got me backstage to meet the diva herself. He bought me a gold-and-garnet pinkie ring (which I subsequently danced right off my finger one night at Studio One — it flew from my hand to parts unknown, and I have yet to receive so much as a postcard from it since). He announced one evening that I was his long-lost son, his Baby Bear (the fact that Sly was quite Caucasian notwithstanding), and we promised we would never lose contact.

Two weeks later, Sly flew to Paris for an extended stay — to write, he said. I didn't hear from him for over three years. (I did, however, read his first novel: *Blue Shadows*, a briskly moving, briskly selling murder mystery starring a gay detective.)

"How did you find me?" I sat cross-legged on the floor, leaned back against the dresser whereon the telephone squatted.

"I found you," Sly said. That would be all Sly would ever tell me on that subject; he did that sometimes — he liked to be mysterious. "I can't talk long," he continued, "I was wondering if you're free for dinner next Saturday night?"

"I don't know. I'll have to ask," I said. I palmed the mouthpiece. "Hey, big fella," I called to the immobile figure on the bed, "an old friend of mine wants to have dinner with me next Saturday night. Can I go?"

"I don't care," Keith said, half into the pillow. Even muffled, I was sure that Keith's "I don't care" was as far from the truth as east is from west; but, in what amounted to a spasm of rather childish selfishness (at best), I chose to ignore it.

"Did your daddy say you could go?" Sly said when I got back on the line.

"Yes" — I let the sarcasm in Sly's voice go by— "he did."

"This guy make you happy?"

"Very," I said.

When I crawled back into bed, I found Keith in his cool, silent mode. Not surprising.

"So who is this old friend?" he asked, his back turned to me.

"An old friend from my bygone college days. He's older. Pushing forty-five by now, I should think."

"Old flame?"

"No," I hedged, "not really."

"Whattaya mean, 'not really'?" Keith's voice was steadily rising in volume. "Didja sleep with him or what?"

"Yes, Keith. As a matter of fact, I did sleep with him a couple of times. That was several years ago."

"Gonna sleep with him next week?"

"That was uncalled for, Keith."

"Maybe," he said. "But let's face it, K.T. — you do have this problem about keeping your clothes on."

"Thanks a lot, Honey," I said, rolling out of bed and onto my feet. I yanked on my jeans and t-shirt, and snatched up my Adidas running shoes. "I'll see you later, okay?"

"Go ahead." Keith rolled over onto his back, propped up on his elbows, his face contorted in anger. "Why wait? Why doncha go find your goddamn Papa Bear right now? Goddamn little slut."

"Hey — fuck you, okay?" Why is it my wit always seems to take an unscheduled leave of absence just when I really need it?

I ran downstairs (I could just hear Keith yell, "Well fuck you, too" as I slammed the front door). I was smearing the tears off my face when I arrived at Snookie's, where I settled in for several cups of coffee and a good long cry.

It was dark when I got back home. I found Keith sitting ramrod-straight in the blue wing chair, staring intently into a two-day-old *Wall Street Journal*. I sat across from him on the couch.

"We really ought to talk about this," I said to the paper. It did not move.

"All right," said a tight voice behind the newspaper. "I don't want you to go. Now *you* talk about it."

"Keith" — I tried not to raise my voice, but it wasn't working — "Sly is an old friend of mine. I haven't seen him in years. I just want to see him, that's all. What is the big fucking deal?"

Keith slapped the paper down to his lap.

"I bet he just thinks you're the cutest thing, doesn't he?"

"What?"

"I bet he's always making over you like you're just the hottest little hunk of meat in all creation, isn't he? Isn't he? You just wanna have your goddamn little ego boosted, doncha?"

Well, boys and girls, he had me there. As a matter of fact, Sly did think I was the greatest invention since the chicken taco, and took every opportunity to tell me so.

"You know somethin'?" he'd often say to me. "You're just about the most beautiful thing I've ever seen." I'd point out some perfect little blond creature, and Sly would say, "Commonplace. Ho-hum. I'll take a beautiful mongrel like you anytime." That's what Sly liked to call me me with my African and French and Indian and heaven-knows-what-all blood — "mongrel." He called me his beautiful mongrel. He claimed someday he was going to marry some woman, just so he could adopt a houseful of beautiful mongrel children.

Damn right I was looking forward to having Sly tell me I was the prettiest thing that ever walked, over a hundred-dollar dinner at L'Hermitage. So what? And here Keith was making it sound as if we planned to go out and eat babies.

I was desperately trying to scratch up a suitable reply, when I noticed the nearly empty martini glass that had formed a wet ring on the uncoastered coffee table.

"You're drunk," I said in my best Bette Davis accusatory tone, hoping to throw Keith onto the defensive.

"Anesthetized," he said, "and don't try to change the subject." He threw the newspaper to the floor and stood up. I sprang up from the couch. "You're good with words, Babe, but you're not gonna talk your way outa this." He walked slowly toward me as he spoke. "Now, it's not as if I don't want you to have friends; you know that's not true. I just don't like the thought of your running off with some guy you used to fuck. I'm sure you think that's very small-minded and old-fashioned, but I'm afraid I'm just not as hip and sophisticated as you and your showbiz friends. I'm sorry." He stood so close the gin on his breath surrounded me. "Now, if you're gonna be with me, then you're gonna hafta be with me. Nobody else, K.T. Just with me."

"Of course, I'm with you." I reached out to touch Keith's face, ready to try and sweet-talk Keith out of his anger (as I often could), but this time he was having none of it.

"No!" he said, and lashed out with his right hand, back-slapping me across the mouth, knocking me to the floor. I grabbed at Keith's legs, and between my blind rage at the taste of my own blood and Keith's drunkenness, I managed to topple him to the floor as well. We wrestled a very brief match on the living room carpet; me crying and calling Keith every nasty name I could remember and flailing at him wildly with my fists; Keith gaining the advantage quickly (even dead drunk, the man was big and strong and over seventy pounds heavier than me). He pinned me to the floor, his fists tight around my wrists.

"Lemme go, goddamn sonofabitch muthafuckin'—" I struggled in vain to free myself from Keith's grip, tears streaming down the sides of my face and puddling in my ears. "Goddammit, Keith, you're hurting me."

"Am I?" he said. "Good. I'm glad I can hurt you, too. You see" — his voice was a raspy hiss; I could feel his arms tremble with rage — "I can hurt you too." A tear executed a perfect dive from Keith's eye and landed cool against my cheek. He let go of my wrists and collapsed against me, his face against my shirt.

"Goddamn you," he cried, "why do you do this to me? I love you, and I just want you to love me — just me — is that asking so goddamn much?"

"But, I *do* love you," I blubbered.

"No."

"I do."

"Then why do you hurt me like this?"

"Because," I managed between sobs, "because I'm a neurotic asshole, I dunno."

I wrapped my arms around Keith's back, grabbed handfuls of his shirt, and we just wept together for a while. Finally, Keith rose up on his hands and looked down at my face.

"Oh Jesus," he said, "you're bleeding. I've made you bleed. I'm so sorry, Babe." He began kissing my face, licking up my tears and blood and snot.

"No, I'm sorry," I said. "I won't go."

"I don't care," Keith said, licking at the tiny wound at the side of my mouth. "Really I don't."

"No, I—" But Keith was kissing me harder, causing some pain against my sore mouth, grunting deep in his throat and rubbing against me. And we made love, fiercely, on the floor.

So I never went to dinner with Sly. And he never called me again.

And I really didn't mind it all that much, in and of itself. Still, the fact that Keith and I had actually come to blows; that blood (and *my* blood, at that) had been shed over my having dinner with an old friend (all right, then — an old flame) disturbed me.

And I began to wonder.

How many other friends might Keith forbid me to see? What might I do to incur the big guy's wrath next? Was he planning to make a habit of slapping me around and then boffing the daylights out of me afterward, a la Stanley and Stella?

I was beginning to feel like a caged bird. I had, after all, relinquished a certain amount of my wonted freedom for Keith. I had become (for him) about as domesticated as I could (I imagined) possibly become. And now I was being told with whom I could and could not have dinner. And if the bars that held me captive were indeed the brawny arms of the man I loved — still, a cage is a cage.

And I began to wonder.

I began to wonder if maybe, just maybe, moving in with Keith Keller might not have been — and, oh, how the dewy-eyed Ronettes romantic in me cried, No! No! Don't even think it! — might it not have been a mistake?

The following Wednesday, Marsha paid us a surprise visit at the Blue Dahlia. She gestured Snookie and me to her table between sets. Our Dahlia shows had settled into an uneasy tedium by this point; and this particular night I was tired, and (as Snookie liked to put it) "something of a bitch," and not really in the mood for my dear manager, she whose most noteworthy accomplishment to date remained the procuring of the Blue Dahlia gig.

"Siddown," she said, "I've got a proposition for you."

"We talkin' television, Marsha?" I asked.

"I'm working on it," she said. It had become an involuntary response, like blinking.

"Seems I've heard that song before," I muttered. Marsha shot me a gonad-withering glance.

"We gonna talk, we gonna argue?" she said.

"Sorry."

"As a matter of fact," Marsha continued, "I'm talking Las Vegas."

"Vegas?" Snookie's face lit up like a slot machine flashing three cherries.

"Now, wait" — Marsha made a fast smoothing-over gesture with her cigarette hand — "let's not get too excited here. Let me tell you what the deal is."

217

The "deal" was that another of Marsha's protegés had been given a shot at two weeks in a Vegas lounge, on a trial basis — sort of a long, expensive audition, really. And in order to showcase her client in the best possible fashion, it was Marsha's wish to employ Snookie on auxiliary keyboards, and myself on backup vocals.

I was skeptical. I was used to working solo. In one. Alone. The thought of being shanghaied into an act not of my own design was less than attractive. Besides, I had never done backup work before, and I was none too sure I wanted to.

"I understand you're a solo artist, Johnnie," Marsha said, "but it might be a good thing for you. You've never played Vegas; you've never done a tour, even a short one. The experience could be helpful. Besides," she added, "Randi's doing backups, too; and heaven knows, she's a solo artist."

"Randi?" Somehow I couldn't imagine that Cajun wild woman stepping back and making with the doo-lang doo-langs for anyone.

"Look," she said finally, "at least come and see Lavinia's act."

"Lavinia?" Snookie said through a snorting laugh. "There's a person named Lavinia?"

"Lavinia White," said Marsha. "She's playing Saturday nights here."

Lavinia White was easily among the ten most beautiful women I had ever seen. She was a caramel-dipped Joey Heatherton. Her hair looked like you could comb it with a feather. Her skin looked like if you bit her, she'd taste like butterscotch pudding. In a cinched-in, backless, strapless, white-gauze potato sack of a dress that would make four out of five women look like a white-gauze sack of potatoes, Lavinia White looked like an artist's rendering of the Original Sin.

Lavinia White was a woman of the utmost beauty, style, and poise — and, it would seem, the barest minimum of talent. She was the basic colored girl pop singer with Diana Ross affectations, right off the rack. Except that she was less talented than most.

Marsha Goldman discovered Lavinia White while the latter was representing the city of Compton in the Miss Black Southern California Beauty Pageant, and the former was (quite inexplicably) a judge. Lavinia placed dead last in the talent competition (her rendition of "God Bless the Child" placed her well behind Miss Black Hawthorne — whose talent entry consisted of displaying the dresses she'd sewn from Simplicity patterns — and reportedly opened every automatic garage door within a two-mile radius); she placed second overall. This dazzling display of image over talent impressed Marsha enough that she immediately signed the girl on as her initial management client.

From the ringside table where I sat (flanked by Snooks and Marsha), I shredded my cocktail napkin in nervous agitation as Lavinia opened her act with a reading of "Love Hangover" that no doubt seriously hastened the death of disco. Snookie slapped at my hand (playfully but firmly) and hissed, "Be nice."

I bit down hard on my plastic drink stirrer when (during the light smattering of applause which followed her first number) Lavinia smiled wide enough to smudge plum-colored lipstick onto both her ears, spread her impossibly thin arms as if to hug the Blue Dahlia in its entirety, and, shouted, "Thank you! You're beautiful! Lavinia loves you!" at a decibel level that made the speakers distort. Lavinia executed a variation on this move after every single song.

When, during her last number ("Reach Out and Touch Somebody's Hand" — natch), Lavinia (in total disregard of her audience's almost complete inattention) not only dismounted the stage and shook hands with fully half the audience (disengaging fingers from cocktail glasses by force when necessary), but even managed to get a couple of the more alcohol-weakened patrons to sing off-key into her microphone, I knew I was in the presence of showbiz success in the making.

Lavinia White was born to play Vegas. She was beautiful in the extreme, marginally talented at best, and as phony as a wax banana in your aunt Hildy's fruit bowl. Lavinia White *was* Las Vegas.

Something told me that a two-week Vegas stint with Lavinia-loves-you would definitely be two weeks for the diary. Like running away with the circus for two weeks — only stranger. Besides (as Marsha had pointed out), I'd never been to Vegas, I'd never been on tour, and (as Marsha could not possibly have pointed out) I dearly needed some time away from Keith, just to think about our relationship without his beautiful, emotional, influential presence.

I tapped Marsha on the arm.

"I'll do it."

"You will?" Marsha smiled nearly as wide as Lavinia — after all, she had very little chance of hiring Snookie for her magical mystery tour if I had chosen not to go.

"You're kidding." Snookie's face simultaneously registered both his understandable disgust at the spectacle we were witnessing and his equally understandable surprise that I would choose to take active part in it.

"Why not?" I said. "We're long overdue for an adventure, aren't we, Snooks?"

Snookie smiled his my-best-friend-is-a-lunatic smile. I shrugged my so-what-else-is-new shrug.

Keith was less than overjoyed about the prospect of my spending two weeks in Las Vegas.

"Do you have to go?" he asked.

"Of course I don't *have* to go. I want to go." I could hear my voice slipping into the patronizing *Mr. Rogers Neighborhood* (I-am-dealing-with-a-small-child) tone I tried so hard to avoid when talking to Keith.

"Why?"

I counted to ten, slowly, in French.

"For the experience. For the fun of it. For two lousy weeks, Keith!" I was hoping this wasn't destined to metamorphose into a full-fledged fight. I didn't want to fight. I didn't want to make trouble — I just wanted to go to Las Vegas.

I decided to go for the soft sell.

"Keith" — I lowered my voice to a Louise Lasser raspy near-whisper — "I'm a singer. You might have noticed I spend an inordinate amount of my time in nightclubs."

"K.T., I know you're a singer."

"Let me finish." I touched a forefinger to Keith's lips.

"Now, as a singer, as a performer, touring is going to be part of my life. Now, if we're going to be together —

222

and I'd like to assume for the sake of argument that we are — then we're both going to have to get used to spending some time apart."

After a short pause, during which my words hung in the air between us like one of Snookie's smoke rings, Keith sucked in a long breath before saying,

"I'm not so sure that's something I want to get used to."

"And just what the hell is that supposed to mean?" Was this *I won't let you go?* Was it *Maybe we shouldn't be together after all?*

"I don't know," he said.

"Oh, Daddy," I leaned my forehead against Keith's chest, "please don't make this difficult for me. You knew I was a performer when you had the incredible lack of judgment to fall in love with me."

He slipped his big arms around my back.

"I knew the job was dangerous when I took it." He sighed. "You're right, Babe. Of course you should go."

My back stiffened just a bit beneath Keith's hands. His reading of the lines "You're right, Babe, of course you should go" lacked conviction. Had I been the director of the movie *The Life and Loves of Johnnie Ray Rousseau,* I would have yelled, "Cut!" through my megaphone. I would have gone to Keith, gestured him aside, and said, "Keith, Sweethaht, about that last speech: it lacked conviction. I need for you to say that like you mean it: 'You're *right,* Babe, of *course* you should go!'" I'd have made him endure take after take until I believed he really meant it.

But I let it go.

Keith was letting me have my way, without a fight, and I saw no reason to haggle over vocal inflections.

"Well," I said to Snookie later on the phone, "I'm going. I don't think Keith is any too thrilled about it, but I'm going."

"Well," Snooks said, "you certainly can't say I didn't warn you."

"Warn me about what, pray tell?"

"About Keith, that's what, pray tell. About his pressuring you about this Vegas trip. About how, any minute now, he's going to be asking you to give up this show business nonsense and take up something steady, like word processing. Let's face it, Honey — he's just not one of us. He's — dare I say it — normal."

"Snookseleh, Snookseleh, Snookseleh, Keith has not — repeat — has not asked me to give up my career. And he's not going to." I hope. "He'll just miss me, that's all. Who wouldn't?"

"All right" — Snookie had obviously decided to concede the point for now — "if you say so. Can't say you haven't been warned. Anyway, I'm glad you're going. We'll have a blast. You're gonna love Las Vegas."

I hated Las Vegas.

I suppose I should have known better. How could I have expected but to hate a town that so proudly glorifies bad taste at its most excruciatingly blatant? A town that boasts more powder blue leisure suits per capita than any other spot on the map. A town whose chief attractions continue to be gambling dens and Wayne Newton. A town where a performer of the caliber of Lavinia White could get two weeks' work as a night-club singer.

Yes, ladies and germs, I hated Las Vegas. From the word "go."

In fact, by the time Snookie and I entered Circus Circus's immense automatic plate glass front doors, I had already hated Las Vegas for several long, grueling hours.

The drive from L.A. was an ordeal comparable to the plagues levied upon Egypt by the God of Israel in His last big fit of pique — matter of fact, a nice plague of boils might have brightened my day. We left early in the morning, while the late-August weather was still reasonably cool and pleasant; but by midmorning, the day had turned oppressively hot and dry, and the drive across mile after endless mile of desert highway was uncomfortable in the extreme. Snookie's Pacer being (as I've mentioned) without air-conditioning, we drove with the windows down, and the hot desert air whipped through the car, the effect of which brought vivid new meaning to the term "hell on wheels."

Somewhere in the vast wasteland roughly halfway between Los Angeles and Las Vegas, the Pacer overheated (I should have known better — so much for learning from our mistakes), to the tune of some ominous-looking billows of steam flowing from underneath the hood of the car (with my vast lack of knowledge concerning the internal combustion engine, I assumed it was smoke — I said my prayers, fully expecting to be blown to kingdom come), forcing Snookie to pull over to the side of the highway and douse the car's decrepit radiator with water, and we waited in the blistering heat as the engine cooled. I huddled in what little shade the stalled car provided, sucking down one of the diet soft drinks we had brought along (which was now tepid and syrupy with the heat), and mumbled curses in a voice not unlike Mercedes McCambridge's voice-overs in *The Exorcist*.

Finally, after what had seemed like hours, we climbed back into the car, which seemed even hotter and stuffier than before, and were — like Willie Nelson before us — on the road again.

The Pacer overheated twice more before finally transporting us safely — if none the better for heat and travel — into Las Vegas.

By the time Snookie pit-stopped into a service station just inside the Las Vegas city limits, we were both hot and dirty, and I, for one, was as mean as a Siamese cat right after you've accidentally sucked its tail into the Hoover. I muttered unpleasantries under my breath as Snookie staggered toward the john.

When he climbed back into the car, Snookie was chuckling softly to himself. "God, I love this place."

"What's up?" I asked.

"There's a slot machine in the men's room," he reported. "And there's a rather rotund middle-aged gentleman in a Hawaiian-print shirt who told me he'd been in there for over an hour, and he wasn't leaving until he hit a jackpot. I love this place."

I smiled what must have appeared a wan excuse for a smile, thinking I had obviously entered a highly unhealthy venue, and I wondered if it might not be too late to turn back.

"Welcome to Las Vegas," Snookie said.

As we approached the immense imitation-wood-paneled front desk, our faces were damp with sweat and smudged with dirt, the overall effect being sort of a mud pie with eyes. My clothes were sticking uncomfortably to several key portions of my anatomy, and were rapidly growing colder and colder in the sudden near-arctic coolness of the grossly over-air-conditioned hotel lobby.

I felt like a bag lady.

The Pacer's catastrophic performance on the highway had landed us well behind schedule, and we were due at a rehearsal and sound check in the lounge within a few minutes.

"May I help you?" A tall, thin praying mantis of a young man appeared behind the desk. His dark hair was brilliantined back in the style of a 1920s lounge lizard, and his upper lip was decorated with a mustache that looked as if he had drawn it on with an eyebrow pencil. From the look of utter distaste on the man's face, I felt assured that Snooks and I looked as scruffy as we felt. He looked at us as if we were the Roto-Rooter man's bootprints. I somehow fought the urge to slap the smug, superior expression off the clerk's face, as we signed into our room.

"Oh," the clerk announced, "you have several messages here from a Ms. Goldberg."

Whereupon, my ears were assaulted by the familiarly unpleasant voice calling from across the lobby.

"Johnnie! Sidney!" I turned to see Marsha Goldman making her trademark double-time baby-stepping way across the lobby toward us, waving wildly and smiling like a jack-o'-lantern. She wore a bright canary yellow sundress, in which her voluminous gozongas seemed to take on lives of their own, with high-heeled sandals on her tiny feet. A huge straw purse hung in the crook of her elbow.

"Where in the world have you been?" Marsha demanded, a miniature Mama.

"Well—" Snookie started to explain, but Marsha interrupted.

"So hurry up, already," she said, gesticulating with her cigarette-wielding hand. "You'll be late for the rehearsal." She tapped her foot impatiently on the durable indoor-outdoor carpeting on the lobby floor. I was sure I could see the desk clerk wince as Marsha flicked her cigarette ash onto the floor next to her red-lacquered toenails. "We're going to be late as it is, and we certainly don't want to look unprofessional, now do we? Make a bad first impression here, and it'll be all over the Strip by morning, and you'll never work this town again, I can promise you that. Now, come on, already," she ordered, with a gesture of her small, childlike hands that suggested shooing baby chicks into the chicken house.

"Have someone take their bags up, will you?" Marsha tossed over her shoulder to the desk clerk, confident that it was no sooner said than done, and skittered off toward the lounge.

"What tornado hit you two, anyway?" Marsha asked, just a bit too loud. "You look like dreck!" She rummaged through her purse, and extracted two tiny foil packets containing Wash 'n' Dri premoistened towelettes. "Here — use these," she said, handing one packet to each of us, "you look awful, but there's nothing we can do about it now, there's just no time." And she skittered on ahead through (dramatic pause) the Casino.

I had never seen anything like it before.

The immense room was blindingly bright with fluorescent lights that flashed and sparkled like a Christmas tree gone berserk. Although Marsha was talking nonstop over her shoulder as she led us through the casino, she was completely inaudible over the deafening din of clanging bells, buzzing buzzers, the mechanical whirr of the one-armed bandits, and the steady jingle-jangle-jingle of coins.

Everywhere I turned, as far as the eye could see, there were people, easily two whole generations of America's Caucasian middle class (the only dark-skinned people I could spot were sweeping up), dressed in blinding synthetic fabrics, intensely engaged in various games involving cash and chance. Men in baggy flower-print shirts, with white shoes and matching belts, gleefully gathered their money (hard earned over a quarter century working the graveyard shift at Lockheed or pushing Kenmore side-by-sides at Sears Roebuck) and stacked it onto roulette tables, never to see it again; ladies with hair of unnatural hues piled high upon their heads yanked at slot machine handles with surprising vigor. I tapped Snooks on the shoulder.

"I've never in all my life seen so many—"

"Slot machines?" Snookie essayed over the noise.

"Wiglets," I replied.

We followed Marsha through the casino and toward a curtained-off area beyond. Tossing the curtain aside with a flip of her hand, Marsha admitted us to the lounge. The room was only dimly lit, unlike the casino, and I was momentarily blinded by the abrupt change in light.

When finally able to distinguish large shapes, I could see chairs stacked upside down on the tiny cocktail tables. Behind the bar, at the rear of the room, stood a good-looking dark-haired animal with a mustache, wiping glasses.

Ahead of us, on a small but workable stage, a rather short, dark man (in what I could scarcely allow myself to believe was a canary yellow polyester jogging suit; seven or eight outsized, gaudy rings; several gold neck chains; and a monstrous pompadour welded together with enough petroleum to lube a '65 Buick) was singing "Quando Quando Quando." If this rendition was any indication of the man's talent, Frank Sinatra could continue to sleep peacefully at night.

The singer (and I'm using the term quite loosely here) was accompanied by what was obviously the house combo — three less interested looking individuals one could scarcely hope to find. I had hoped to encounter a higher grade of talent in Las Vegas, even in a lounge.

"I'm going to be violently ill," I whispered to Snooks. "Now, quit."

"Oh, good," Marsha said in what she probably considered a whisper, "Johnny's still rehearsing, so we're not late."

As Johnny What's-His-Name tore into a swing version of "Lover," with an energy and fervor quite unmatched by vocal tone quality, I spotted Lavinia White, seated at one of the half-dollar-size tables in the very center of the room; a vision in a snow white sweatsuit,

230

matching jogging shoes, and those funky little short-short socks with the pom-pom at the heel. Her hair was wrapped under a white scarf in a Hedy Lamar-ish turban effect. Her face was nearly obscured by the oversized Foster Grants she wore despite the darkness of the room.

She was stirring absently at a Styrofoam cup from which dangled the tag end of a Lipton Flow-Thru teabag with one hand, and tapping a testy little drumroll on the tabletop with the other. She was every inch a star.

Among the people seated at, perched upon, and leaning against three or four tables surrounding Lavinia's, I spotted half a dozen or so young men whose long, unkempt hair, spandex tank tops, and unhealthy postures made them immediately recognizable as musicians (I remembered a couple of them from Lavinia's Blue Dahlia show — the others were obviously late recruits). There were also three good-looking young black women in pastel sweatsuits whom I later learned were Lavinia's makeup girl, Lavinia's wardrobe mistress, and Lavinia's hair stylist. As I recall, one, two, or perhaps all three of these ladies were named La Wanda.

Sitting alone (an overflowing ashtray her only company), sucking a cigarette like tomorrow had just been canceled, wearing a t-shirt with the Equal Rights Amendment printed across the bosom and the look of a woman who has just heard on the six o'clock news that her brand of feminine hygiene spray has been found to cause cancer in laboratory animals, was Randi. I stopped to say hello, as Snookie went to check on the stage setup and Marsha to confer with Lavinia.

"What's up, Lady?" I pulled the second chair from off the tabletop and seated myself astraddle it.

"Shit" — Randi managed to squeeze three or four syllables out of the word — "Ah'ma kill that little bitch."

"Am I safe in assuming we refer to, um, our star?"

Randi turned up her nose as if she had just dropped her peanut butter sandwich into a cow cookie, and nodded.

"Might I venture to ask why?" At this point, I had yet to actually meet Lavinia White. Randi and I had rehearsed together with Lavinia's musical director and (I assumed) boyfriend (Tyrone, a tall, handsome copper-colored gentleman with chemically straightened hair and a penchant for pimpish attire and too much cologne); this rehearsal would be the first time we actually sang with the diva herself.

"She sends Marsha over here to tell me to make sure I don't sing too loud, or move too much, or upstage her in any way." Randi stabbed her cigarette into the mound of butts in the ashtray. "Fuck, I could upstage that little bitch if I was dead and buried. Plus" — she lit up another Camel filter — "plus, she says I gotta wear a dress. A *dress!*" You'd think she'd been ordered to have her entire body tattooed. "Shit, I don't even own a dress. They're gonna make me wear one o' hers. I swear, I don't know how I let Marsha talk me into this shit. I need this like hemorrhoids."

"Now, Randi." I decided to play Mr. Blessed-Are-the-Peacemakers — maybe running into someone even more seriously pissed off than I was took the wind out of my sails. "Maybe we should cut Miss Lavinia some slack here."

"I'd like to cut her some throat."

"No, really." I laid my hand somewhat tentatively on Randi's. "Lest we forget this is Lavinia's Vegas debut, almost undoubtedly the apex of her career thus far. She really needs for this gig to be a success, and she's a little nervous. And, you are, heaven knows, one very strong performer. She's probably just a little bit afraid of you. Who wouldn't be?"

"Yeah?" Her expression softened a bit.

"Yeah. Let's give the diva a chance. She's probably not such a bad egg."

At which point Marsha approached our table.

"Okay, kids, let's get started, shall we?" She leaned in close between Randi and me. "By the way, you two: Vinnie was giving some thought to having the backups sing from the wings."

I saw Randi's eyes and lips fly open in tandem; I can only imagine mine did the same.

"From the wings?" Randi tried to whisper, but did not quite succeed.

"Offstage?" I attempted an air of cool detachment, and failed miserably.

"Uh-huh." Marsha pretended everything was just hunky-dory. She wasn't fooling anybody. "Just a thought," Marsha called over her shoulder as she rushed toward the stage, "just something to think about."

Randi shot me a see-what-I-mean look.

"Forget what I said," I whispered. "This is war."

As it turned out, Randi and I were not relegated to the wings. We were, however, placed as far upstage of the diva herself as was humanly possible while still remaining onstage — one would have thought we were carrying at least one highly contagious disease apiece. Randi and I decided during the rehearsal to do everything in our combined power to blow Miss Vinnie right off the stage. Hell hath no fury like a pissed-off performer. We sang at the very top of our capacity (which, for both of us, was considerable); when the sound man all but turned off our mics, we improvised some rather distracting choreography during the ballads. Neither of us was overly surprised when, immediately following the show, Marsha cornered us and let us know in no uncertain terms that if either of us even considered pulling a stunt like that again, not only would we both be out of a job, not only would we never work in this town again, but Marsha promised to personally execute the manual removal of our spleens if we attempted to undermine Lavinia's act.

Not that we would have. It wouldn't have been any fun anyway. Because, our admittedly childish prankstering notwithstanding, Randi and I did fancy ourselves professionals. And because, much to our chagrin, Las Vegas seemed to love Lavinia nearly as much as Lavinia claimed to love Las Vegas. It was S.R.O. in the little lounge for Vinnie's every performance. By her third night, Marsha was negotiating with the hotel management to have Lavinia held over for two additional weeks. We were a success. And whether or not I found Lavinia White personally sick-making, and her act the very epitome of everything I find abhorrent in show business, I have never been so stupid as to sabotage any success in which I play a part, regardless of how small that part.

That my part in Lavinia's show consisted almost entirely of standing far upstage in almost complete darkness, wearing a pair of pegged tuxedo pants and a powder blue ruffled shirt, singing "takin' it to the streets" over and over for what seemed like hours, made clear to me something I should have known all along: I like being center stage. And I really hate being in the background. Listening to roomful after roomful of people enthusiastically applauding Lavinia White's anemic renditions of Diana Ross hits and much of what truly sucked in the seventies (musically speaking) made me miserable. By the third night, I was perfectly morose. So, I might add, was Randi. We required no words to express our shared misery — the utterly defeated look in our eyes was sufficient.

Snookie, by contrast, seemed to be having the time of his very life. Since he'd done very little other than my shows for nearly two years, I'm sure the change of scene was good for him. Besides, within the first week of our arrival in Las Vegas, Snookie had won over two hundred dollars at the roulette tables; developed an unrequited but obviously enjoyable crush on Lavinia's drummer (just the sort of shaggy, stringy musician type Snookie fell for every time); had what he termed a "truly transcendent one-night stand" with the handsome lounge bartender; and discovered the hotel's subterranean spa, where a well-muscled masseur pummeled away at Snookie's shoulders and (for a mere five-dollar tip) treated him to what was later described as a "better-than-average hand job."

Snookie suggested I loosen up and have some fun, as I was in Las fuckin' Vegas for cryin' out loud. And although I really wanted to loosen up and have some fun, the facts of the matter were that I truly hated singing for Lavinia White, and (as I'm sure I've mentioned) I hated Las Vegas.

In Las Vegas, I found, time has no meaning. As anyone who's ever been there will tell you, the Strip is designed so that all of one's waking hours are spent indoors, away from windows, watches, sundials, ancient Aztec stone calendars, or any other reminder that time waits for no one, it passes you by; reminders that somewhere, the sun was rising or setting, that somewhere someone was sleeping. The obvious rationale being that nobody gambles while he sleeps.

I found Las Vegas's perpetual artificial high noon utterly disconcerting. I quickly came to resent the fact that I could look at my watch, read three o'clock, and have no immediate environmental clue as to whether it was three in the morning or three in the afternoon. All the lights were blindingly ablaze, the casino was a manic hornet's nest of activity, and the games went on, day and night, a.m. or p.m. I found this state of affairs plastic and unhealthy — like Cheez Whiz.

It scarcely took me the time required to lose seven dollars worth of nickels to the one-armed bandits to figure out that I was definitely not the gambling kind. With very little else available in the way of daytime entertainment on the Las Vegas Strip, I spent my days in the hotel room I shared with Snookie, watching old movies and used car salesmen on TV, reading magazine after magazine, cursing my fate, and missing Keith.

A week into our engagement, right after the show, I called Keith at home.

"Mmmfh?" he answered. Being wide awake and somewhat wired after the performance, I hadn't considered that for some, it was nearly three a.m.

"Keith?"

"K.T.?"

"Did I wake you?" Duh.

"Nah," he lied. "How are you?"

"I'm all right," I lied. "God, I miss you."

"I miss you too, Babe. I wish I could hold you, kiss you. Jeez."

"What?"

"I'm getting hard."

"Me, too."

"We better talk about something else before this conversation enters the realm of the obscene."

"Okay," I said. "I miss you."

"I miss you too, Babe."

We laughed.

I sat for a long, expensive moment, smiling foolishly to myself and caressing the telephone receiver.

"Babe?" Keith finally broke the silence.

"Huh?"

"Was there something you wanted to say?"

"Oh, no. I just wanted to hear your voice."

"Then we better hang up: this is undoubtedly costing somebody some money."

"Oh, yeah. You go on back to sleep, okay?"

"I love you, Babe."

CHUNK

a-chunk-CHUNK

a-chunk-CHUNK

"I love you, too."

 The rest of that week was a grayish blur of discontented monotony, just eating and sleeping and doing Lavinia's shows, and waiting to go home.

The last night, a few minutes before the last show, I sat backstage with Randi. We crouched in a corner on the floor: there was scarcely an empty chair or unoccupied square foot of space in or around the lounge, such was the draw Lavinia White had become. She had been held over for four more weeks; Randi, Snookie, and I had politely declined the offer (relayed through Marsha) to stay on. In the two weeks we'd sung behind her, Lavinia had never once spoken directly to me or Randi.

"Glad this one's almost over?" I asked Randi, quite rhetorically.

She snorted a cigarette-smoky laugh.

"Yeah, you could say that."

"I guess we just chalk it up to experience, huh?"

"Sugar," she said, shoving out her cigarette on the concrete floor, "this little girl is so fuckin' tired, excuse mah French, of chalkin' shit up to experience..." She lit another cigarette, exhaled a haze of gray-white smoke, and stared into it for a moment. "You know" — she

turned to me suddenly — "I've been singing profession-
ally since I was twelve years old."

"You're kidding. What—"

"What am I doing in fuckin' Las Vegas, sittin' on the
floor in somebody else's too-tight black dress, about to
go sing behind some little no-talent black bitch?"

"Okay." I conceded the spirit, if not the letter of my
question.

Randi shrugged, turned up a well-lipsticked mouth.

"I owed Marsha a coupla favors. She wanted to use
my boys for this gig. Besides, a payin' job's a payin' job,
huh?"

"But you're so good," I said. "One of the best I've
seen around town. I'd expect you to have a recording
contract at least by now."

"Oh, Sugar, I had a recording contract, four, five
years ago. Cut an album. It never got any push, never
even got any kind of distribution. It was a shitty deal all
round. I was young and stupid — didn't even know
enough to get a good lawyer. They said recording contract and I just signed."

She looked straight ahead for a moment, as if reading
some writing on the opposite wall.

"Marsha done anything fuh you?" she asked.

"Oh, yeah," I said. "I mean, she got me the Blue
Dahlia gig, of course. And she's promising to get me on
the Griffin show."

"Oh, she'll do it," Randi said.

"How do you know?"

"She got *me* on."

"Really?"

"Coupla times."

"Oh."

239

"Don't tell me," she said. "Let me guess. You been runnin' around thinking you were gonna get on TV and make show business history. National exposure, the phones start ringin' off the hook, and your career is made. Am I close?"

"Damn close." She put a pudgy nail-gnawed hand across mine.

"Sugar-pie, take it from a woman who knows. It just don't work that way. I understand where you're from. I mean, I watched all those Ruby Keeler movies on TV, too. But it's just not like that. What it's like is a whole lotta work for a whole lotta years, a whole lotta Marsha Goldmans, a whole lotta gettin' fucked over by people don't deserve to wipe y'ass.

"And maybe you make it. I mean really make it. But more likely you'll find yourself thirty-three years old, with your kid at home, and you in fuckin' Las Vegas singing backups for Lavinia White."

We just sat for a moment, holding hands. I'd been royally beaned with the high-and-inside pitch of reality, and I was a little bit dazed.

Randi took her hand from mine, mussed the top of my head.

"Don't let me get to you, Sugar. I'm old and bitter and it has not been a wonderful two weeks."

"I hear you, Sister."

"Will you two please get up off the floor!" Marsha stood close enough to inundate us both with her Estee Lauder body splash. "We go up in five minutes, now let's get the lead out!"

Randi stretched her legs out in front of her, clicked the heels of her black patent leather pumps together, and said,

"There's no place like home, there's no place like home."

There's no place like home.

Keith met me at the door, and we kissed. We kissed like I'd been gone two years instead of two weeks. We kissed like Solomon and Sheba. We kissed like that very first night. My suitcase had barely touched the floor before we were in bed, doing our level best to make two weeks worth of love.

After sweaty and spent and a little bit sore, I snuggled as close to Keith's big warm body as I could without becoming a tattoo on his chest. Being with Keith again was sweeter than ever. I could hardly hold him tightly enough, kiss him deeply enough. My heart beat the drum line to "Doo Wah Diddy Diddy." My veins ran melted butter. I couldn't stop smiling. I was home.

How could I have thought staying with Keith was a mistake? True, he was jealous of me, more than a bit possessive of me. What greater compliment (I thought, wiggling my butt against Keith's resting dick, feeling it stir) than that this big, strong, beautiful monster of a man should be jealous of me? Only a prize asshole could but be delighted at the prospect of being possessed by such as Keith.

And if our career goals and temperaments did not always dovetail, what of it? Did not opposites attract?

241

Most assuredly they did (I thought, studying Keith's big, pale arm against my darker, smaller one), indeed they did. And if Keith was a notorious homebody, much more likely to be in his own living room, reading Norman Mailer by the fireside on a Saturday night, than on either side of any nightclub stage, was it not possible that it was this very trait that made Keith exactly what I needed in a husband? Just what the doctor ordered, as Clara used to say.

Someone to see that I didn't get too far out there, even as I made sure he didn't become too stodgy. Someone to keep my feet safely on terra firma, even as my head was in the sky. Someone to give my life balance as I balanced his. Someone to be my anchor. To be my home.

Keith gave me a hard, full-body, all-over hug.

"God, I missed you," he whispered.

I could scarcely remember ever feeling so good. It was going to work out. Everything was gonna be all right.

Good day, sunshine.

And so the weeks following Las Vegas quickly began to bear a striking family resemblance to the weeks that had preceded Las Vegas. I went to work. I came home. I sang in clubs. I loved Keith. This was my life. And I was happy. Tired, but happy.

And I assumed Keith was happy too.

I suppose this was something of a large-scale assumption on my part, but what could I do? He never told me he was unhappy, and what choice had I but to take his word for it? True, I was as often away from home as before. More often, since we were hired on for Thursday nights at the Blue Dahlia as well as Wednesdays. But I spent as much time with Keith as I possibly could, running home right after gigs, keeping rehearsals short, spending less and less time just hanging out with Snookie. Our lovemaking (when we could schedule it) was better than ever, Keith clutching me to him as if he never planned to let me go.

Maybe I was just slightly less than observant of Keith's feelings, of his moods. Maybe I was a tad insensitive. Perhaps I should have taken more notice when Keith grew less communicative, taken a minute to ask myself if something was wrong, instead of telling myself the big guy was just having his period, and running off to rehearsal.

I don't know.

Maybe I had no right to be surprised when, one October Saturday morning (as I was frying eight slices of bacon for breakfast, feeling as contented as a Carnation cow), an orange juice glass fell (or perhaps was pushed) to its demise on the kitchen floor; and as I turned, startled, dropping the fork I was using to turn the bacon strips, Keith said in a voice perfectly brimming with portent,

"This isn't working."

Maybe I shouldn't have been surprised. But surprised I was.

"What isn't working?" I knew good and well what, of course; I'd simply been taken way off guard, and was stalling for a moment to regather my equilibrium, which lay shattered among the shards of glass on the floor.

"This," Keith said, his voice barely audible. "Us."

I picked the fork up off the floor.

The bacon burned, and I slid the frying pan from the fire.

Keith swept up the fragments of the orange juice glass (it had broken cleanly in two) and dropped them into the paper bag beneath the sink.

243

I knew this was the end, even as Keith and I moved like prizefighters to opposite corners of the kitchen. I knew what Keith would ask of me. (Hadn't Snookie warned me more than once? Hadn't I come to expect it myself, even as I told myself everything was fine?) And I knew I was in no way ready to give it to him.

We seemed to be speaking lines from a play we'd rehearsed for weeks, or a movie we'd both seen several times.

"I miss you so much when you're gone," Keith said.

"I miss you too."

"I need to have someone here when I'm here. I need you. I need you to be home."

"Keith..." The utter futility of this conversation struck me even as we were having it. Why didn't I just pack up now and save time. "You know that it is the nature of my work that I be away from home sometimes. Maybe a lot of the time."

"I know," he said. "I just want you home with me. I just do. What's the use of having a lover if I'm going to be alone?"

Uncomfortable pause.

"So." The distance between my corner of the kitchen and Keith's seemed to lengthen. When had my life become a German expressionist film? "Just what are you asking me here?"

"I don't recall asking you anything."

You've been with me too long, I thought. You're beginning to retort like me.

"You want me to quit singing, don't you?"

"I wouldn't ask you that."

"But you want me to—"

"Yes."

"And you know I just can't do that. Not now."

244

"Yes," he said. "I guess I do. I must admit I had allowed myself to fantasize your saying, Hey Keith, who needs show business, all I need is you. And I'd take you into my arms, and we'd kiss; fade to black. The End." A little smile raised one corner of his mouth. "No, huh?"

"Oh, Keith, I—"

"Was it incredibly naive of me to hope I could be enough for you?"

"Keith."

"I'm sorry" — he put up a shielding hand — "that wasn't very fair, was it? I know your singing is important to you, it's just that—"

"Oh, Keith" — I turned and faced the wall, braced my hands against it — "you know my singing is important to me. Good. Did you know that I've wanted to be a singer since I was seven years old? That I knew even then that's what I had to do, what I had to be? It's all I really know." I turned back to Keith. "If I'm not a singer, I just don't know what the fuck I am."

"You're the guy I love."

I looked at my big, beautiful lover, and I wondered what kind of an asshole would give up such a man for the dubious privilege of calling himself a nightclub singer. My kind of asshole, I guess.

"I'm sorry," I said. Amazing how empty words can sound.

"Me too, Babe."

That was it.

Over.

Slow fade to black. The End.

And, as I recall, it didn't really hurt at first. I mean, I didn't cry. I didn't actually feel pain. I felt empty. I felt alone; but I'd been there before.

"Hold me," I said.

And when Keith gathered me up into those big arms of his (for what in any Hollywood movie would have been the very last time), a wee small voice (the voice of relative sanity, some might say) whispered to me, Now's the time, Fool.

Tell him. That. You're never gonna leave him. Tell him — tell him — tell him. Tell him right now.

So tell the man, already.

Hey, Keith, who needs show business — all I need is you.

Remember?

And I suppose anyone in his right mind would have said that. But I didn't. I just said,

"I do love you."

"I know," he said.

I don't believe we ever had breakfast.

Concerning the rest of that day, the next day, indeed the next several weeks, facts and details maddeningly blur. My memory — famous trivia receptacle and detailmonger that it is — short circuits, and pictures smear like those old Polaroids when you didn't separate them just right.

I remember the odd mixture of sympathy and smugness on Snookie's face when I told him Keith and I were breaking up.

"Well," he said, "you know I'm much too good a friend to say I told you so," which, of course was as much as saying I told you so. He offered me the use of his lumpy (but reasonably comfortable) couch until I could find a place of my own. I accepted without hesitation.

I remember suggesting to Keith that, although we obviously could not live together, that perhaps we could remain lovers, maybe date. Keith smiled with one side of his face and said at twenty-five years old, he was well past the desire to date.

I remember kissing Keith good-bye at the door (my few belongings already having been moved to Snookie's). I remember our combined concerted efforts to part friendly if not friends. I remember our unconvinced, unconvincing smiles and attempts at casual (even jaunty) postures; all transparently futile attempts at striking a tally-ho, carry-on, you-win-some-you-lose-some Noel Coward sort of attitude while watching Passion and what we'd both chosen to name Love walk out the door with their suitcases in their hands and shuffle away like Charlie Chaplin and Paulette Goddard into the black-and-white sunset.

We kissed like madmen, as if to kiss one another enough to make up for the rest of our lives of never kissing one another again; Keith's massive arms clutching me so close he hurt my ribs, kissing me so hard I tasted blood; I grasping one handful of Keith's shirt, another handful of his baby-fine hair, biting into his lower lip as if to eat a part of him, and so have him in me always.

"I want to fuck you," Keith whispered. As I recall, we had barely touched since the morning we'd called it a day, and I'm sure at least a week had elapsed.

"I want it too."

He fucked me like a lover, and like a rapist. As if to give me every shred of love he had inside him once and for all; as if finally unleashing all the hurt and anger we both knew he felt (but which he was so careful to keep inside) and beating me into a bloody jam for taking his love and leaving. I dug my fingers into the skin of his powerful flanks, and wept puddles into both my ears.

I bunked in with Snookie for five or six weeks, roughly the time it took for me to find a livable, affordable one-bedroom apartment on the West Side; roughly the time it took for me to stop using "Who cares?" and "What's the difference?" as my stock answers to every conceivable question; roughly the time it took for me to stop having to drink myself to sleep.

I went back to work, of course, with what people used to refer to as a vengeance. For a while, my act reverted back to my French Dirge period: I dressed entirely in black. I did entire evenings of heartbreak ballads ("What Now, My Love" followed by "Non, C'est Rien" followed by "It's Over, Good-bye"), sometimes singing "Stay with Me, Baby" every single set until my throat bled. Marsha finally got me into an armlock and made me promise to put some up-tempos back into the show — seems some of the Blue Dahlia's customers were pairing off and making suicide pacts — and Snookie gently informed me that wearing all-black clothing was all well and good if one happened to be Johnny Cash, but was otherwise to be avoided.

And I got better. Let's face it: after six weeks of wearing black, heaving profound sighs, and carrying calla lilies, I had to get better, or Snookie would have had me embalmed. I never even tried to fool myself that I would ever completely lose the nagging feeling that I had made the wrong decision (I would have had that no matter what my decision), or that I could ever forget about Keith (I thought of him nearly every spare moment of the day, and not a night of drugless sleep passed that did not include a dream starring Keith). I simply pressed on. What could I do? I had rolled out my sleeping bag (as Snookie put it), and now I must zip myself in.

"I Will Survive" became the recurring background theme for the movie musical that was my life, playing incessantly behind a fast-moving quick-cut montage: Johnnie Ray plunking down three hundred dollars to learn the NBI System 3000 word processor. Johnnie Ray handing in his resignation at Troy Nelson. Johnnie Ray working a succession of temporary word processing jobs. Johnnie Ray singing rock at Tom Sawyer's, singing Top 40 at the Blue Dahlia, singing "When Sunny Gets Blue" against the white baby grand at Tony Roma's in Beverly Hills. Johnnie Ray as the Lead Player in an itsy-bitsy theater workshop production of *Pippin* in deepest Holly-wood; Johnnie Ray grinning in pleasure and surprise when the production rates a one-paragraph review in the *Times,* and one Johnnie Ray Rousseau is described as (quote) a cut above the production itself, with a sweet-as-honey tenor (unquote). Johnnie Ray, smiling and laughing and pretending to quaff Pepsi at the beach with a group of clean-cut all-American youth in a television commercial whose residuals paid Johnnie Ray's rent for over a year.

If by chance you saw (and, heaven forbid, remember) the above-mentioned Pepsi commercial, it might be of some interest to you that, among the group of clean-cut all-American youth portrayed in said commercial, separated from yours truly by one small, pretty, pigtailed black girl (who was no doubt cast lest anyone believe the black boy with the biceps might have designs on one of the three blonde girls in the group), wearing a pair of baggy madras bathing trunks and his habitual caramel-apple suntan, was none other than Louie.

He was the very first thing I laid eyes on upon entering KTLA studio "C" for the cattle call. The call for "clean-cut boys and girls, 18–22" had, of course, been blurbed in *DramaLogue* and *Daily Variety;* consequently, every living thing between the ages of fifteen and thirty-five had been there since daybreak for a nine o'clock call, composites in their hands and Vaseline on their upper front teeth. I was by this time almost twenty-four, but I could easily pass myself off as a mere lad of twenty or twenty-one just by dressing in whatever the college kids were wearing that week, breathing through my mouth, and clearing my mind of all conscious thought.

I wasn't sure if I should go over to Louie and say hello — I hadn't treated the boy as well as I might have, after all — and while I was deciding whether or not to just turn tail and run (I'd never been cast in a commercial before — what made me think I'd be cast in one now?), Louie spotted me, elbow-and-shouldered his way across the crowded soundstage toward me, smiling like the young Roddy McDowell as Lassie came home.

"Johnnie Ray," he said, as if it were a complete thought.

"Hi."

It had been the better part of a year since I'd last seen Louie. In that time he had managed to lose much of his baby fat. Judging from the newly delineated upper arms that stretched the short sleeves of his pristine white alligator shirt, Louie had taken to working out. He was wearing his hair shorter than I remembered. He was affecting the style of dress that in L.A. was passing as "preppy"; although dressed like a native Californian's idea of an Ivy League schoolboy, he still managed to look like a snapshot of Mortal Sin. He could model swimwear for J.C. Penney's, or model in the buff for *Blueboy* magazine, or simply slow traffic to a crawl in West Hollywood in the summertime.

In short, ladies and germs, one extremely beautiful boy. "How've you been?" he asked.

"All right," I said, "if you don't ask for details."

"You still playing Sawyer's?"

"'Fraid so."

"Still with that big guy?"

Schmertz.

"No."

"Should I say I'm sorry?"

"No. I guess not."

"Good," he said. "You're a free man again, then?"

"If this is freedom, then I guess I am."

"So after this thing is over, you think you'd maybe like to have some lunch with me?"

"Yeah. I think I'd like that."

So Louie and I went to Hampton's and had turkey burgers, large ice teas, and a good long chat.

"Why'd you quit Sawyer's so suddenly?" I asked, my burger dripping a gruesome-looking yellow-and-red puddle onto my plate. "You never even said good-bye."

"I got cast in a little theater production of *A Midsummer Night's Dream*. Lousy production, but all my life I'd wanted to play Puck. Anyway, I had to quit working nights. Besides" — Louie tongued a mustard smudge off the side of his mouth — "I had sort of fallen in love with this colored guy one Friday night. And next thing I knew it was you and the big guy. I didn't think you'd notice I was gone."

He looked at me over his turkey burger, and I noticed for the very first time that Louie's eyes weren't blue at all. They were hazel.

"You broke my heart," he said. And he smiled, as if to say just kidding, leaving me somewhat at loose ends. I made a big deal out of pulling the tomato slice out of my burger and slurping it up into my mouth, before saying (as much toward the tabletop as toward Louie),

"Think you might like to come home with me?"

He said, "Uh-huh."

Two weeks later, Louie moved his clothes, his Schwinn ten-speed bicycle, and several large, framed theater posters into my apartment.

He stayed for nearly two years.

To call my relationship with Louie a love affair would be to stretch the truth. It was more like roommates *a la carte* with a side order of sex. Fuck buddies. Louie's lifestyle and mine seemed supremely suited to one another. Our ambitions were similar and so were our business hours — Louie worked part-time during the day in a chi-chi greeting card shop in Westwood Village, and was generally in some little theater production or other at night. So we understood each other.

We both liked Jane Olivor and David Bowie and tuna sushi; we both disliked red meat, white shoes, and Wagner. We liked one another. We enjoyed each other's company and each other's body. On the rare occasion when we were both home at the same time, we made energetic (almost athletic) love.

We had a silly little ritual that (as I recall) preceded most of our lovemaking sessions. One of us would approach the other, and stand or sit so close that noses nearly touched. Maybe I'd kiss Louie, a little sucking kiss on the side of his neck, or maybe Louie would look at me with that wet-lipped look that made me poco loco and rub his hard little front against me; and one of us would say to the other,

"Do you want to?"

More often than not, we wanted to.

And I'd pull my knees to my chest and watch Louie's face go all closed-eyed and slack-lipped, and watch Louie's stomach muscles bunch up and relax over and over (like an accordian playing "Lady of Spain" double-time) as he fucked me. Or I'd do Louie, holding one of his small, perfect feet in each hand, sucking his slightly cheezy toes as I worked. Or we'd beat off in each other's face, talking dirty at one another like the boys in the blue movies ("Yeah, Baby, beat that thing!"), and laugh self-consciously afterward.

It was very good sex, by and large. Uncommonly good sex. So good, in fact, that it was surprisingly seldom that, while loving Louie, I saw Keith's face.

I don't remember sleeping with anyone else during the time Louie lived with me, and (as far as I know) neither did Louie. Still, our relationship was more personable than passionate, more satisfactory than satisfying.

When, about twenty months after moving in, Louie informed me that he was moving to New York ("There's just no *theater* here," he said, and how could I argue?), I removed his Angela-Lansbury-in-*Mame* poster from the bedroom wall and wished Louie all the luck in the world.

We kissed good-bye and we promised we'd write. We still do, if only Christmas and birthday cards.

I told him I'd miss him.

And I did.

More than I ever would have guessed.

Did I mention that I did finally play the Griffin show? Oh, indeed I did. Marsha Goldman was a woman of her word. After over a year of "I'm working on it," some singer (Julie Budd, if memory serves me — it usually does) canceled out at the last minute and, as they really like to open the show with a singer (and no, Merv doesn't count — have you heard him lately?), Marsha called me at the downtown law firm where I was working part-time hammering out precis into an IBM Displaywriter.

"This is it, Kid," she said. No further explanation was necessary.

Any elation I felt (and I admit there was some) proved premature. The Griffin people refused to pay the Boize scale; the Boize, naturally, declined the opportunity to appear on even a nationally syndicated television show for jack-shit nothin'. I was leery of the house band's ability to do my material justice — Merv was opening the show with rather bizarre big-bandish arrangements of "No More Tears (Enough Is Enough)" and the like — so I chose (over Marsha's threats to dismantle me with her bare hands) to sing to Snookie's piano accompaniment only.

Then my dream of exchanging witty talk-show talk with Merv ("Oh, Mervyn, I'm *already* a star — I'm simply waiting for the public to catch on!") was shattered: I would not be interviewed. At all. It was one song, and off.

So I did the show. And to say that pop music history was made would be to exaggerate. I opened the show ("My first guest tonight is one of the fastest-rising young singers on the pop music scene today..."). I sang "Unchained Melody" with Snookie on piano, bowed and smiled, and got the hell off the stage. Never to be seen or heard from again.

Needless to say, this appearance did not make my career. Oh, Marsha managed (as would any manager worth her salt) to parlay it into a couple of fair-to-middlin' club bookings; but if I'd had any delusions left about stardom coming a-knocking the day after the show (and I admit to some residual delusions, at least), they died of natural causes in the weeks following the show.

The day after the show was aired, I boarded the Freeway Flyer for work. I wore my Ray-Bans and braced myself for the appearance of the autograph hounds and adoring stage-door Johnnies. Halfway downtown, I was confident that my privacy was only too safe. As I got off at my stop, a middle-aged man in a gray suit and a sizable paunch stopped me with a hand on my shoulder.

"Hey," he said, "didn't I see you on the teevee last night? Griffin show?"

"Why yes," I said, fighting back a smile and hoping my face and posture projected just the right blend of cool nonchalance, slight irritation at being recognized, and the noblesse oblige of the true star. I reached for the ballpoint pen in my shirt pocket, prepared to scribble an auto-graph ("It's for my daughter — Ralph") and register humility at the man's lavish praise ("Y'know, only two or three truly great pop voices emerge in a generation...").

"Yeah," the man said, "I thought so." And walked away.

I saw Keith today. And strangely enough, I didn't even recognize him right away.

I'd been wandering the second-floor men's wear department of Neiman Marcus, just wasting time. Knowing good and well I couldn't afford so much as a handkerchief, and taking a perverse sort of pleasure in picking up pure silk pleated-front shirts and Italian-made pegged trousers that cost more than my rent, and then turning up my nose and tossing the merchandise aside as if it just wasn't my cup of tea.

As I shopped, I noticed the big, dark blond man perusing ties a few yards away, and the thought skipped across my mind (like a small, flat stone across a steam) that there was something about the guy that reminded me of Keith. But, after all, the woods are crawling with big, dark blond men who look vaguely like Keith; besides, I hadn't seen Keith even once in all the time since we'd parted company, and the time had long since passed when my heart leapt up into the roof of my mouth at the sight of any and every large, big-armed white guy.

So when the guy suddenly turned (as if feeling my eyes on him), and I recognized Keith, and he, me, and he smiled right at me as if he meant it; my heart leapt up into the roof of my mouth and stuck there like a mouthful of dry peanut butter sandwich.

"Long time no see," he said, walking toward me, right hand extended. I took his soft, cool hand in mine, and managed,

"How are you?"

He had hardly changed at all. His hair was just a bit thinner than when I'd last seen it, his waistline just a bit thicker. And he had grown a beard — neatly cropped close to his jawline, and a good deal redder than the hair anyplace else on his body. It made him look like a Viking, or a Nordic Jesus. Otherwise, Keith seemed to be much as I'd left him; his hazel eyes just as clear, his physique (in alligator shirt and Calvin Klein's) just as imposing.

"I'm just fine," he said. "And yourself?"

"Good," I rasped. "I'm just ... good."

"You're looking very ... healthy."

Healthy, I thought. Healthy? Why you awful sonofabitch, I look terrific. I didn't say anything.

"God, K.T., how long has it been?"

Hearing him call me by his pet name for me was like an arrow through me.

"Almost four years," I said. Seems like a mighty long time. Shoo-bop shoo-bop, mah baby.

"You look good." He seemed to be repeating himself somewhat. "You're still working out."

"Uh-huh."

"Me, too."

No jive, I thought, fiercely fighting the urge to lick his Adam's apple.

"Only once or twice a week these days," Keith continued, "but I'm still at it."

"Well, there you are!" A woman appeared from out of nowhere (as if one of the Armani leather jackets had

260

suddenly given birth). A big-boned Nordic type of the general Liv Ullman ilk. When she attached herself to Keith's arm like a mosquito to your uncle Elmo's bald spot, it occurred to me that the lady looked enough like Betsy to be her sister. I suddenly needed a Di-Gel.

The woman smiled in my general direction; one of those wide-open, all-encompassing smiles worn by the kind of woman who smiles at fire hydrants.

Keith introduced us.

Her name was Debbie. What was it, I wondered, with Keith and these big blonde chicks with the baby-doll names. Betsy. Debbie. Sheesh!

Debbie offered her hand, and I accepted with some reluctance. Her grip was surprisingly delicate for her size.

"So where do you and Keith know each other from?" she asked.

I used to fuck the living daylights out of him, I thought.

"College," I said.

"Oh." She bought it.

She was not unattractive. She looked healthy and strong, good breeding stock. Nicely dressed, nicely groomed.

I hated her guts.

I wanted her stripped naked, covered with Karo syrup, and tied securely over an anthill.

I smiled at her in what I hoped would pass as the good-natured manner of an old college chum, rather than a lonely homosexual musician who wanted nothing more than to shove her into oncoming traffic and sodomize her boyfriend on the floor of the men's department at Neiman's.

As we made the most mundane of small talk ("How 'bout the prices on these lamb-suede walking shorts"), I

261

took the liberty of undressing Keith with my mind. Remembering the size of him, the arms and chest and body-building hardnesses of him, the warm weight of him. I found myself absently tying the sleeve of a $200 French-made shirt into a double half hitch.

And I found myself wondering, was she good in bed? And was he the same sort of gonzo, abandoned sex animal with her that he'd been with me? And did he ever absently grope between her big soft thighs looking for something that just wasn't there? Looking for me, maybe?

Tacky, tacky, I thought, mentally rapping myself upon the knuckles.

For some reason, Keith asked me to have lunch at the Club Room with him and Debbie. Like a fool, I said yes.

We made more small talk over drinks.

"So what have you been doing with yourself?" I asked Keith.

"I just moved back from the City."

"*The* City?"

"San Francisco. The bank moved me up there just after — just after I saw you last. I love the City, but it's good to be back in old La-La. How about you? Did the album do well?"

"You know about the album?"

"I happen to own a copy," he said.

"You're kidding." It pleased me more than I hoped I was letting on. "You may own the only copy. Hang on to it — someday it will be quite worthless."

"It's very good, you know."

"Yes, it is," Debbie chimed in. "I've heard it. I didn't recognize you from the cover."

Shut up, bitch, I thought.

"Thank you very much," I said. "I liked it too. But the record company didn't push it, hardly distributed it re-

262

ally. And it died a thousand deaths. Didn't so much as brush the charts, and has taken up permanent residence in bargain bins across the country."

"When do you do the next one?" Keith asked.

"What next one? It was just a one-album deal. It was a bad deal from the word 'go.' I should have known better."

"So what are you doing now?"

"Clubs. Still. I even do Sawyer's now and then. It's more or less a name club now; a lot of the new wave kids go there. I do a small tour now and then — opened for Joan Rivers in Atlantic City for three weeks last year — the apex of my career thus far. I keep at it."

I stabbed absently at a salade nicoise. I picked up the scent of Keith's hair from across the table. I remembered (as I usually only remember when I'm alone at night) the feeling of Keith's hands on my skin, the taste of his cool, wet kiss on my tongue.

And I got hard.

I was glad we were sitting down.

After a while, Debbie excused herself to the ladies' room. (I imagined we were boring the poor girl to tears. I didn't much give a fuck.) Keith and I shared a few moments of gawky silence while a pretty blond busboy cleared the dishes and poured coffee. (You know you're in a class joint in L.A. when the busboys are Caucasian.)

"She's nice," I said finally.

"She's very ... good for me."

"Good for you," I said, trying to sound at least semi-sincere, knowing I was failing.

"She stays home," he said.

"Touché."

"I didn't mean that like it sounded," he said, staring down into his coffee cup.

Keith started to say something, then stopped short.

Then, leaning forward, he whispered,

"You're still so beautiful, K.T. I hoped when I saw you again, I wouldn't think so anymore."

"So are you," I said, "you sonofabitch." We just sat and stared into each other's eyes for a minute or two, grinning foolishly (the way young lovers do), before Keith said,

"Do you have a — are you seeing any—"

"No. Not for a while now."

"Do you think—"

"Yes." Anything. Ask.

"What?"

"What?"

"What were you saying?"

"Nothing," I said. "What were you saying?"

"I'd like to — see you — again."

"I'd like that, too." So much for trying not to appear eager.

"Well, here..." Keith pulled out his wallet, extracted a business card, handed it to me. "Give me a call; we could have a drink together or something — that's right, you don't drink much. Dinner maybe, or, something."

I didn't say anything.

I just took the card.

"Could I have your number?" he asked.

"I've just recently moved. I don't have a phone yet." That was what Clara would call a bald-faced lie. And, frankly, I'm not exactly sure why I lied. Maybe I just wanted to maintain some control over a situation which (for me) was rapidly flying out of control. If I called Keith, there was some small chance of maintaining some semblance of cool. If Keith called me, I knew good and well if he asked me to meet him at the ends of the earth for cocktails, I'd be there with my good shoes on.

When Debbie returned from the ladies', we all took it as a signal to adjourn.

Keith insisted upon paying for lunch. And I let him. He was, after all, a successful young banker, and I a poor struggling nightclub performer with a part-time day gig and an album that stiffed.

I walked with the happy couple to the sidewalk in front of the store. As we shook hands, Keith held my hand just a little longer than was truly necessary, looked into my eyes, and smiled a smile I hadn't seen in way too many years. If Debbie noticed anything, she didn't let on.

And as they walked away down Santa Monica Boulevard, as I watched their backs grow ever smaller and merge with those of other shoppers and passersby, I realized that in my left hand I still held Keith's card.

I started to tuck it into my pocket, but stopped short.

Who was I trying to kid? I thought. So I call Keith up, and we go out for drinks or dinner or ... something. There was still this woman, this Betsy II, probably the latest in a veritable parade of Betsys. Besides, it hadn't worked between Keith and me before — what said it was going to work now?

I held Keith's card in the palm of my hand for a moment, then crushed the stiff little paper, slowly and deliberately, into a little crinkled ball. And dropped it (with a little flip of my wrist) into a convenient trash basket. And walked away.

But not before committing Keith's telephone numbers (both home and business) to memory. Like Clara used to say: I may be crazy, but I ain't no fool.

Sure, it didn't quite work out with Keith and me before, and there's a good chance it won't work out now. After all, it's been nearly four years since I lived with Keith. An awful lot of Kool-Aid under the bridge. I'm older now, of course, and (I should hope) perhaps a bit wiser for wear and tear. And I'm tired.

Tired of the standard operational showbiz bullshit. More than a little bit tired of show business in general. Tired of living from hand to mouth, from one gig to the next, from one temp typing job to the next. And, as Brother Al Green used to sing, I'm so tired of being alone. So I figure, what have I got to lose?

And so, as I sit here inscribing Keith's numbers in my little red book, wondering if one hour after seeing him is too soon to call, I am reminded of that great old song by easily the least talented of all the girl groups, the Marvelettes:

"Beachwood four, five, seven, eight, nine." Remember? You can call me up and have a date, any old time.

Snookie once said the entire spectrum of human experience is covered in the lyrics of girl-group songs. I tend to agree. A subject easily worth a chapter in the book, don't you think?

CONTINUING TALES IN THE LIFE OF
JOHNNIE RAY ROUSSEAU:

Larry Duplechan's
CAPTAIN SWING

$16.00, cloth

Johnnie Ray Rousseau's life is at its lowest ebb. The love of his life was killed in a hit-and-run, and now he's been called to the deathbed of his hateful, homophobic father. There he meets Nigel, his second cousin, who looks like mortal sin in Levi's and tank top, and who offers a love that Johnnie is none too sure he ought to accept.

"*A beautifully written novel, whose rhythm pays homage to Junie's (and Nigel's) love of jazz; its words sing of home, family, hurt, and, most of all, need.*" —BOOKLIST

"*Duplechan's novel is marvelous, sentimental but not sappy, pensive but upbeat, and told with a slow, sassy wit that will keep readers hooked.*" —LIBRARY JOURNAL

"*A low-key charmer that quietly captivates.*"
—PUBLISHERS WEEKLY

"CAPTAIN SWING *mixes humor and pathos into as tasty a dish as Aunt Lucille's down-home boudin.*"
—*Victoria Brownworth in* LAMBDA BOOK REPORT

"*Makes the southern Louisana characters come alive in the steam of the bayous and the bedrooms. Duplechan writes with a grace and humor that lets the reader walk slowly through life in the small Black and Cajun community.*" —ALABAMA FORUM

African-American titles...

B-BOY BLUES, by James Earl Hardy, $11.00. Mitchell Crawford always wished, hoped, dreamed, and prayed for a Ruffneck — a hip-hop lovin', cool-posin', street-struttin', crazy crotch-grabbin' brotha. And he finally finds one in Raheim Rivers, who is a vision of lust: six feet tall and 215 pounds of mocha-chocolate muscle. Mitchell knows Raheim will take him for a walk on the wild side, especially between the sheets. But he doesn't count on getting behind Raheim's mask — and finding someone he can love.

"A lusty, freewheeling first novel ... Hardy has the makings of a formidable talent." —KIRKUS REVIEWS

BROTHER TO BROTHER, edited by Essex Hemphill, $9.00. Black activist and poet Essex Hemphill has carried on in the footsteps of the late Joseph Beam (editor of *In the Life*) with this new anthology of fiction, essays, and poetry by black gay men. Contributors include Assoto Saint, Craig G. Harris, Melvin Dixon, Marlon Riggs, and many newer writers. Winner of a Lambda Literary Award.

A HUNDRED DAYS FROM NOW, by Steven Corbin, cloth, $19.00. Dexter Baldwin and Sergio Gutierrez are wildly successful — both professionally and in their relationship. But Sergio is closeted, both to his family and in his business. As his health begins to erode from AIDS complications, he gambles on an experimental bone-marrow transplant that may help him, or may create new complications. It will take a hundred days to determine if the procedure is successful — a hundred days that are filled with secrets and revelations.

FRAGMENTS THAT REMAIN, by Steven Corbin, $10.00. Skylar Whyte, a critically acclaimed actor, is the eldest son in a dysfunctional African-American family. *Fragments That Remain* explores the dynamics of a family in which the lighter-complected child is favored over his darker brother. It examines the subtle and sometimes not-so-subtle layers of racism within an interracial homosexual couple, and in the gay community at large.

> *"A blistering novel. Corbin imparts a stinging poignancy to the harmful, obsessive behaviors repeated in successive generations of a family."* —PUBLISHERS WEEKLY

IN THE LIFE, edited by Joseph Beam, $9.00. When writer and activist Joseph Beam became frustrated that so little gay literature spoke to him as a black gay man, he did something about it: the result was *In the Life*, an anthology which takes its name from a black slang expression for "gay." Here, thirty-three writers and artists explore what it means to be doubly different — black and gay — in modern America. Their stories, essays, poetry, and artwork voice the concerns and aspirations of an often silent minority.

...and assorted others

GENTS, BAD BOYS, AND BARBARIANS, edited by Rudy Kikel, $10.00. Thirty-nine new gay male poets write about love and lust, death and healing. These exceptional new poets include prizewinners from prestigious quarterlies (the "gents" of the title), denizens of the 'zine scene (the "bad boys"), and rogues of the performance and poetry "slam" worlds (the "barbarians").

SCHOOL'S OUT, by Dan Woog, $12.00. Author Dan Woog interviewed nearly three hundred people — students, teachers, principals, coaches, counselors, and others — for this exploration of the current impact of gay and lesbian issues and people on the U.S. educational system. From the scared teenager who doesn't want his teammates to know he's gay, to the straight teacher who wants to honor diversity by teaching gay issues in the classroom, Woog puts a human face on the people who are truly fighting for "liberty and justice for all."

ONE TEACHER IN TEN, edited by Kevin Jennings, $10.00. Gay and lesbian teachers represent one of the last professions to come out in large numbers. Here, more than thirty educators relate their experiences of fighting for justice in their own lives, while also trying to make the world a better place for young people.

THE MEN WITH THE PINK TRIANGLE, by Heinz Heger, $9.00. Thousands of gay people suffered persecution at the hands of the Nazi regime. Of the few who survived the concentration camps, only one ever came forward to tell his story. This is his riveting account of those nightmarish years.

MY FIRST TIME, edited by Jack Hart, $10.00. A fascinating collection of true, first-person stories by men from around the country, describing their first same-sex sexual encounter.

MY BIGGEST O, edited by Jack Hart, $9.00. What was the best sex you ever had? Jack Hart asked that question of hundreds of gay men, and got some fascinating answers.

GAY SEX, by Jack Hart, $15.00. This lively, illustrated guide covers everything from the basics (Lubricants) to the lifesaving (Condom care) to the unexpected (Exhibition-ism).

REVELATIONS, edited by Adrien Saks and Wayne Curtis, $8.00. For most gay men, coming out is a continuous process, but often there is one early moment which stands out as a special and crucial time. In *Revelations*, twenty-two men tell their stories.

THE PRESIDENT'S SON, by Krandall Kraus, $6.00. When a popular president seeks re-election, his advisors agree that his son's homosexuality must be kept secret at any cost.

SUPPORT YOUR LOCAL BOOKSTORE
Most of the books described here are available at your nearest gay or feminist bookstore, and many of them will be available at African-American and other bookstores. If you can't get these books locally, order by mail using this form.

Enclosed is $_____ for the following books. (Add $1.00 postage if ordering just one book. If you order two or more, we'll pay the postage.)

1._____

2._____

3._____

name:_____

address:_____

city:_____ state:_____ zip:_____

ALYSON PUBLICATIONS
Dept. J-55, 40 Plympton St., Boston, MA 02118

After December 31, 1996, please write for current catalog.